PRAISE FOR *Perp*

"With *Perpetua's Kin*, M. Allen Cunning
he is one of the bravest and most talented novelists writing today.
His prose sings with a rare kind of poetry, even as the story sweeps
you along with its dark mystery and heartbreaking tension. With
each page we gain the greatest gift of fiction: an insight into our own
trembling humanity."   — EOWYN IVEY
author of *To the Bright Edge of the World*
and *The Snow Child,* Pulitzer Prize Finalist

"*Perpetua's Kin* blew me away with its stark, astonishing music. I've
never seen the raw devastations of war brought alive in language
so uncannily beautiful, so powerfully strange. This is a flat-out
brilliant book."   — LENI ZUMAS
author of *Red Clocks, The Listeners,* and *Farewell Navigator*

"A tour de force performance…a novel that materializes — almost as
if by magic — as both a sprawling epic and a series of exquisitely
wrought miniatures…Cunningham transports the reader across the
continent, through multiple eras, and into the souls of his charac-
ters. *Perpetua's Kin* is an aching meditation on solitude and connection, and the vast American landscape that breeds both."
— JUSTIN HOCKING
author of *The Great Floodgates of the Wonderworld*

"*Perpetua's Kin* is beautiful, reminiscent of *The Green Age of Asher
Witherow*…takes the reader right in…Cunningham gives us a book to
savor — a fulfilling, substantial book, and a joy to read."
— JANET BORETA, founder of Orinda Books (CA)

"Cunningham has once again raised the bar on the art of the novel.
Perpetua's Kin may be a distinctly American portrait, but the over-
arching themes are universal. I walk away from a reading like this
ruminating on the largeness of life."
— NANCY SCHEEMAKER, Northshire Bookstore (NY)

"With a vast scope and penetrating psychological depth, *Perpetua's
Kin*…mak[es] the past not only vividly real but essential to our
understanding of the complicated present. Cunningham's novel takes
us on a journey into our messy and violent American legacy and
offers us a pathway out, confronting brutal truths and embracing
hard-won compassion."   — SCOTT NADELSON
author of *The Fourth Corner of the World*

"Deliciously dark, emotional…swept me off my feet…writing so rich and haunting that the novel is still begging me for a second reading …One of the best contemporary novels I have read to date."
— NANCY SCHEEMAKER, Northshire Books (NY)

"Seven years later, the images still haunt me…Cunningham's prose is perfect—he writes dialogue and sentences that beg to be read aloud."
— GAYLE SHANKS, Changing Hands Bookstore (AZ)

"Classic. A story of such powerful magic, sorrow, disaster, and illumination that it is impossible to read this book without experiencing profound emotional and spiritual modulation…A fully formed, timeless American writer."
— Square Books (Oxford, MS)

"Remarkable…a feat reminiscent of William Styron's *Lie Down in Darkness*."
— *Foreword Reviews*

"An amazing first novel, and a refreshing revival of an earlier literary mood."
— *Rocky Mountain News*

"Disturbingly convincing…too compelling to put down…unpolluted by careless word choice, emotional flourishes or manipulative clichés …Cunningham's novel haunts."
— *The Salt Lake Tribune*

"Combine[s] a strikingly beautiful prose style with an unerring instinct for storytelling."
— ROBERT OLEN BUTLER, Pulitzer Prize winner

"Compelling and artfully told."
— *Saint Louis Post-Dispatch*

"It's like this guy is 200 years old, he gets it so right."
— TOM FRANKLIN, author of *Crooked Letter, Crooked Letter*

"One of the finest debut novels I've ever read."
— STEVE YARBROUGH, author of *The Unmade World*

"Dark and foreboding, vivid in character…An impressive and satisfying debut novel."
— *San Jose Mercury News*

"Breathtaking…impeccably imagined, sensitive and real…convincingly shatters the equation of childhood and innocence."
— *BookBrowse*

"Superb…a beautifully conceived, adroitly executed novel that defies simple categorization…It is wonderful. Don't miss it." — *New Pages*

"Spins a deceptively simple tale from a language as delicate as lace."
— *Rain Taxi*

"From the very first pages I knew that I had something special in my hands...I could not bear to put it down...gritty and magical, fantastic and authentic. It is one of the best books I've read this year."
— Susan Swagler, *The Birmingham News*

Lost Son:

* A Top 10 Book of the Northwest, *The Oregonian*
* A Featured Hardcover at the Village Voice Bookshop, Paris

"Powerful...the perfect amalgamation of imagination and research."
— Annie Blooms Books (Portland OR)

"Gripping and beautifully written...incredibly ambitious."
— Strand Books (NY)

"Awe-inspiring...in the depth of understanding [it] reveals regarding Rilke's life...Cunningham has painted a rich portrait."
— Steve Turnbull, Joseph-Beth Booksellers (Lexington, KY)

"Vivid, melodic, and retaining a lyrical beauty throughout...seamlessly infusing fact with fiction...a vast monument to the power of the creative spirit."   — *Curled Up with a Good Book*

"Beautifully expressive prose...you'll want to savor every word."
— *Historical Novels Review*

"Cunningham has taken risks...and he has succeeded in producing an offbeat and absorbing literary work."   — *Library Journal*

"Lyrical and moving."   — *Booklist*

"[You] feel gradually, in joy and astonishment, the magic of Rilke reach out from every page. *Lost Son* is at once a subtle and signal imaginative achievement."
— IHAB HASSAN, author of *The Dismemberment of Orpheus*

"Beautiful and fluid. I found myself torn, lingering over passages and yet eager to rush on...mesmerizing."   — *The Oregonian*

M. Allen Cunningham

PERPETUA'S KIN

M. Allen Cunningham is the author of the novels *The Green Age of Asher Witherow, Lost Son,* and *Partisans,* as well as the short story collection *Date of Disappearance,* an essay collection entitled *The Honorable Obscurity Handbook,* an illustrated work of cultural criticism entitled *The Flickering Page,* and he edited and wrote the introduction for *Funny-Ass Thoreau.* His work has been shortlisted for the Indie Next Book of the Year Award, a Finalist for the Flann O'Brien Award for Innovative Fiction, a Semi-finalist for the American Short Fiction Prize, and has appeared in many national and regional literary outlets including *The Kenyon Review, Glimmer Train, Tin House, Alaska Quarterly Review, Catamaran, Boulevard,* and *Epoch.* The recipient of residencies at Yaddo and multiple fellowships, Cunningham is a contributing editor for the literary journal *Moss.* He teaches creative writing in Portland, Oregon and elsewhere.

MAllenCunningham.com

M. Allen Cunningham

PERPETUA'S KIN

[*a novel*]

ATELIER26 BOOKS
Portland, Oregon

Cover design by Nathan Shields
Book design by M.A.C.

Perpetua's Kin
(Fiction)
isbn-13: 978-0-9976523-7-6
isbn-10: 0-9976523-7-3

Library of Congress Control Number: 2018906678

Atelier26 Books are printed in the U.S.A. on acid-free paper.

ATELIER26 BOOKS, an independent publisher in Portland, Oregon, exists to demonstrate the powers and possibilities of literature through beautifully designed and expressive books that get people listening, talking, and exchanging ideas. We've quickly become recognized for the excellence and idiosyncrasy of our titles, which have been honored by the 2018 PEN/Bingham Prize, the 2016 PEN/Hemingway Award, the 2015 Balcones Fiction Prize, and the 2014 Flann O'Brien Award, and cited on numerous Best of the Year lists.

Atelier26

Distributor: Independent Publishers Group (IPG)

Atelier26 is grateful for grant support from the Oregon Community Foundation.

For the crucial support of a Project Grant, the author thanks the Regional Arts & Culture Council.

RACC

Atelier26Books.com

for my mother and father

for my son

Looking back I wonder if I can write about it and emphasize the things that should be and rather gloss over the things that I wish was not in my life — but have concluded to tell it as it was as no one but myself will ever get to read it and if they could who would?

— G.T.H., around 1954, age 88, San Francisco

Can you punctuate yourself as silence? You will see the edges cut away from you, back into a world of another kind — back into real emptiness, some would say. Well, we are objects in a wind that stopped, is my view.

— Anne Carson, *Plainwater*

It is interesting that communication once again is becoming dominated by telegraphy. This page reached your browser by telegraphy.

— *The ElectroMagnetic Telegraph,* an online paper by J.B. Calvert

i. (IOWA, 1886)

Seeing she would not live out the night, Benjamin's mother made it known in the household, so the young man found himself alone at her bedside. It was July the thirtieth. He would be twenty-three in about a week.

She clutched his hand. Time had come sure enough. Her gaze once green seemed to swim with silverfish now.

"Forgive your father," she said. "Understand him."

She then set him a task to follow her going. He was to tell nobody. He listened close and gave his promise to do it.

She said, "I'm sorry to go before your birthday."

She drifted an hour in husky sleep. Her death as it came seemed terribly small, noise in her throat like a stifled hiccup. Then silence, huge in consequence, his life wrenched off course.

He sat alone in his room with her words. Stay at home. She knew that she alone could win his vow in this. But how strange to bind him from past the grave — she had guarded his freedom while she lived.

He went to the barn that night as she'd instructed. It was very late and the summer darkness just coming full. He did not carry a lamp. Slow, he fumbled through blackness, the shut-in musk of straw, alfalfa, wagon grease, manure. The goat's bell clinked. He heard her rustling to rise in the stall. He hushed her going by and she gave murmur and fell quiet. He could hear the horses breathing and shuffling in the farther darkness.

13

His eyes were changing and now he stared through dim cobwebbed light from the window. He moved past the halfwall to where the canning bench was, cluttered with tins and tools, old currying combs, lamp oil canisters long since emptied, sawblades, axehandles, shingles. Cautious of rusted nails he felt about. A packet was all she'd said. His fingers tugged through chrysalises, sticky spider sacs that whispered like static. He rubbed knuckles and palms on his trousers, then withdrew the candle he'd brought and lit it, turning to keep the glow off the window.

In candlelight he tipped back the tins and canisters and looked underneath, behind. Nothing. He crouched to the shelf below. More cobwebs. A grain funnel, rusted. His father's old mackintosh boots deep in dust, kept as if the man clung to hope of regaining the leg lost years before.

Along the bench's underside he noticed the torn gossamer. He put the candle forth and looked into the upper recesses. Gossamer sizzled and vanished with a faint deathly odor but no smoke. Where the spider's canopy parted he could see something wedged between wall and scantling. He reached.

His hand came back holding a thin packet bound with twine. He bent each envelope back. All bore dates within the year. Each was addressed to his mother Harriet Bauer — her maiden name — care of the Postmaster at Albia, the town to the north.

Their town was called Perpetua and it had its own post office: the Wabash Depot where Benjamin himself had worked as errand boy, messenger, and finally novice telegraph operator for nigh on eight years. It was not a half-mile's walk from their house. The Lorns, including his mother, had never lived in Albia or anywhere beyond Perpetua's platted dirt streets. But these letters, whatever they were, had held secrecy enough to call her clear to the next town on several occasions — and to make her use her maiden name. Benjamin wondered how she'd managed to slip north so often without the notice of the men in her house. Or under what excuse?

He stowed the letters in his shirt and carried them inside.

ii. (ONE YEAR LATER)

Benjamin stares at a photograph of his father. He has two in his keeping, ambrotypes almost identical. John Manfred Lorn sits middle-aged before a false pastoral with hair oiled and arms gartered. Icy spectacles hide his eyes, wires drawn tight behind his ears. His L-handled crutch slants at the chairseat.

The man suffered in his time. Ghosts plague him still. With his wife's brother he'd gone to enlist in the War of the Rebellion. They'd known each other from boyhood. They were both about nineteen and only J.M. survived to come home, a cripple. Benjamin was born by then, conceived before his father went away. For a long time this was everything Benjamin knew of the past which lurked large in the house and trailed the limping man through every turn. It wasn't much to know but it made J.M. Lorn a doubtless authority.

Now, motherless and almost twenty-four, Benjamin studies his father's lined face and no longer wonders what beyond the leg got hacked from this man's younger self in war. Forever refusing to be a cripple, the father has never told what maimed him. Over his hearthstone a tasseled silver cutlass hangs in honor, its hilt marked C.S. The sword signifies things only he can know.

Lorn & Son, the father's harness and leather shop, stands proudly on Perpetua's town square. In the fragrant brownwood interior J.M. Lorn has long sought normalcy, vacant trouser leg swatting the crutch clumping aisle to aisle across the floors. All through Benjamin's boyhood that crutch-noise sermonized. Always the man was overtaxed by the mute past that unlegged him. Even in privacy at home he guarded his amputation with Edenic shame and raged should anyone but his wife pay the naked stump a glance. Benjamin remembers once straying too close to his father's bath and the fists of foam that sent him off rubbing soap-stung eyes and crying. Nothing could threaten J.M. Lorn so much as indignity. Benjamin's mother caught up the boy and held him saying "Shhh." But it was an error he never made again. After that, in dread of something that marked the world of man, he determined to stay a child of woman.

How he's tried to banish this father from his mind. Benjamin sees this when he holds the ambrotype and memories bubble from blackness. It's become his lifelong task.

In his bedroom the night his mother died Benjamin untied the twine that bound the letters and sat with his back against the door. Forgive your father, she had said, as prelude to telling this secret. Understand him. But what in these letters could redeem the hateful father? Benjamin read.

Miss Harriet Bauer
Albia, Iowa
Dear Madam —
I beg pardon for so long delaying answering of your letter, the moreso because of the nature of your queries. I fear I must disappoint in telling you that I was not acquainted with your brother Alfred Bauer, although my regiment the 77th Ohio joined his in frays for the Union

cause under General Steele's ill-starred expedition into southern Arkansas, including our attempted defense of the supply train in Moro Swamp, where Fagan's cavalry overwhelmed us terribly.

There were as you likely know some 1,400 seized prisoner that day. Having been struck down about midway through the engagement it was my strange good fortune to number among those presumed dead and be left in that mire to meet my fate. This, you will note, I failed to do. And though I still suffer my wounds, by blessing I never had to suffer marching at the point of Rebel bayonet to that awful Texas stockade where they herded my compatriots, your brother presumably included.

I am glad however to inform you that you are not amiss in writing to me, for a loyal friend of mine was among the surviving prisoners at last exchanged. He survives today. I have forwarded him your letter at his home in Dayton Ohio. I pray he may furnish you what answers I have failed to. I wish you all luck.

Cordially,
Jasper H. Slea
Columbus

Benjamin stared at the letter awhile. He folded it away and withdrew the next from its envelope. He read till the late hours.

Next morning he would wire the Postmaster at Albia: *Harriet Bauer deceased. Upon receipt of letters notify B. Lorn at Wabash Depot, Perpetua. Do not forward. Strongly prefer to collect in person.*

PART ONE

An American man is one who has outgrown his
father.

— Thornton Wilder

1. (THE LORNS OF PERPETUA)

Perpetua was Benjamin's birthplace as it was his father's. Benjamin's grandfather Thornton Hanson Lorn first brought the family name there around 1842. The town was in its infancy then.

Thornton's parents were born and bred in the damp northern climes of Germany, both the offspring of modestly landed farmers, and it was there they sired Thornton. He was a child just learning to walk when in 1822 they secured passage to America.

Coming late to the harbor at Kiel the Lorns found their ship the TAGESANBRUCH embarked. But within a day or two a different vessel, the SCHATTENBILD, brought them down off the roiling Baltic Sea into a chasmed Atlantic. The steerage stank. The decks squirmed. There had been quarrels in the crowd, oaths and tussles, and many had taken sick. The waves were green at morning, blue at midday, red at dusk. They'd heard there were things to die of in America: beasts, Indians, the like. Their families, wishing they'd stay at home, had striven to give them fears. Though not doubting the dangers, Lorn and wife supposed America would offer things of promise as numerous. Unlearned fears made them emigrants.

So the fourteen-month Thornton Hanson Lorn took his first steps over the deck of the SCHATTENBILD as she hissed through phosphorous night. By time of landing at New York the boy had learned to travel upright unhelped, though the ship's floating lent him a peculiar idea of balance. Between his parents he lurched from the rancid dockyards into the hemorrhaging avenues of Manhattan. Like many his age he would keep a swaying gait his whole life.

Alighting in America the Lorns could hardly yet suppose it but they were to grow old there. They went down to Pennsylvania where they lived and farmed and let years abrade youth. The toddling blonde-haired Thornton, like his siblings after him, grew up and at twenty he moved west to stake claim in the rolling hill country of southern Iowa. There he set up house in the seedling Moravian village of Perpetua and harrowed farmland all his own, walking the earth with nautical stride, harnessed to a moldboard plough that was harnessed to a draft horse. He walked again behind the harrow and took joy to see the dark clods of earth his disks bladed soft.

At an early harvest dance in the Perpetua Grange Thornton held a girl's hand through the courtesy turn, the curlicue. She'd recently come with her family from Vermont. The bones of her fingers were small and light as cinnamon sticks. Thornton felt his boots stumping at the boards. Straining for gingerness he shifted to his toes. During the sashay he caught whiff of her and his mind bloomed with thoughts of balsam or birch or delicately leaved northern trees.

He called at the girl's home soon after. Her people were called Lighty. She was Frances. She played the English flute. In the parlor they sat, he and Frances and Mr. and Mrs. Lighty. He held his hat on his knees. She asked had he ever heard the tune of Glenlogie, then pursed her cheeks and blew and her fingers were quick at the stops. In the melody's Celtic windings, half sprightly, half melancholic, he watched her lips at the mouthpiece and fell in love with her embouchure.

Thornton and Frances courted three months and married.

New Lorns were soon begotten and grew faster than their parents could reckon.

Thornton's ploughshare dulled. The disks of his harrow dulled. With strops and stones he honed them. The strops thinned and snapped and the stones softened beyond usefulness. Other strops and stones followed. Thornton's aging draft horse began to stumble. An aging farmer in his furrows he shambled after. His farm had yielded scores of crop in its time: corn and potatoes and oats, fruit in smaller portions. It was a croft farm, little else.

One morning Thornton awoke to a quarter-century gone. The summery sprigs on his neck had whitened, their nap thickened: impassively his mirror showed him so. Surely he'd noticed before but it felt the first time.

At forty-three Frances took to deathbed. For weeks her cough had clattered in the house. She oughten have cleared the clothesline in that wet weather, scolded Thornton. Then she left him to the widower's immemorial grief. *Widower*, he said to himself, and repeated it every day for weeks.

In those days forty-three did not seem too young to die. It was no injustice. Still he stood betrayed by her absence. Time had cheated him some way, although taking account he found every year in place, no fewer than any man his age. Indeed, he'd had twenty-five with Frances. Her death had defied preference but didn't any death? So Thornton, griefstricken, concluded he owed the world and the rules of things no bitterness.

History is brisk. You are baffled to begin a story only someone else may close. These were the beginnings of Benjamin Lorn's.

2. (BENJAMIN — chief events of his youth in Perpetua & circumstances of departure)

Benjamin's earliest memory shows him his mother at the dining room window with water pitcher in hand counting out seconds after a blast of lightning. Small at table, his supperplate forgotten before him, he watches her watching on his behalf.

He's learned to pretend at numbers, seeing elders tick their fingers. So he lifts hands above his plate and starts. He doesn't know the order but pretending is comfort. Then comes noise like the ceiling ripping away. His water glass shakes.

"Thunder," says Mama. "Not to worry. Can't hurt you."

Lightning though is different.

We'll keep counting Mama and me till it's gone.

His first worded thoughts. One needn't know numbers to remember. But words, words are necessary.

Early on Benjamin saw fixity in the world. Daily came the dawn, nightly the dusk. Mornings Mama kissed him awake and there was bread to eat warm from her oven. Nightfall brought parlor hours and fire in the hearth. Out his window every day the boy saw vegetable patch, garden fence, the scorched mound of the refuse pile and, beyond, cornstalk seas of neighboring farms. Every stalk tall as a man, they massed themselves up to each dooryard. In town his father's store stood firmly at the corner of the square. The carved signboard had read their family name forever. Benjamin noticed no weathering in the painted letters for wear could not be clocked. On Sundays Perpetua's red brick church stood in place as always. It was eternally there, walls well mortared and granite cornerstone aglitter with feldspar and mica. The church steps were immovable when you trotted up them into the sanctuary and you knew that the high wooden steeple of the belltower stretched doubtless above, foul weather or clear.

Benjamin could note the turning of days, riffling of seasons, transits of sun and moon, but these told no loss. To the contrary they bore out order, recurrence, permanence. He could not have imagined what the blacked-in calendars of grownups betokened.

Evenings by the hearth, curled on the checkered chesterfield or stretched on warm hearthstones, Benjamin listened to a tale his grandpa told. Old Thornton Lorn lived in the house then. His mystic stride trailed glamour into every room. In that presence J.M. Lorn's halting movements spoke subtraction — the stolen leg sapped him of stature.

Beside the fire Grampa recounted the day in his youth when he beheld a circular rainbow. *Ya, a perfect ring with the blue heaven in its center!* He couldn't remember where the vision had come to him. Maybe aboardship when he'd first learned to walk, maybe above the wilds of Pennsylvania. *Can't say, can't say. But you see, what matters is the vision itself. What matters is I should see it in my mind's eye all the days after.* What mattered, Grampa insisted, was the thing he'd known beyond doubt ever since that moment: *My life would never close! The symbol guaranteed it!*

Every one of Benjamin's boyish drawings made use of the varicolored ring as his grandfather described it. For years that symbol was more than a figment of an old man's religious faith. It was the boy's own vision and its meaning was his.

Nature dubs the child immortal at birth — but she undoes her mistake. A summer night and the boy shook from a waking dream. A voice had told him he was going to die. He padded down the cold hallway in darkness. Woke Mama to tell what he'd heard. Beside her J.M. Lorn slept on without care (or was it in heavy resignation?). Harriet Lorn led the child back to bed. Sitting in the dark she dealt him the usual motherly tenderness. No use. The fear would not go. At last he drifted off to sleep his fear.

From then on Benjamin walked alert to the creaking of floors. Every evening the sunlight, instead of hiding under covers or going to sleep, gave out altogether. Benjamin learned to tot up the loss. Though morning brought new light, now it was just that: new. Not the same light and could never be.

From the Book of Ecclesiastes Benjamin learned that the living know they will die while the dead know nothing. *They have no more reward and even the memory of them is lost.* The churchhouse boomed with talk of blood, sacrifice, every man and woman's last retreat from the world. The pastor's words made the churchgoers cry aloud. Benjamin saw now. The gift once given would be taken back. You were mortal and mortals must pray.

Every Sunday night in church the benches were dragged about to make a square and as the voweled noise of a Singing erupted he would sit amid caustic harmonies.

> *Our life is ever on the wing,*
> *And death is ever nigh;*

The moment when our lives begin,
We all begin to die.

Soon birds in whirling chevrons brought home the close of passages in the boy's days. He understood Mama's marking time by flowers that bloomed and withered on the sill. And the harvest taught him. The hordes of corn blanched a yellowish white. Clattered when the wind moved over. Skeleton sea. Then the corn was cut and looking again Benjamin saw stubbled black fields. They broadened the horizon but now it was desolate, uncolored, and the snows fell.

See all nature fading, dying,
Silent, all things seem to mourn;
Life from vegetation flying,
Calls to mind the mould'ring urn.

His parents and fellow singers held the heavy songbooks open in their laps but seldom looked down. Their hands swung like pumphandles meant to work up from depths a fresh and bracing water.

Benjamin learned the hymns and took to singing the treble part with Mama and the wives, voice bright with belief. Across the squared pews he could catch his father's eye. Though John Manfred boomed bass with the singers around him, his eyes never gleamed to match Mama's. Mark the difference. Were belief and passion woman's domain? There was no doubting women knew of reckoning, grit, getting by, like men did — but unlike men they knew in a sinless sort of way. The fairer sex they were called. While men seemed sinners to the last. Men bashed, brooded, grudged, raged, and racked up hurts. How many times already had Benjamin watched Uly Turner, town inebriate, lope from rear of the church to sinners' bench, hair askew and waistcoat undone, grimacing sin? And how many whiskered farmers and cattlemen had stood in Lorn & Son for mended bootsoles or saddlehorn, splattering the spittoon and grunting oaths like pleasantries?

From the time he entered school Benjamin was made to wash for supper outside. This was his father's decree. On all but the bitterest frozen day he stood barechested with J.M. Lorn in the dooryard rear of the house. By turns they bent to splash and shiver at a basin of chill water. Mama and Grampa washed inside. "For their frailness," said his father. "But you and me are none so delicate. These hard bodies need cracking, they're shelled with sins." He demanded the boy enumerate each sin committed since last night's washup. By this penance Benjamin earned privilege to return indoors and partake of the meal.

I tossed rocks at a cow in the Edsburg pasture. I coveted Will Cummins's new jackknife. When the teacher said the prayer I thought other things.

Failing to name the day's trespasses he must stand in the weather till one returned to mind. He didn't know if his father would let him freeze. Didn't care to know. In the end, always, he longed to prove obedient.

Whenever Mama protested the regimen, as she did often enough, his father rebuked her. "Don't I stand freezing beside him? Don't I tell my sins too? A man repents to save his fellows same as himself. The boy need learn this."

"Once learned oughta serve, John."

Bonewhite and shirtless, shivering, J.M. Lorn swung the boy a hard grin. "Own soul's so clean she pities us."

Benjamin, sensible of his gender's curse, returned the grin. The custom continued. He'd learned to ledger each action and thought against its likely wickedness. Your soul will defy you except you tame it by will, discomfort, repentant shame. The heart, heart's wishes, are Iscariots. Women need not fret these things.

I took matches from the tinderbox and burned sticks behind the livery. I cussed in the schoolyard. I told Will Cummins maybe there's no Jesus and no Devil.

"Lord forgive my sinful boy and me," said J.M.

3. (THE PACKET)

Miss Harriet Bauer
Albia, Iowa
Kind Madam,
Some days ago I received from my longtime comrade Jasper Slea your letter inquiring about your brother's death at Camp Ford prison in Texas. It will I hope relieve you to learn that I know a little of the events relating to that misfortune. Since he served a different regiment entirely I was never familiar with Alfred Bauer. It was not therefore your brother's name that drew up my memory but rather your question "Can he have taken his own life as rumored?"

The sad day's events transpired at the very close of our imprisonment and of the war itself, which only sharpened their bitterness and thus burnt them deeper into memory. For a crude account I may tell you this: In January 1865 your brother, myself, and the near one and a half thousand like us having suffered capture in the swamps of Arkansas had for nine months endured imprisonment and abuse at the hands of our Rebel overlords. Many were sick in this time, other men died, the Camp being accoutered in just the lowliest way, and there being some six thousand prisoners altogether. Still other men attempted escape and if captured, as most of them were, met with merciless punishment by Lieutenant-Colonel Borders the Rebel commandant. In that New Year your brother with an accomplice undertook escape and was waylaid before gaining three mile's distance from the pickets. This was in the depths of a bitter January night. I and my hut-mates were bestirred by the guards' trumpet and rousing we discerned the noise of dogs in chase. Shortly thereupon the Rebel drumroll summoned every prisoner into line for rollcall. Standing forth we were counted by the guards while harking to the commotion in the woods of the Rebel pursuers and their hounds. Whispers circulated that two of our fellows had fled. To stem any conspiracy afoot our prison masters saw fit to keep us at rollcall. Thus we stood in our thin wrappings shivering to every man and awaited the outcome in the woods. For a term of perhaps an hour all grew quiet. Finally the hounds were heard again, and the hollering of guards, and these were followed by a succession of rapid shots, the dogs in uproar for a quarter hour after. Another single shot rang out, frightfully distinct as I remember, and still, very soon after, another. We remained in lines, more than six thousand, listening. No further shots were fired.

By and by the pursuers came in again, carrying in their midst their captured fugitive, one of our comrades, a bedraggled leftover of a man with one leg blown apart below the knee. That was the Rebels' pretty work. In their Camp Hospital such as it was they relieved him of this leg before dawn struck. The second fugitive we soon learned had dispatched himself rather than suffer capture. It was said he used a pistol obtained by stealth some time before from a tinker licensed to sell and trade to men let out in the woods for work detail. This was avouched by the second unfortunate escapee.

The fallen man was your brother Alfred Bauer of the 36th Iowa Infantry Company C. Though only some had known him, your *brother's fellow prisoners mourned him his ill destiny myself included. The good of it lay in considering him paroled to a better place than our pesthouse of a prison.*

I pray this gives you a fuller picture of your poor brother's demise, and by that may your grief be eased and not aggravated. If you should wish to learn something more whatever it be I hope you will think me your servant in the matter.

I send my late condolences.

> *Yours,*
> *Barrett Burnham,*
> *First Lieutenant 77th Ohio*
> *Infantry – Dayton, Ohio*

4.

Old Thornton, growing ever older, continued his talk of circular rainbows. But words warped. You heard a voice whose sap had run out.

Thornton Lorn's hands rattled, gray hair shook, and how brittled the bones that caged the birdlike life. "Help Grampa up the stairs," Mama said many a night. "Stay close behind and give him your hand on his back." A fit of coughing seized the old man. Hand cupped to watery mouth, he spent himself in shakes. When he'd caught wind again he spat in the fire and resumed talking. But the bright image had fizzled.

—*Do you see, boy? The symbol guaranteed it!*

No. We all shall tumble down the stairs, the bonecage break and let fly.

Soon Thornton marked the change in his listener and

ceased to tell the story. Grasps at immortality embarrassed him now.

Almost as soon as Benjamin stopped drawing circular rainbows early that autumn, he took to making a different shape. One day the boy was scratching in the margins of a letter his mother had received when Thornton came upon him.

"Mm," said the grandfather, stooping. "Will you be a reverend?"

Benjamin didn't look up. "A reverend?" He was pulling his mouth in concentration.

"Ya, to draw all those crosses."

Benjamin grunted a laugh. "Not crosses, Grampa. Look."

Thornton bent closer. The boy had hemmed the letter's news with lines of fence. From cross to cross they ran in doubles neatly parallel. He thought the boy had drawn the posts too tall but then he saw. "Ah. The wires, are they?"

At the copper-edged counter in Perpetua's Wabash Depot Benjamin had stood with his father, sometimes his mother, and watched Mr. Mueller, depot man, postal clerk, and operator, tapping signals into the wire by use of a trim lever key. The key made glottic clicking sounds and Mr. Mueller's green visor glistered as he canted his head to listen. His tapping formed no clear pattern but a body could speak to anyone in the country — even as far as California — by that method. Or so Benjamin had learned. It seemed pure conjuration. It offered wonder even grownups could not foreswear. The boy could think of no other thing with such a claim, whose magic would not die no matter how aged or wise a person got.

The humming wires followed King Street along Perpetua's town square and continued west to the track by the depot.

From there they trued themselves to the railroad. Standing in his father's store or at the depot platform Benjamin watched them bellying pole to pole and onward to distances unreckoned. Twice, three times a day the trains thundered through that way, to vanish at the narrow place on the horizon. It always left the wires swaying overhead, droning sorcery. "Wind makes em hum," his father told him, but Benjamin would not believe this. At heart he knew the sound to be voice of a secret energy. Already he felt eternity in the wires. He knew he might walk for hours and come nowhere nearer that pinpoint where those wires and all else disappeared.

One cool Saturday Thornton Lorn announced he was going to the depot to send a message. Would Benjamin care to come along?

Saturdays the Wabash was quiet, trains running scarcely at all. They found Mr. Mueller shuffling cards in his ticket window.

"Boy likes to draw the telegraph," said Thornton Lorn. "Might you show him some things, Ed?"

Mueller let his cards lie and Benjamin found himself led from the small passenger gallery through the glass-paned door stenciled AGENT and into the office. Drawers and cubbies rose to heights all about him stuffed with wonderful papers. Inkstamps and punchtools, cardfiles, luggage tags, signal lamps, and a pair of bronze scales watched him arcanely. A minute later he was sitting in the operator's chair. And there before him bolted to the desk lay the signal key, fabulous in shapely brass and coiled wire. The lever ended in a glossy disk the size of a silver dollar.

"What'll we send?" said Mueller, crouching behind.

Benjamin turned, at loss to answer. But his grandfather was already jotting a message to a friend Gavin Robley, away to see relations in Osceola. "Pick a word for him," he told the boy, "to say when he comes back."

Benjamin mused. "Just anything?"

"Anything Christian."

After some thought he chose Watermelons. So the message read:

> *Howdy Gavin. This from my grandson trying the wires.*
> *Tell him Watermelons upon your return. —Thornton*

"Ready?" said Mueller. Covering Benjamin's hand he guided it to the key.

Tap! tap! tap! tap! tap! tap!

The sprung action gave Benjamin much happiness, the lever surprisingly taut. Close in Benjamin's right ear Mueller was reading aloud while in his left came the brisk tattoo from the sounder box, a wonderful crackling.

Tap! tap! tap! tap!

And suddenly it was done.

"There she goes," said Mueller. "She's off."

The agent's hand came away but the boy's still hovered above the key. Benjamin was listening — for what he wasn't sure. Did he hope to hear a diminishing clatter as the message went forth, like a train? He looked up to find Mueller and his grandfather grinning.

"Well?" said Thornton.

But caution overcame the boy. He nodded at the men and made a smile but didn't mean it. Some unfledged part of him feared this day should serve for further lesson in the impermanence of magic. Had the wires carried his message or had they not? He must get proof before he could rejoice.

Gavin Robley was to be at Osceola for three more days. In the Lorn household the parlor clock turned torturous. The boy checked the one on the mantelpiece upstairs but it too had deigned to punish him. He would draw no telegraph wires to pass the time. He dithered about. Apparitions of circular rainbows converged at his heels. He wondered would anything ever win his belief again should the telegraph disappoint? He felt how absurd his suspicions were, what an elaborate fiction it would need for wires to be raised and people to mimic transmittal and receipt — but he demanded verification.

Finally it was Tuesday and Mr. Robley had come home. Benjamin alerted his grandfather at breakfast. Old Thornton glanced up forgetfully from the porridge he was stirring. "Oh Gavin? He'll call after church."

Which would mean four more days of purgatory. Intolerable.

The Robley home was four or five miles distant by the Hillcrest Highway, just over the narrow Chariton River. Benjamin set off that morning walking south through sunglare and dust. He trailed no stick and kicked no stone as he went. His motive had matured him already. Like a man he traveled bent upon destination.

He could feel the season in the air cooling and very still above the fields of corn and sorghum where the harvests had started. The country's summer gold was tarnished ochre now. The hay lay piled in enormous green-yellow mounds by the waysides but he was not tempted to climb them and play at balancing. He hurried along the road through the tinny babble of insects. He came to the Chariton and crossed the muddy current by a farmer's plank bridge. A footpath wound upward along tree-shaded banks to the small settlement of Dennis. He turned down a drive and stood before the Robley place.

He realized he'd never pursued what was fearful to him. Drawing his breath he mounted the porch steps determined to face the thing.

He knocked. He thought he heard a voice calling from within. He laid his cheek to the door. When the call came again he gripped the latch and stepped inside onto a looped brown rug and stood alone in the Robley foyer.

A pendulum flashed in the glass belly of a grandfather clock. From a pinecone newel post a banister ascended and curved behind a wall. Benjamin did not know the motions from here. He waited.

There came another call. Outside he'd guessed it a woman's voice originating deep within the house but now he knew it for a child's call from a neighboring room.

"Didya come in?"

He turned. A double doorframe led into a parlor on his right. He made to step that way just as a little girl skipped through and bumped against him. She gave a small gasp and backed off. She was in brown pinafore and barefooted. Red curls sprang about her face.

"Excuse me," he said. "Is Mister Robley at home?"

Her pink feet carried her in a curtsy-like hop. He'd outgrown those gestures himself — of bubbling energy, needless motion.

"You mean my grampa," she said.

"Is your grampa Gavin Robley?"

She retreated beneath the parlor lintel, glaring. She was scant more than a baby and had a child's fickleness of trust. He took her for an irritant in the way of his task. She lowered her eyes and plunged past him around the banister and up the stairs. The steps challenged her stride, knees caught in her skirt. She called ahead. "Grampa!"

Again Benjamin stood in the clock's noise. The pulse of the pendulum behind its glass seemed to challenge him and he nearly questioned the purpose of his errand now. But no, he was here. Then above he heard a descending tread. Old Mr. Robley appeared in the stairwell.

"Ah, the grandson Benjamin, is it?"

"Yessir. Hello."

The clock continued as Robley came down. This man had called on occasion at the Lorn home to summon Benjamin's grandfather to the society hall or solicit a match of chess. And like most men in Dennis and Perpetua he'd called frequently at Lorn & Son. He stopped at the foot of the stairs. He was in shirtsleeves. He had a wiry robust look. One hand gripped the banister and he waited.

But Benjamin was unsure of his own part.

They stood.

At last a click as the old man's jaw unlocked. "Ah, it's business brings you, I see."

"Yessir."

"That telegram, is it?"

The boy's hope welled. "Yessir. The telegram."

"I see. Hmm." Robley leaned his head as if to discern some falsity of motive. "Thought you'd come to call on my granddaughter Alma."

"No sir."

Robley buried a grin. He was tedious as the many old farmers Benjamin was bound to nod to about town, though the boy knew he was a miller.

"What age are you, Benjamin?"

"Seven, sir."

"Mm, well Alma's a bit younger."

This was sagely remarked and Benjamin bristled at the condescension, but "Yessir" was all he could reply.

Half up the stairway behind the old man the girl reappeared to sit in skirts on the steps. She'd found a dolly and was hugging it in the crook of one arm, thumb stoved in mouth and baby teeth gnawing. Robley noticed her.

"Alma, this is Benjamin Lorn. He's son of the man keeps the leathery in Perpetua. He's seven."

Alma considered him anew, fearless from her place on high and with her grandpa between. She withdrew her thumb. A thread of silver saliva drooped and broke. "How do you do."

Old Robley smiled. Benjamin blushed.

"How do you do."

It vexed him being pushed back to child-talk.

"Well, to the matter of that wire," said Gavin Robley. Stepping forth he crouched to level gray eyes on the boy. His hand came heavy on Benjamin's shoulder. Stale breath like Grampa Thornton's. Gravely he said, "Watermelons."

Benjamin breathed and felt Robley swatting his arm, old man chuckling pompously in his face. But no teasing could trouble him now.

Returning down the Robley drive toward the Chariton, Benjamin's steps were jaunty. Little Alma skipped at his heels. Some whim had permitted her to like her guest. Her feet were quickly dirtcaked.

"Wheresa waddlemelons?"

"No place," he said happily. "It was a message. Why, you like watermelons?" He was feeling generous toward her now.

"I like spittin' a seeds." She dropped her dolly in the drive.

He stopped to help her dust it off. "What's she called?"

"Avis. Like my auntie."

He held the doll ceremoniously before him. "There you are, Avis. All better."

He returned it to her and she took it with a stare. "Are you a daddy?"

He laughed at the scandalous notion. She joined in though she didn't seem to understand.

"Goodbye Alma Robley. Goodbye Avis."

At the end of the drive she stood hugging the limp thing, watching him go.

Benjamin fairly loped over the Chariton and down the highway toward home, mind ahum with mysteries, distances, the enigmatic beauty of electricity and its infinite reach. From the highway shoulders in both directions the low country coursed away in slopes and fields. His gaze roamed those expanses and he felt his first vastness wondering how men could keep at home while spaces opened all around.

Send! commanded the operators with a twitch of the hand — and flash it was done. Lightning could zoom through a wire. A soul could go anywhere.

5. (1887)

Recounting that day on this July afternoon many years later, Benjamin tells Alma Robley: "I never felt restless till then."

They're seated together in the shut parlor of her parents' house, bathed in late daylight. Benjamin is nearly twenty-four.

He says, "It's restlessness, you should know, makes me a traitor in my father's eyes."

"Are things so bad between you?" she asks.

"Yes. They won't improve. Not now."

"Can you be certain?"

"Afraid so." He wants no pretense about the matter. Best it

comes out clear from the start. He knows he needn't worry in telling her, for there's nothing demure about Alma, no fragile sensibility needing protection.

She's a peculiar creature, peculiarly pretty: loose red curls combed up and pinned off her neck. Tiny ears. A fair, near invisible downy fuzz along her jaw beneath the earlobes. Beauty of a gentle, pleasingly brittle kind — but some straight strength augments it. No daintiness there. All this carries plainly through her voice too, which is clear and bright and sweet.

"Do you like your tea?"

He swirls the remainder in his glass. "Delicious."

"Was in the sun since this morning."

"I can taste the very beams." He's gladdened to win her smile.

He asks may he pour her some. She declines without excuse and he thinks how he likes that directness.

She's wearing a viridian cotton dress and small jacket-top to match, its high collar frilly and peach colored. She smells of powder, which thrills him. He feels the warmth of privacy brimming between them clear to the parlor's picture rail and he's flooded with an unaccountable druglike sensation. He wonders if he's sitting altogether upright. How is it this girl throws him into such a wooze?

He unpockets his kerchief to dab at the sweat beneath his chin, around his collar. Why did he not wear a hat? Two undershirts but no hat only to arrive all but drenched after the walk from the station. Pressing the mother's hand to introduce himself, he'd had to beg use of a towel. Since seventeen he's been an awful perspirer. He was shown to the mudroom at the rear of the house where he blotted himself, fretful of his poor impression. *Sopping hog from Perpetua comes to call on your daughter.* How it smarts in any who wishes to author himself to feel thoroughly authored by others. All this before Alma came down to greet him.

"I must've been very small," she says, "that day at my grandfather's house. I always remembered the Lorn boy towering over me."

He smiles. She's a head shorter than him even now. Clasping her exquisite hand in this parlor half an hour ago he felt himself an ogre before her. His grip could enclose that hand twice round.

She asks further about his family and Benjamin does his best to describe them, thinking amid the awkwardness how it must be simpler for most people, this custom one uses to become known to another. Stiffly he tells of his father and grandfather, of his father's store, of his own employment at the telegraph and what treachery his father takes that to be. Then tells of the loss of his mother last year and how quickly her absence unkiltered the house. At this last Alma looks hurt somehow. She glances to the floor and slowly fans her hands across the green pleats of her skirts. Bones of birds in those hands, something in their motion amazes.

"And now you're going away West, you say?"

"Yes. Oregon. Washington."

They sit silent for a time. The house is very quiet, the sun at a steep slant through the window now.

"Oh look at the light," says Alma at last. "Would you like to walk out awhile?"

Down the porchsteps into purpling light. The built up heat of day stands cured across the sky, maroons and mauves. The hard sun that at noontime sends you scurrying for shade goes kidskin soft at evening and invites. It surprises Benjamin how this Sunday has hurried to a close. She consented to his visit last week by letter and a long six days crawled toward the date and now, already, the nearer country is gelled in darkness and their feet tread pale shadows.

Alma walks a pace ahead. Watching her, Benjamin cannot reckon whatever luck has brought him to this moment, stepping out in magical light with this Dennis girl so unlike other souls in Appanoose County. It fills him with a strange kind of joy, which he believes must be wonder.

A week ago he found himself beside her in a crowd of massive number on the public square at Centerville. It was July the Fourth and the happy mob had come "to make the welkin ring" as the *Daily Iowegian* implored. He'd never seen so many people in one place. There had been a grand parade that morning followed by Rev. Bartlett of Centerville's thundering recitation of the Declaration of Independence, then toasts beginning at noon led by the county's distinguished Union veterans, a free-for-all footrace around the square at three o'clock (First Prize $5.00), climbing of the greased pole at 3:45, a blind wheelbarrow race and sack race at half past four, and amid the gleeful havoc an all-day platform dance on the courthouse lawns in the heat of the square. At nightfall the celebrants waited in their thick numbers for the culminating fireworks display their paper had promised: "THE HEAVENS ABLAZE!", "JUPITER OUTDONE!"

Benjamin's parents had been married in Centerville on a July Fourth years before, a knowledge that raised the sting of his mother's absence. Not that he'd wish her to suffer his father anymore, only that he himself had never lost her. He was in a bitter temper. Benjamin's old schoolmate Will Cummins had coaxed him out early that afternoon, Benjamin irascible from the time they left Perpetua. But he liked Will's dependable gaiety. You could brood and grumble and never dent the fellow's charm. A good friend, to abide you being a bad one.

Will wanted to prowl the festivities for Gracie Carmichael. He'd dreamt of turning her about the grandstand under festoons of red-white-and-blue. You couldn't call Will Cummins debonair, not theatrical or cavalier — actually he was all but ordinary — but in his presence girls always smiled. His confidence in the goodly order of things made the order of things good. To Benjamin this was freakish, but never imagining that he himself could spark any girl's attention, let alone her smile, let alone her affection, he learned to make the most of standing by while Will set off lights in their eyes.

"Why, Miss Carmichael!"

Just a quarter hour on the square and Will had delivered them through the swarm. There she was, cooling off in the shade of a great chestnut tree. Though by odds she might have been there on another fellow's arm, she wasn't. And God be staggered, she was happy to see Will Cummins. Promptly she'd threaded her arm in his and off they went to climb the platform stairs into handholding music exactly as Will had dreamt it. Will did not gloat — he never did — and for that Benjamin was grateful.

Though Gracie Carmichael did not remember Benjamin when she pressed his hand, he had served her in his father's store some years before. Her family had lived a few months in Perpetua but soon moved on to Centerville. He didn't bother to recall himself, and couldn't begrudge her. Why remember a tubby puddingfaced fellow, once the puddingfaced young man in apron and garters who'd priced you a yardage of burlap? As it happened, Gracie had come to the square with a friend, though the latter girl was busy at dancing most the day.

Always feeling too big in his clothes, too heavy about the legs, Benjamin shied from dancing and today his low spirits were no encouragement. He spent half the afternoon listening to speeches. He found Captain Gedney's toast to the men of the 36th Infantry rousing: "We were their brothers unto death. And they are ours unto eternity!" Benjamin thought of his mother's brother as he raised his cider.

Later Will fetched him back. He said Gracie and friend awaited rear of the courthouse lawn, rumored best spot for the fireworks show. Benjamin weaved after him through elbows and coats, a blurring crush of bodies. Arriving at last, he watched Gracie's little blue gloves clasping at Will's shirtsleeves and his early bitterness returned in force. For the first time ever he resented his sure-footed, lucky friend. It was Will's world. Well, let him have it.

Gracie's friend was small in brown dress. A thread of sweat glittered along her reddish hairline. She put out her hand, not awaiting introduction, and Benjamin pressed it. He hardly heard her name, then the crowd shifted to jostle him out of place and behind. All the better. He would stand apart.

Soon Lucky Boy and Gracie were laughing and chattering with Gracie's friend. Benjamin couldn't figure how to insinuate himself amongst them. He knew the thunderhead he seemed amid their sunniness. So he dug the slim copper case from his waistcoat and plucked a cigarette and struck a match with his thumbnail. He was surprised a minute later to find Gracie's friend standing close eyeing him through his screen of smoke.

"You'd snuff that if I asked, wouldn't you?"

He coughed and hurriedly stubbed the cigarette upon his bootsole. He could feel himself coloring. What an oaf. His presence offended.

"Oh but I didn't ask."

"You—I thought you meant to ask—"

"I'd hardly the chance. You ought to give a person a chance. What if I was being theoretical?"

He knitted his brow, feeling very ugly. "You meant to get a theory first and then ask me to snuff it?"

The girl studied him. He thought she was making sport of him. His unsociableness flared and he turned from her, as seemed acceptable in that crowd. But he felt her gaze.

Darkness had fallen and a corn-yellow moon floated above the square. All stood watching for the chalky verticals of the first rockets to shoot from the courthouse cupola. It was then that she recalled herself to him. Gavin Robley was her grandfather she said.

"Of course, of course." He cringed to remember so late. "That was a long time ago." Cringed again at this hackneyed excuse.

A green light surged high, blossomed overhead in dazzling canopy. In the gleam the crowd's true numbers leapt forth, a figure even greater than Benjamin reckoned. That made her attentions the more generous. The first boom came after great delay, immense. He saw her flinch and then the light pulsed out. The crowd hummed pleasure.

"Sorry I didn't recollect," he called. "You were awfully little." But rockets were flying now to steal his voice. He couldn't know if she'd heard.

She was little even still, she came only to his chest. Remembering her the child who'd dropped her dolly in the road he felt a quick compulsion to protect her. The booms rolled above like a Titanic drum corps. Alma Robley ducked her head, hands at her ears. But she was smiling. He stood closer, a gesture of permission. That she might be guarded from that thunder if she wished. Yards overhead cinders sizzled and fell.

. The following morning Benjamin sat down to a sheet of letter paper:

> *Dear Alma Robley,*
> *No doubt it will surprise you to get this.*
> *Truth be told I surprise myself writing it.*
> *That you kept memory of me at all, let alone*
> *from many years ago, seems a wonder. But*
> *I'd flatter myself to think you may recall our*
> *meeting at the Fourth Festival beyond a day*
> *or two. This is why I write today…*

Now they walk out at the edge of the Robley farm, past the last cornrows and across the road to the raised lip of the millcreek. Half a mile off at the foot of a slope the Chariton flows under bowering trees, its lisping audible where they stand. They continue to talk in the ginger manner of the parlor — about the small sayable things that define them, the shapes of their lives so far.

Born in Appanoose Co.? Yes, both.

Parents born here? Yes, Benjamin's father was, though his mother came from Indiana. Alma's parents both from Illinois.

Like life in these parts? Both unsure. Sometimes yes, sometimes no (mustn't say too much too soon).

Intend to settle here? Both unsure (he cannot speak all his thoughts), but the world is large and enticing, agreed.

Religious? Neither terribly so though both attend church, she the Dale Church near the highway.

Ambitions in life? Of course, both, though neither can yet name them.

They stand. Farms and hills stretch dimly away, the country's limits lost to dark. In the western sky a spatter of pale stars. Against that, aglow by a nearer sourceless light, her profile appears to Benjamin a silhouette cut from silver.

"I want to thank you, Alma."

"Thank me? Whatever for?"

"Letting me call today." He does not shrug. He wants her to see he means it. "I was not at my best you see, on the square that night …"

"Oh, aren't you a guilty one. But sweet. No need to thank me."

"I want to though. I'd thank God or Fate if I happened to believe in either one but I'm afraid I don't. Not altogether." He listens to his own voice, hardly knowing what he'll say next. "And I allow that's a lack in me, it's what puts me in tempers like on the Fourth. Maybe that's hard to understand. But … you're standing right here, see? I can believe in *you* so you get my thanks."

The stars have started to shiver. In corn and pasture, crickets form a chorus. Benjamin wonders has he ever felt so peacefully alive? — his senses woven together and thrown like a net on the world. No sound, sight, scent escapes. Alma makes no move from this standing place of theirs, and he loves that about her.

From the depths of a long thought she says, "Don't believe in God? My!"

He loves this too, despite his agnostic mien, how this girl can find no reason to disbelieve.

"I'd like to say another thing, Alma."

"Of course."

"It seems to me that you and I … We seem, don't we, like we could be great friends? And I want you to know why I say this now. Why I don't care to wait and say it later." Suddenly he understands himself. He knows what he couldn't have known just hours ago riding the cars from Perpetua.

"Yes Benjamin?"

"When I leave here, Alma, it's for far away. They say there's good work out there, good wages, and lots of country to be wired, and I don't know how long till I come back or if I'll ever come back to stay." In absence of a hat to fondle his hands are playing at his jacket cuffs. "Alma, I want to know if I may write to you."

She stands veiled in darkness now, but he can just make out her mild mouth and chin. She's looking at him.

"If you'll have me," he says, "for a correspondent. A friend in words and thoughts at least."

"Is that treachery to your father? That you're going."

"Yes. And I'll tell you plain, I break a vow to my mother too."

"You told her you'd stay?"

"Yes. She urged it of me. To stay and tend to my father's store like he always wished. She didn't want to die knowing things were bad between us. I said I'd do what she wanted. And I've done it for a time — this whole year matter of fact. Now I just can't anymore. There, I've told you. Will you think me a traitor?"

"You meant your promise?"

"Of course. She was in deathbed. I wouldn't lie to her."

With a rustle her glance breaks away. "Something's changed for you then, since she died? Something makes you feel you have to go?"

"Indeed."

He falls silent. He doesn't mean to evade. He will tell her if she wants to know. He will tell her the sort of man his father is. But she doesn't ask.

"I go and it's treachery. I'm glad you know it now. And I

hope you don't fear me for it. I may be many … regrettable things but I'm not dishonest." And now he feels more sorrow than bitterness to add: "But I cannot stay."

6. (THE PACKET)

Dear Miss Bauer,

You have me right. I am the same Woodson who served in Iowa's 36th Infantry. It does seem a wonder you'd send for word of me clear to New York, even being unsure if I am the one you seek, while there are likely yet men surviving in Appanoose whom you might more readily query. Nevertheless, I won't have your troubles be for naught.

I ought to let you know from the first that I kept no careful records from the war. I have in truth endeavored to leave most of it forgotten. We in the Infantry did our part for all it was worth, which to me appears very little. But I nurse no anger about it. Moreover, I have lived these twenty years in the east, maintaining but thinnest of ties to Appanoose and Wayne Counties or to Trillium. After the war I never felt at home in that town and left the place within a year of my return from the horrid prison in Dixie. Folks in Trillium as you likely know were never Unionists. This made for unhappy living after the war. I was one of many to leave. Today I am surprised to think we ever raised a soldier there at all. But yes, once we'd come home they routed us. And during the war did we not route the so-called Rebels much the same? These matters of home, history, ownership, honor, loyalty, look the more absurd as the years draw on. Do we fight for matters so immaterial? Or do we seek pretext for fighting which our natures would provoke of us anyhow? We did not fight to free the

negro, as many a lad among us believed. No, that was done by chance
— and mainly to weaken the Rebels.

But forgive me, these are not your questions. As to those, I will
answer the first that, no, I did not know your brother Alfred Bauer.
We were in different companies, myself in Company I, first as private
and later as orderly under Capt. Gedney. Alfred Bauer's death
however I do remember. No doubt many a survivor of Camp Ford
does. Are you yet in correspondence with any others?

Seeing as you have the main points of that night's events in hand
already, I will not retrace them but only add that this failed escape
was to me most disheartening once I laid eyes upon the recaptured
man, a Pvt. Lorn of your brother's company. This man was
something of a roughscruff, a rabblerouser. Though I was spared
interaction with him I knew him from my first months in the 36th, as
did most the Appanoose men, for a principal instigator of the riot at
Keokuk before the regiment embarked downriver to Dixie. That later
night in Texas the Rebel guards dragged him back to the stockade
with one leg blasted, and while noting the fellow's broken state I yet
pitied his dead chum much the more, deeming it likely how this devil-
may-care Lorn had led that other to early doom but weeks before we
might all be granted freedom (the fighting was almost at its close).

The war, you see, taught me of little but its own senselessness. I
am now sworn to lifelong neutrality.

I regret how little I've furnished you in this. Still I send it in
hopes that your pains in reaching me should not come to nothing.

> *Sincerely,*
> *Isaac Woodson,*
> *New York*

7.

In milder seasons while Benjamin was still a boy there came to Perpetua and Centerville itinerants of every stripe: magicians, thespians, jugglers, snake oilers or snake handlers, boxers or sword swallowers or traveling Turks. They would arrive afoot, by wagon, maybe trailing a team of sad-necked burros, and could be counted upon to number at least five individuals and three or four troupes in fall, twice that in summer. So Perpetua was granted amusements, medicinal anodynes, or instructions in matters eternal — and certain spectacles mingled all these in one. A Perpetua Meeting was always such an event.

Twice each year the white tents billowed up on the edge of town. Beneath the vast canopies ululations arose as everyday Perpetuans went off in trances, young children muttered in tongues, and souls were scoured clean. These Meetings drew everyone in town. People came from Albia, Iconium, and Unionville too. Even the tottering aged and shut-ins would venture out, maybe the first time in the year, on chance of being mended. The atheist and agnostic also came, if only for the thunderous Singings, or to gawk at mildmannered housewives in Pentecost rending garments and tearing at their loosened hair. Snakes were brought forth from burlap sacks to writhe and snap in the dusty floor till men of God made them glassy-eyed and docile as worms.

Nightly for a week the people would unfasten themselves in shouting and song and then resume their orderly lives redeemed. The last prayer said and last hymn sung, the tents

— come to seem very permanent for housing so much spirit — would be struck of an afternoon, leaving pastures shorn to perfect circles of bald earth.

During one of Benjamin's boyhood summers a blind speechmaker arrived in Perpetua following that season's Meeting. A lean man, furrow-faced, he wore a beaver top hat. Frayed sleeves hung high on his wrists. He carried no baggage save a slack duffel in which angular items jutted and clanked mysteriously. From the Wabash Depot he wavered forth along Chariton Street to the square. Door to door he inquired if he might post notice of a speech. A long cane swept before him.

Benjamin watched the man from a window of Lorn & Son with the tidy shelves behind him chockablock in talc and leather oils, cheekstraps and cavessons. The blind man came past along the boarded walk to the shop's door. The bells jangled as he came in. He called out greeting and shut the door and stood listening.

Benjamin hung back in his aisle. He watched the man's strange eyes. The sealed lids twitched.

"I say hello," the blind man called again. His cane arced and tapped and his thin shoes went soundlessly over the floor for two or three paces. He stopped in the middle of the store. Inside his duffel something scraped and settled.

Benjamin cinched his breath. He'd practiced piping greetings to customers all morning but was dumb now. His father had gone next door to see the cabinet maker Major Farrows.

The blind man stood waiting, head tipped back and shut lids astir, membranes more of hearing than sight.

Finally he pivoted and walked to the door — but stopped as his hand met the latch and said, "Needn't fear a sightless man, son," then turned to show Benjamin his face. A dollop of flesh drooped from the bony nose. The gaunt head swayed.

In fortitude Benjamin said, "I didn't."

"What didn't you, boy?"

"Didn't fear you."

"Oh, but didn't answer either."

Benjamin shrugged defensively, then felt foolish for it.

"Is't thy pa runs the store, boy?"

"Yes."

"And has hopes you'll take after'm does he?"

Benjamin almost shrugged again but he'd learned better. He was silent.

"Beware the shopkeep's shuttered soul, boy. Beware the pencil behind the ear."

A red tongue wormed at the mouth's corner and then in brisk patter the blind man began to pour forth.

"Tabulation calculation incrustation oh but so it goes and all the time we know these ledgered lives be Lethian yea we do mine friend because our world is other than this is it not? is it not? oh we are but guests of ancient time."

These words pooled darkly above Benjamin's head. The voice had diminished to a breathless drone before the blind man stopped. Benjamin watched the thin shoulders heaving in their ill-fitted coat. Still the haggard nose was nosing the air.

"Well, listen young prodigal. I'm to make a speech come eventide on the morrow. I'd hoped to beg a little of thy pa, see if t'wouldn't please'm to post a notice here. Will you take it and let'm have it?"

"Yessir."

The blind man held forth a tube of paper. Stepping to receive it, Benjamin caught whiff of the fellow's reek. His nails were a thorny yellow.

The notice was no mere handscratch but a proper broadsheet in bold lettering. Benjamin stood reading as the blind man shuffled out.

> **TO TRANSPIRE UPON TOMORROW'S EVE:**
> **A SPEECHMAKING BY ONE WELL-PRACTISED IN THE ART.**
> **SUBJECTS TO INCLUDE:**
> the imbedded questions of existence; matters of faith in time of science; man's self-augury and other squandered propensities; the alembic qualities of mind; the soul's locomotion versus locomotive industry; alliterative soothsaying; epistemic epigrammatizing; and telling of the times.
> **THIS AND MORE COMMENCING UNEQUIVOCALLY COME DUSK IN THE BARE PLACE WHERE THE REVIVAL TENTS STOOD.**

The boy still had the notice unscrolled when his father returned. John Manfred came thumping crutchwise over the floorboards.

"What'd that roustabout say to you?"

"Who?"

"The babble talker."

"The blind man?"

"Do you mean to answer me or not? Blind. Huhn. He pilfer anything?"

"Left this is all."

His father snatched the notice.

"Will you post it, Pa?"

"Who's asking, boy? You or he?"

"Him, father. I never saw him before now."

"Oh no? Well, he sees everybody. Some sort of doomsayer, knows everyone everything. Pshaw."

Benjamin didn't understand. He stared at his father's big

fingers crumpling the edge of the notice. J.M. Lorn grimaced down his spectacles at the words.

"Came nextdoor just now that beggar, wavin his cane like to be blind as a whipsnake, stinkin brimstone, and gets to gibberin at Major Farrows and me, his tongue droppin half out his jaw. Well he kept spittin and I say I'll be goin now and then he stops and takes awful pains to listen to me pass. Even puts out a hand to keep me. Looks at me with those eyes shut closed as can't fix a glarin thing and says 'I know you sir.' Well do you now, I say. 'Why yes,' he says, 'I've just parlayed with thy boy. And you sir were in the War of the Rebellion were you not? Aye, and myself the same. Maynard Rifle took my sight. Percussion powder blasted my eyes away. Yes, but I need no eyeballs to know another soldier when near one.'"

The father's stare gripped the boy.

"You tell any dirtcaked stranger of your pa, Benjamin?"

"No, father. I don't. I wouldn't, I mean."

The notice fell from J.M.'s hand. It slid to the floor and skated weightlessly beneath the bootshelf, but his stare did not break. Benjamin watched the paper but didn't move after it. To move could be folly when J.M. Lorn's eyes had this commanding glaze.

"You mind your business, boy."

"Yessir."

"You keep private matters private."

"Of course, father."

J.M. nodded, his jaw working slowly. "Don't you noise your father's affairs anywhere."

Years later Benjamin would recall this admonishment, wondering what his father could have meant. Didn't he know that his boy knew nothing of his private past?

"Yes, father."

"Now get down and get that paper."

"Yessir. Here it is, father."

J.M. took the notice and crutched himself to the counter. "*Parlayed*. With *thy* boy. What hogwash did that lunatic *parlay* you with, Benjamin?"

Benjamin was twanging with guilt though he didn't know why. "You say he's a beggar?"

"You mean to answer me or not, boy?"

"Yessir. He talked some rhymes was all. I couldn't make him out."

"But you saw he kept his devil fingers off these shelves, yes?"

"Yessir."

"I'll not be pilfered, Benjamin."

"No sir."

"Nor will you be. It's your honor too in these goods. You share the name on that sign. Say it now. Nor will you be pilfered."

"Yessir. Nor will I be pilfered."

He watched his father wad up the blind man's notice and drop it in the pail.

Next night at supper Benjamin asked his father, "You suppose the speechmaker travels most the country?"

Out the window the sky was a paling blue above the corn. Light slanted through the glass to fall upon the table in watered tones. His father's face looked waxen, every feature overcarved. His lenses winced and flashed.

"Speechmaker?"

"Yes, in the store yesterday."

"Oh. If you mean does he have a proper home, I'm sure he doesn't."

"Does he want a home, you think?"

His father had bent to his plate gnawing a cob. He came away licking at kernels clinging to his lips. "Want a home? What's this ingratitude, boy? Shall I believe you do not *want* the home you live in? You'd as happily make a bed in dirt as the warm blankets you've kept to since before you could crawl?"

Often his father's look would take this darting gloomful cast and the boy would scent rebuke. He might not gather why his father rebuked him but would nonetheless sit silent, rebuked as expected. He did so now.

His mother, beside him, touched his arm. She was smiling down at him. "I'd wager he goes about the country coast to coast." Her voice was a golden softness like her hair. "They roam all over usually, this blind man and his kind."

"They're entertainment folk," said old Thornton Lorn. "I once knew a monologist had been everyplace you could think. Chicago, Saint Louis, the capital Washington, San Francisco, even on up into Canada. Could say any great book by memory almost. Why, he—"

"Men like these," said his father uncollaring his napkin, "this blind liar and his like, they sleep in dirt and beg two cents for every bit of jerky their minds can spit out."

"Liar?" said Benjamin.

His father nodded cruelly. "That man was in no army. And I'd wager against it bein powder blinded him. If blind he is. Someone poured whiskey in his eyes more like."

"John. Such roughtalk."

J.M. roared. "Better the boy hear that than hold to illusions, Harriet!"

He was reaching for his crutch where it leaned at the wall.

He sent it falling and it clattered under the table out of grasp. His shouted oath shuddered the dinnerware.

Benjamin had pushed out his chair and was already crabwise beneath the table. Down there his father's leg bent from his seat, lean and staunch. Next to the knee his stump bulged the blue houndstooth of the tablecloth. Dutifully Benjamin retrieved the crutch, busy preserving the image of Mama's smile. Her smile made him feel a kind of invincibility.

J.M. Lorn grunted and looked away as the boy passed him the crutch.

Come twilight Benjamin stood on the big disk of bare earth in a pasture at the edge of town. A number of Perpetuans had gathered, twenty or more, men and women. They stood about with arms or ankles crossed. Some teethed upon long sprigs of grass.

The blind man took stance at their center. He wore the same ill-tailored suit as yesterday. To the boy's eyes he did look a beggar now.

Above the blind man, demurely magnificent, domed the Perpetua sky. Its colors were letting loose. Pasture and speechmaker were tinged a bluish gold. *And yet,* thought Benjamin, *he won't see the glory there.*

The speechmaker had drawn from his duffel a cuspidor of dented bronze. This he'd placed carefully in the dirt at his side, and now with chest thrust forth he began exhorting and waving his arms.

"We stand at this place cause here did God His Unreckonable Self with huge and scrupulous broom ascour the field down to earth — that for weeks to come shalt every instinct of propagation lay razed from this soil where blooded sins have spilt and scattered round like seed."

At intervals, as though roused to froth by a special pungency in his words, the speechmaker jerked his head aside and spat with an air of hard punctuation at the cuspidor.

Benjamin heeded the speech as best he could though the better part of it flurried past him. Endless journeying had burdened this fellow with a message, clearly. It was no message like what the boy heard in church.

"The rotted cob will blast its wholesome brother and whom I pray thee will mulch and ripen the kernel to come? Oh beware thy fears and loathings yea for in strife to gain of something other thou drawest the first thing nigh."

He hocked and the cuspidor chimed.

"Our saints beheaded did smile upon that martyrdom all their days but lo thou shalt see them in statuary ever after and they shalt hold thee fast with grim and rueful eyes and yea those stones tell true."

Again he hocked.

"Loves grow of strange desires friends and it may be thine countersoul would quarter thee close and ah this be wonder and yea its torments are the beauties of the earth."

The land grew dark. Fireflies arrived to spiral about the speechmaker in differing flights. *Those also he will not see.*

By and by the listeners began to disperse. Each before going dropped a coin or two in the blind man's hat. Benjamin remained among the last but the dark drawing down meant risk of a scolding once home. He was sorry to go without payment but he hadn't thought to bring any. He crept away feeling himself a cheat, and passing among the lit windows of the houses on Church Street he could still hear the blind man's voice ringing from the pasture. It followed him as he climbed the porchsteps. Then he closed the door after him and realized the voice was in his mind.

He lay awake with a candle that night, fidgety, following dashes and dots in his book and tapping out fervid messages. It was a telegraphy manual the operator Mr. Mueller had lent him. His fingers were constantly tapping — at desktop, at supper table, at church pew. Day or night the telegraph's electric tendrils clasped his thoughts. The bewitching science of wires. Ohm's Law, that fundamental of electromagnetism, discovered in the manual's scientific preface:

ENERGY = VOLTAGE = ELECTRICAL CURRENT X RESISTANCE

The law scarcely made sense but he felt elegant secrets in its brevity. Resistance would become a watchword in years ahead, for Benjamin's father wished to pour his own desires into the boy. As J.M. Lorn saw it, the son's destiny was doubtless. It had been etched in their proud signboard for years. But Benjamin's thoughts roamed, hands jittering at his imaginary key. *Dit, dah, dit, dah.* He didn't bother to wonder where his stuttering messages flew. The key was the knocker upon a door. He was dreaming of unknown country as he rapped at that portal. Already he yearned to travel.

In this night's strange ardency Benjamin felt his body rising to his hand. Then he himself became the key his fingers coupled and he was drumming deep a code he'd never yet discovered, frantic on his back at frequency with the stars that twitched and glimmered on the windowglass above. Who ever could have told him how a child may wire his limbs to infinite space? — what journeys enjoy out there?

J.M. Lorn groaned in the parents' bedroom down the hall. The boy heard him up and thumping his crutch. Often at night the stump would smart. Benjamin snuffed the candle and feigned sleep as the father klok-kloked past his door.

That man's compass was broken. In the limits of a dark house he jabbed and staggered. Had he ever once felt longing for a vaster country?

8. (TEXAS, 1865)

It stinks of meat. It drones of flies.

Too many in Camp and too many in hospital. He lies soaking his cot, a paltry tourniquet cinching thigh below the groin and lower down the leg a spill of red and black and bone. Some moments it bloats to sausage and some it shrivels, his vision going furry his neck lolling loose and the head very heavy like someone sliced the tendons.

They'll make him wait. Hoping he'll drain just dribble away through their weak knot at the thigh into puddling Union stuff on the raw floor. Their blue-bellied pig neatly slit and fit to empty while they watch.

A guard stands by. Hell for? Does he look to leap up and run?

Count yerself lucky, advises Guard, a boy at best. Pink cheeks no whiskers yet and his cap set jaunty. Dogs hadn't gotcha ol' Chilicothe's boys'd of shot ya down.

Did too, he groans, near unintelligible. Gave me dog and bullet both.

Words slur away in an animal garble.

That leg'll go but yer here. That's lucky.

Chilicothe the devil. How that name was bandied in Camp for

men of blue he'd hunted and shot in wood and swamp beyond the pickets. Chilicothe sped the dogs before him each cur kept starved in Tyler and trained upon no game but man so they knew the scent and taste and hungered to have at it.

From his cot he sees the beasts again how they hurtled down the thicket hardly touching earth at all four to six at first and then a second wave of equal number they broke the bracken and swarmed him with their teeth. Snarling man-eaters rabid at his wound while Chilicothe through the woods behind came slow with gun barrel smoking. Expert tracker. Was said he could out-Indian Indians — and here was proof of that sharpness. Seemed several minutes before the dogs were called back. By then, under their teeth, he thought them his death. At the rifle's report they scattered. He waited heaped in bloodied leaves to be collected or finished off.

And Alfred bleeding in leaves back in the shadows over the ridge, what of him? Was he finished?

They scooped up J.M. and dragged him back alone. In that J.M. had answer.

Private Lorn, goddamn. In comes the surgeon in soiled butcher's white. Goddamn, you've given a hellfire's try, ain't you son?

He tries to answer. Only gurgles come.

And now everything's on edge and twirling, a stained white sheet in a billow and his parts out dangling as he's carried ...

Come sight again it's the surgeon's whiskers dark spikes like

boar's hair flaring in whale oil glare and then the sound of steel
the swish and chime of blades. And light comes spoking off
those knives — it sticks the light like glue in his eyes — and
Surgeon's mouth whiskered in grimace or grin with yellowed
teeth cropping from bottom lip the lip all crackled does he bite
it while he saws while he severs man from himself upon a table?

Oh you'll do, says Surgeon's mouth, and it's a smile after all but
lip closes quick and he turns that toadsticker in hand and goes
to work and there's noise in somebody's throat the throat going
K-K-K-K-K like a spigot let to flow…

9.

At school Benjamin studied maps of America showing territories almost too many to count. They spread to the ocean in the West. Their dark edges met in fascinating geometries, each colored piece cluttered with names, varicose rivers.

The boy could locate his own Iowa pictured in yellow or pink. Always the wobbling hems of the Missouri and Mississippi sewed it in place. His eyes explored the centimeter-thin area below Des Moines. That smallness of scale became vastness when he walked outdoors — hard to grasp a nation's immensities — and was there anyplace in the world as big as America? As ever he watched the wires soaring pole to pole. To think they linked the principalities of the globe.

He became a regular expert in the Telegraphic Alphabet. Via mail order from a Kansas City bookdealer, with help of his mother's purse, he procured a different volume called MODERN PRACTICE OF THE ELECTRIC TELEGRAPH, published years earlier by F.L. Pope, a famous telegraph engineer according to Mr. Mueller who'd recommended the book highly. The Pope manual's elaborate technical illustrations were a treasure. Benjamin took pains to keep the pages unsoiled and corners sharp.

About this time he made a practice of composing coded messages and dropping them about the house. Found upon sideboard or between pantry jars these bullets and slashes were riddles to his elders, and Benjamin would be called upon to decipher.

His father was first to sour of the game — his discoveries soon went straight to the rubbish can. Two or three times Benjamin retrieved them and tried anew, but finally came to see the sabotage and quit baiting the man. Meanwhile the boy's mother and grandpa indulged him. Each would sit to watch as he changed his glyphs into layman's letters.

Benjamin cherished most these moments with Harriet Lorn. Decoding on her behalf he could keep her at his side, curling close. Bath powder, rosewater, cake soap: her glorious smells engrossed him. He would slow his hand and feign consideration of a word. She troubled him with deep and primitive joy.

His missives were strange. Though he'd authored them he couldn't account for them.

> *Paper is wood, water is air, and a boy is*
> *neither and also more*
>
> *Should they climb to nowhere, the steps of a*
> *stairway are always beauteous*
>
> *Yesterday is tomorrow, what shall today be*
> *before it's done?*

"What ideas!" said Mama. "Are you a poet?" She kissed his hair and a flood of warmth colored him to the ears. How could a person be newly beautiful each time you looked upon her?

Stay, you moments of nearness.

Telegraphy became an eccentric brilliance in Benjamin. To the Pope manual and other guides and histories he applied an ardor unmatched in his readings of different subjects. He was a middling student at school. This rankled his father and grandpa, but his mother saw his diligence. For his fourteenth birthday she funded him a subscription to THE TELEGRAPHER. The kindness would martyrize her.

Saturdays Benjamin was to man the counter in Lorn & Son. His father came in one week to discover him reading. The crutch swung, hacking the magazine away.

"Are you any use, you dreamin whelp?"

Benjamin could remember himself, no more than four, going one day to Mama's pantry to discover a fleshy black thing clinging to the wall. He touched it and it scurried. He shivered. Was this splayed thing one of God's creatures? He went to ask J.M. Lorn. A minute later he watched the man smash the spider with his crutch.

Now he watched the magazine flutter down and drew throbbing knuckles to his chest.

Harriet Lorn suffered her husband's rebuke. The crutch beat the floor as he stalked their bedroom.

"You coax illusions, woman!"

In bed down the hall, taut beneath blankets, Benjamin listened. As wife Mama never argued.

"He makes believe talent of distraction and do you curtail it? Why no, you goad it on! Dammit woman, do you think?"

In later blackness the boy awoke to the squeal of the doorlatch. His mother slipped through the room to his bed and drew back the covers and lay down in her nightshift beside him.

"Haven't you slept?" Her whisper boomed hot in his ear.

He lied that he hadn't. It made him guilty to know the punishment she'd taken. The lie won him her tight embrace. Again came breath in rich static against his ear. "My sweethearted boy."

Benjamin resolved to quit his father. Next day he went alone to the Wabash Depot and offered Mr. Mueller his help.

To J.M. Lorn this was audacious betrayal. The store sign mocked him in absence of his son. He could have forced the boy's return but didn't. Better to be shed of one so feeble in character — J.M. would have Benjamin see this. And if the boy's mother would support such disloyalty, then J.M. would mete out — if not punishment — a pointed counterstroke. Now while washing for supper in the frigid dooryard behind the house, Benjamin must not only say his sins but add in mantra four times over, "I betray my father."

Benjamin touches his shoulder where it slopes to leave a slackness in his shirts, and remembers his father's violence. That mantra seemed too much at last. One night after J.M. berated his wife concerning the boy, Benjamin turned defiantly dumb.

"You'll not say what I tell you?"

"No sir."

He remembers the man leaning away from the crutch, the crutch-tip leaping from pebbled dirt where the chickens scratched — then splintering heat falling like an axe at his numbness as he flinched and turned.

"Father!"

And the father's red eyes as Benjamin wheeled to accuse him.

"Agh! Father my shoulder's broke!"

But it was the collarbone — and fractured, not shattered, which seemed, in that senselessness, lucky.

Mama nursed him with horrified love. Things went hard between her and his father after that. They spoke shortly and seldom and their eyes would not meet at table. A new chill of danger hung in the house.

He'd not understood his father's fury till then, but saw that he must scuttle like a spider now. The man's shadow would not fall to catch him.

10.

Benjamin swept the trodden floors of the station house. He straightened and ordered the stamps, parcels, and forms at the agent's window. Mainly he lurked at the signal desk where veiled in mindless abstraction Mr. Mueller received transmissions and tapped out others in turn. At Mueller's feet the ribbons of coded paper lay unspooled from the tape drive in heaps like tangled snakes. He hardly ever read them, taking most signals by ear, pencil transcribing as the sounder clicked its crazed rhythms. Because it transmitted too softly at times he'd jury-rigged an empty tobacco canister for amplification. A Pony Sounder he called it.

To Benjamin, though he knew his code, the wire was a garble, all rattle and snap with but the slightest modulation. At best he could hear a kind of far off clip-clop and this made him think of the horse messengers once relied upon to carry, through all weather and terrain, the dispatches that now sang pole to pole across mountains or cable to cable under oceans in matter of moments. He read somewhere that Englishmen were telegraphing Bombay — and receiving answer — in little above four minutes.

What the boy got from his books was augmented by Mr.

Mueller's knowledge. The agent, so thoroughly a man of his trade, was a natural teacher.

"Benjamin, do you know 'The Victory'?"

Benjamin admitted he didn't. He watched Mueller's gaze drift upward as if to draw down thoughts hung in the dusty rafters. Slowly, recalling, Mueller said, "One morning he made him a slender wire. As an artist's vision took form and life. While he drew from heaven the strange, fierce fire. That reddens the edge of the midnight storm. And he carried it over the mountain's crest. And dropped it into the ocean's breast. And science proclaimed, from shore to shore, that time and space ruled man no more."

He said they were lines from a poem in honor of Samuel Morse. By then Benjamin knew well of Morse — and Morse's colleague Alfred Vail. The words of their first historic transmission hung like a pennant in his imagination.

A PATIENT WAITER IS NO LOSER

They sent the message across a New Jersey factory loft using a spiraled copper wire two miles long. Parts of the wire had come from hat factories in New York. Their later transmission from Washington to Baltimore was more famous — and Biblical:

WHAT HATH GOD WROUGHT!

But Benjamin had never heard this poem. He asked Mueller to say it again.

"I'll write it out for you," said Mueller. "Now see Mrs. Main gets her wire, will you."

The boy tucked message in pocket and hastened along on his errand.

Later Mueller did write out the poem as promised. Benjamin folded the paper carefully and tucked it into his watch pocket. He would carry it in that place for years.

. . .

Edwin Mueller was not convivial or garrulous but was always kind. He was a widower and father of two grown sons who did not care to become railroad men. They knew telegraphy of course, and would work in the Wabash from time to time when their father and his half-retired predecessor Mr. Lyle were both indisposed — but the Mueller boys had found their talents elsewhere. They had jointly opened a hardware store in Buxton, a coal town to the north populated entirely by Swedish and negro miners. They'd made it a flourishing concern. They even bade their father quit the Depot and let them fund him a life of leisure. This prospect he amiably refused more than once. All this was known in Perpetua. Though Edwin Mueller was just forty it was taken for granted that he would clerk the Wabash ticket window, tag the luggage, rehearse cordialities with passengers in the woodpaneled waiting room, and operate the telegraph till eternal glories called him home.

He was a trim, genteel man. In all aspects of his profession he prized courtesy and civilizing restraint. He was scrupulous in dress as much as manner. His cuffs and collars were always impeccable and he cleaned his spectacles several times each day with a pale blue handkerchief shaken from his pocket, which he would restore to a neat rectangle before stowing it away again. Nothing could ruffle him, and it seemed to Benjamin that nothing lay beyond his abilities. Courtliness, decorum, and breadth of knowledge lent the agent an entrancing air. Not that Mueller seemed more than human. Rather, he had a skill so ingrained, so well expressed in every undertaking, that it substituted for the more particular personality he seemed to lack. He was the kind of operator they called First Rate and that was the *what* and *whom* of him. But if Mueller was always

71

measured, never effusive, never fond, still he had no heir among his sons, and he seemed pleased to find something of the kind in Benjamin.

In the dank heights at one end of the Depot atop a narrow set of stairs ascending from the luggage gallery, there was a loft with a pallet bed, a grimed windowpane, and an ancient dressing trunk with shaving mirror propped atop it. Time to time Mueller would sleep the night up there, usually in order to meet a belated train but sometimes for reasons less obvious and maybe more personal. He seemed on some nights plain unable to leave the building. A kind of lonesome peace kept him. He stretched himself out in darkness neighbor to the flies nesting in the eaves, while pieces of luggage and freight stood rowed like sleeping orphans in the open room below. True men of the railroad, Benjamin understood, dwell and dream alone amid other men's property. Possessionless, unfamilied, they are yet glad. Were they born to this even temper though, or was it a blessing come of their labors? Only time could teach Benjamin his answer (the answer could be only his, it differed for every man).

Over and above his countless duties as station agent, Mueller was Wire Chief, Night Chief, Superintendent, Batteryman and even Lineman which sometimes meant Pole Climber. It fell to him to mend breaks, tend to the green-caked grove cell batteries oozing in the musty cabinet below the signal desk, and locate the cause of any "Escape," or dip in voltage making for poor connection. But amid these duties he did not fail to bait his young assistant. Working for Mueller, Benjamin only grew in the conviction that the telegraph was a chimerical business.

"Do you know, Benjamin, what Samuel Morse's main achievement was?"

The boy was up on a stepladder cleaning an oil lamp. He thought a moment. "To transmit intelligence with electricity," he said. His books put it this way.

"Well, yes. That was achievement, most certain. What I meant to ask is, can you say what he discerned that made it possible to send messages using a wire?"

The boy stood staring from his perch, blank, shy to venture again.

Mueller had been tinkering with a small handtool at the signal key. He swiveled on his stool and sent a browing glance over the rims of his spectacles. "The interruption of the electrical signal," he said. "That was Morse's first big notion. A signal must be interrupted, mustn't it now, if it's to become communication? Think about that, young man. Without interrupting the signal, what have we? A wire's noise."

Benjamin, open-mouthed, nodded.

"A message comes through," said Mueller, "and it falls to us to interpret the whole — all the broken signals as one, yes? We tune ourselves, you might say, to the music entire and not the separate notes. The whole and not the parts. Understand?"

Benjamin did understand. He felt understanding permeating him. It was like the wire's surging current. He nodded again.

Mueller had returned to his handiwork.

11. (1887)

Traveling is living. They call life a pilgrimage, after all, and he is going. Twenty-four this year, his whole life so far elapsed in Perpetua in his father's house but now, who can say, is he bound to stay away for good? Isn't one's first departure forever, whether he comes back or not?

The wheels grind at the rails. Benjamin glowers in the sweltering car, gazing out at stands of corn scrolling past. These farms he's known forever. His face floats translucent over the scene. He seeks resolve in the eyes — and it's there, he finds it. Perpetua, cosmos till now, flees along the track behind. Back there his father swoops across the bitter floors of Lorn & Son with his klok-klok-klok as always.

Shiftlessness, ingratitude, disloyalty — these, in sum, are that man's charges against him. So be it. Knowing his father now in a manner his mother never could, Benjamin won't loiter to serve as the man's deliverance. Twenty-four years hasn't done it. J.M. lathering in the dooryard: *Say your sins, boy, and let me say mine.* A man may accumulate mountains of tiny confessions but these cannot serve for justice while more massive sins stay unspoken.

From the Postmaster at Albia, last week, Benjamin received notice of new letters arrived for his late mother. He went at once to retrieve them. And wrote yesterday his second letter to Alma Robley:

> *News came to me very lately by which I am given a fuller picture of things I thought I'd understood, and see how wholly I was in the dark. This makes it impossible to honor my mother's request and stay at home.*
> *Strangely, having once long wished to go I now find myself driven away.*

"Do you suffer melancholia, Benjamin?" asked Doctor Whitlow upon examining him day before last.

Benjamin looked at him square. "Yes Doctor, I suppose I do."

A crutch had swung and beheaded his ease with the world. What doctor would mend that? While Mama lived he had borne the disfigurement. No more. The late-coming letters, though she will never read them, leave no doubt. Benjamin sees John Manfred Lorn for what he is. Her death has shone a light.

How Harriet Lorn's eyes had bleared in those days last year. What quick fear it put in Benjamin's heart as he sat with her in the sickroom tipping water to her lips, quenching her brow with cool rags and, when she seemed restful, reading to her the Psalms. From the glaze of damp sheets she listened, mouth agape. Her throat rattled softly.

It was a kind of cancer. She never described its rooting place and he didn't wish to know. There had been an operation the year before to cut some of it away. She had rallied from that but now it was loath to release her. In the spring it grew. As summer came on she lay sweating in the midday heat of the house.

Benjamin noted the preoccupied way his father moved about the rooms. The man's entire frame looked clenched. Walking, sitting, dining, sleeping, J.M. Lorn was tense with avoidance, never staring the thing head on, never talking of it. Dominator though he was, his hushed house now suppressed him. He would not allow that his own sense of the world's disorder could be verified like this.

Old Thornton Lorn, blanched with submission to these things, could proffer no shrewd counsel or comfort. Failed oracle. He sent Benjamin discreet inquiring glances.

Something was astir. In sickroom, stairwell, kitchen,

Benjamin breathed a dread air. But curiously, as though his eyes had been washed, the world stood forth with glaring clarity. Mounted on the wall above the mantelpiece there was suddenly a silver cutlass. Even as he realized the cutlass had hung there all his life he realized he'd never truly seen it. What was its provenance? Its hilt of bright bronze bore a confederate marking, a red tassel hung from the pommel. He asked his mother, was it a relic from his father's war? She said it was and had belonged to a Rebel officer. She winced and with a strange conclusiveness she'd never shown said to ask his father. He saw that her strain in answering was more than physical — and he remembered her brother dead in that war. *The dead have no more reward and even the memory of them is lost.*

Of course Benjamin could never ask J.M. Lorn about the cutlass. Sure Mama knew this, he thought her answer strange. He watched relieving sleepfulness come upon her. He sat attendant to her breathing and would not believe that she would abandon the men of her house to their warring ways.

He continued to go to work at the Wabash, seeking the fixity of the Depot and Mr. Mueller's long tutelage, as if by this diversion he would forestall what he couldn't face.

Mr. Mueller stabled a horse in the barn behind the small section house. A pair of saddlebags carried most every tool required for maintenance of the lines. Some days when Mr. Lyle sat operator and Mueller's second son worked messenger Benjamin rode out ensaddled behind the Wire Chief to check the lines as far north as Albia and south to Centerville.

The poles were thirty feet high and stood twenty-five or thirty to every mile. Felled and milled, each had lain out a six-month term to drain of sap. The pole was then burnt and tarred from the six-foot mark to the base to guard against rot. Finally it was sunk five feet in season-soft earth. If the job was good, Mueller told Benjamin, the pole would never rot, not in a man's lifetime. Poles such as these could stand a century or two, maybe more, provided no vandal or storm came to level them. Just so durable in design was man's life itself, Benjamin reflected privately — and yet as vulnerable to forces unseen. With his mother ailing he found a runic message in everything around him.

Because Mueller was expert in all aspects of electricity — wires, materials, conditions, tools, &c., — his talents were often sought to aid the outfits prospecting new right-of-ways throughout the region. In these minor expeditions he served a role beyond his official station, more the auspice of engineer or electrician. The happy consequence for Benjamin, looking on, was to adopt a range of skill far exceeding a mere operator.

I betray my father. I betray my father. I betray my father.

The mantra still beat in his brain though he'd not uttered it submissively since before the night J.M. Lorn tried to scythe him down. No more forced penitence — Benjamin had come into a man's body and would not stand for it. In the household he and his father held to a compact of kinds, like wounded generals at an armistice. But daily the mantra beat — and as Benjamin came full-fledged at the telegraph the mantra turned deliberate. A message he would send ahead of him into his future, his freedom: *I betray my father!*

Seeing she would not survive the night, Harriet Lorn made this known in the house. J.M. summoned Dr. Whitlow, eager to show her mistaken. Within the hour the doctor arrived toting his satchel of vials and secret instruments and entered the sickroom. He came out only to confirm the patient's suspicion. Murmured condolences. Over to Vermilion township a baby was coming and he was in a hurry. Gone.

Benjamin stood with his father and grandpa in the hall, rebuffed at the news, feeling the affront the doctor had visited upon the house, for they did not wish to think of Harriet Lorn lying alone beyond the door nor the thing she lay alone with.

They took turns going in, ill-practiced ceremony. First his father crutched forth, the trouser leg swatting as always. A half hour and he emerged with grim rictus face, avoiding their eyes. Grampa bowed his head and entered. He was also very brief. So Benjamin found himself alone with his death-strung mother.

Her hand groped for his and squeezed. Something was making her hurry. She seemed to want to rear up from the pillow but lacked strength. He knelt. She was whispering. He bent his ear to gruesome breath. She talked with weird fluency as though she'd rehearsed the words. Then her breath grew very scarce.

And hours later he was sitting with his back against his bedroom door reading the packet from the barn.

12. (THE PACKET, CONCLUSIVE)

Miss Harriet Bauer

Albia, Iowa

Gentle Lady,

*I am glad to receive your letter. You are correct that I served the
Confederacy at Camp Ford. Under Colonel Robert T.P Allen and
later under the disgraceful Lieutenant-Colonel Borders I was second
aide de camp in that stockade.*

*Your deigning to send word across lines to one whom in time past
should count an enemy to your brother and your people — this I
recognize as gesture of a noble and forgiving spirit. Truth all told I
wish more of my countrymen down here would study the traits of high
character such as yours. Long before my duty to the South was done I
was full-up and satiated with war. It originates in wickedness and
develops more wickedness at every step. What soldier North or South
would say otherwise? Wicked as we were, we must reconcile all of us.*

But to the subject of your letter.

*I recall the events you describe though I have nothing to add to
accounts already given you. My office that night as far as I remember
kept me horseback at the business of Camp roll call. This anyhow
would have been my function on occasion of any escape (and escapes
were frequent, especially so under Lieutenant-Colonel Borders). I do
recollect the return that night of one fugitive only, a wounded man
later amputated of a leg. My account must end there.*

*I recommend that you contact a man named Livingston, or
Littleton. This man was a guard at the stockade and would have been
one of several charged to pursue escaped prisoners. I fear after these*

years his true name is lost to me, but I know he lived following the war in Marshall, Texas and no doubt may be found by inquiry there if it happens he still lives.

I wish you a satisfactory outcome and greet you and your relations in a spirit of concord and comradely mutual respect.

Sincerely,
Davis Karp
Ingersoll, TX

Miss Harriet Bauer
Albia, Iowa
Dearest Madam,
Our Postmaster in Marshall gave me your letter two days ago, recognizing in its description the person of my late husband Beau Linnington. I'm afraid I've been widowed these two years else you'd receive an answer in Beau's own hand. A very thorough answer that would be too, for Beau in his time was much accustomed to correspondence relating to his war service. I am confident of what his wishes would be regarding your letter. I'm therefore sending yours on to Mr. Stark in Longview, Texas, a compatriot of my husband who also worked at the prison in Tyler.

Adele Linnington
Marshall, Texas

Harriet Bauer
Albia, Iowa
Dear Miss Bauer,
It appears you've been led to believe I was in a search party sent out after your brother in his flight from the war prison at Tyler. I'm sorry to tell you this is false. I was never in a search party though I did serve as guard at the prison in the last part of the war, this apparently being the reason Mrs. Linnington saw fit to forward your letter.

I have checked my memory of the night in question and while I remember some of its happenings there's nothing in them of interest or help to you in understanding your brother's death. Rumors no doubt run aplenty about this night's capture as they do with all else pertaining to life at the prison, escape plots, punishment of prisoners, nature of the command, et cetera. Very few of these rumors I assure you are worth repeating. This anyhow is my view. For every day the sun rose and set on Camp Ford a body can find any number of renditions of person or event depending only on whom you talk to. Therefore I would advise you leave matters at rest so much as you are able, else run the risk of opening old Pandora's Box.

We lost dear ones all of us in those times, we each have our own remembering to do. But forgetting isn't wholly undesirable either, and we ought let things be forgotten when we may. If the matter at hand is no such thing for you, you must of course excuse me speaking out of turn. All the same I can be of no assistance.

Cordially,
Ezekiel Stark
Longview, Texas

Harriet Bauer
Albia, Iowa
Dear Madam,
Since sending my letter some months ago I have found cause to correct myself. I now write with news which may be of interest or use to you after all. I conferred of late with an old friend from the war who served as did I in the guard at Camp Ford prison. I related the substance of your letter to this man whereupon he immediately recalled to me the events about which you inquire. Though I couldn't have known it he was one in the very party to go in search of your brother and his accomplice. As my friend does not care to take up

correspondence on this matter I have secured permission to pass along what he told. I do so in good faith for while rumors are rampant as I warned in my last, I believe the man's word to be wholly an exception. This comes to you "straight from the horse's mouth."

Upon their escape your brother Alfred Bauer and accomplice were tracked from Camp Ford and captured in but little more than an hour. Both were wounded by gunfire in course of pursuit, your brother struck first. As to your question, Can he have taken his own life as rumored? My comrade is certain he did <u>not</u>. He has cause to know this, being among the first to discover the fugitives in the wood, at which instant he saw your brother's accomplice fire upon the fallen man and flee onward alone. This my comrade observed from short distance back. His party arrived presently to find your brother deceased, shot in two places, once by the guard and more conclusively by his friend, who'd left his empty pistol there.

In the opinion of my comrade the finishing shot was intended for a merciful act. And so it would have been too, for the commandant Col. Borders would surely have punished the fugitive with precious little mercy or perhaps death, having issued an order in those late days that all prisoners attempting escape be shot. Alfred Bauer's accomplice himself was spared, I surmise, only because of his lost leg, its removal judged punishment enough. Later, as my friend and I both recall, that captured prisoner claimed Alfred Bauer had fired his own fatal shot all by himself and of his own power. There seemed some design in this to put off the ire of fellow prisoners for the captured man was not well liked all around.

This is everything I can learn or know of the matters pertaining to your inquiry.

Regards
Ezekiel Stark
Longview, Texas

[end of packet]

In the dark early hours Benjamin finished reading. His mother's plea still haunted his ears: Forgive your father. Understand him.

By these letters, clearly, Harriet Bauer Lorn had learned to forgive. Her husband had paid a cost they could scarcely grasp — it made small matter of his indelicacies.

And Benjamin felt he could begin to understand now. He could. And he'd stay as Mama had wanted. And maybe, now knowing his father more fully, he too would forgive the man in time. Yes, if he stayed at home as she wished, the day would come.

He rose and looked out his window. In that July night of Mama's death the dark had new dimension. The stars roared a golden anthem.

It was this following July, days after standing in the glow of the fireworks with Alma Robley, that Benjamin retrieved the two new letters at Albia. Returning by rail to Perpetua, he read them aboard the cars.

Miss Harriet Bauer
Albia, Iowa
Dear Miss Bauer,
I've been traveling for many months away from home and found your letter upon my return a fortnight ago. I hope I may help you even yet by this late reply. I can appreciate your wish that matters be kept in confidence. You have my vow to speak of it to nobody. I am myself much like your near relations, customarily of a mind to let what's past pass and not beg many questions of history. That the terrible War of the States is long behind us satisfies me enough. However, your letter's heartfelt entreaties are impossible to refuse. What little use my

memories are to me, it may be that they prove useful in relieving your "torment of wondering." The ways of Providence are mysterious, and for purposes all wise.

The account you relate concerning Alfred Bauer's presumed suicide accords with my own recollection of that winter night. And the circumstances of our regiment's capture as you have learned them are correct also. What else I remember of Pvt. Bauer is this:

From our company's earliest days mustering at Camp Lincoln, he kept company with a second soldier of same age and hailing from same township — a Pvt. Lorn whose first name escapes me.

In the cold first months of 1863 the 36th Iowa set up in the garrison at Helena Arkansas. It was around Feb. or so that an episode occurred which gave me cause to remember Alfred Bauer well. Mid month or later he and Pvt. Lorn put on before all the company a fistfight like few had ever seen. This rousing contest transpired in the freezing day and lasted the best of an hour, both fighters down to shirtsleeves in the icy air. Your brother, a very gifted fighter, was the clear victor in this match. I for one have never since that day seen superior display of fisticuffs. I recall him moving blithely, a kind of pitter-patter — but he struck like a viper. Electric though it was I thought the bout a show of sportsmanship or diversion for the men — until its pitiful close. Later I learned as did a few of my comrades that rancor had spawned the fight. As I had it put to me, one of the boxers had revealed himself to be something of a Copperhead making remarks of a nature which the other, a fiery patriot, could not abide, so the latter man set himself to patriotize the former. This anyhow was rumored later, and where each one's allegiance was said to fall I cannot now recall. We had our first fight with the Rebels soon after, and such matters of camplife were to a considerable degree made moot.

Later of course the regiment was ambushed in Moro Swamp and its survivors marched to Camp Ford in Texas.

On the night of your brother's attempted escape it was Pvt. Lorn who sought flight by his side. Thus whatever grievance had brought them to fists at Helena was I reckon repaired by then. And it was Pvt. Lorn who came back to the stockade in Rebel chains, crippled by our captors, to report the suicide to those in camp.

This is what I may tell in answer to your questions. I hope it may assist you.

With Respectful Good Wishes
Wallace W. Hart, 36th I.V.I.
Chicago, IL

Miss Harriet Bauer
Albia, Iowa
Dear Miss Bauer,
I wonder if I shall write this to its close and tell the things that are in my mind, or whether I shall send it if I get so far as that.

You do not know me. But having lately learned of your study last year into the cause of your brother's death during the War, I was touched to the quick and perceived how I might put myself at last to The Great Mercy, if it exists. I fear I have wronged you Miss Bauer, you and your relations all. Wronged too my onetime Lord and Savior whose ministry, in the gory filth of my hands, I failed to fulfill during the War that bereaved you of your brother.

Oh Lord let me come to it now recompense be damned. I was a chaplain in the Army when we fought the Rebels, and with many others of the 77th Ohio was in April of 1864 ambushed, captured, and marched from Moro Swamp Arkansas to the Rebel prisoncamp in north Texas. Your brother and his comrades of the 36th Iowa were, as you know, marched and stockaded alongside us. With parts of other regiments we numbered near 1500 in capture and later 6000 in prison.

I was, as were most of us by the time of our surrender, fed up and sickened of fighting. What kind of Christian, I wondered, could be a party to such things? And I may tell you frankly that I have ever since been no kind of Christian whatever. Already in those late days my faith had greatly atrophied, such that I considered myself, privately of course, all but cured of God and of War. And yet to the men I was still, by rights, their chaplain. Whatever my disillusion I had comrades in need of pastoring, of Sunday sermons, of Biblical counsel, and yes, of a trusted confessor. Could I leave them to flail after all they'd seen and sinned? No, I girdled up my doubt, disbelief, and devilish scorn, and forked my very self into Soul and Tongue. In the mud, freeze, and sun of Camp Ford Prison I made a church, and loathsome Saul played at being Paul.

For that fraud I suffer but little remorse. Whatever blasphemy in my thought and spirit, I did not betray my fellow soldier. Surely God, if he works at all, has learned to work through broken instruments. What I <u>have</u> suffered these long years, Miss Bauer, is the knowledge of having shirked, in the malady of my Atheism, a task plainly human. And here is where I come to the matter of your brother.

I never spoke to Alfred Bauer in our ten months in prison or before, but in winter of '64 I became aware of him through the person of Pvt. J.M. Lorn. The latter man, having heard report in camp of my chaplaining, sought me out one day — a December morning as I recall. He was like most of us a woeful sight, all bones and beard and in rags of little comfort for the weather, and he was in a kind of high agitation — a condition, as I would learn, that had increased over many months and was now become all but unbearable to him. He told me at once he wished for my confidence and asked, being 'no kind of believer' as he put it, if he would have it. We went alone into the hut I used for church. We were in discussion there for what seemed half an hour or so. Having won my assurance that all was secret between himself, myself, and God, he told me straight out that he had wronged his regiment by a terrible deed. When I asked had he meant to do the awful deed, whatever it was, he thought for a time before answering No.

Pvt. Lorn was by this point greatly wrought up, wringing his hands and shaking, his eyes wet with tears. It is hard to say, and I could not then tell, whether this was fully remorse or more a letting off of a burden he had carried in silence till now. He added, at no prompting of mine, that in two years of Army life the 36th Iowa had been made to bear a maddening uselessness, indolence, and waste, that their endless posting at Helena Arkansas and especially their futile travels down the Yazoo Pass were, he believed, perfect explanation for the lunacy that had overtaken him. But now he was in terror of the shameful death he must suffer should his deed become known. His words, I remember, were, "They will hang me proper" — and this he repeated a number of times.

Having expressed himself, Pvt. Lorn fell quiet and sat for some moments lacing and unlacing his fingers, still agitated, albeit now more broodful than overcome.

I had long since become, by the rigors of my office, an apt pupil of men and temperaments. I observed that Pvt. Lorn was a cowardly sort of man. But cowardice in him seemed to prompt a quickness, a violence, where in most others, especially in the face of War, it rather dispelled these to induce resignation or flight. For this I found him repugnant, unnatural. I suppose he would have been pitiable too, but that I in my Spiritual injury was so resigned and could not reach to this fellow-feeling.

Had I been the man of Faith I purported to be I might have pressed him to seek God's forgiveness. I might have taken him underwing and nursed him toward repentance and renewal. In time I might have coaxed him to weigh the matter of a confession to the command. As it was, I judged my ministering complete. I had heard him out, acted his confessor, and would keep his secret safe — it mattered precious little to me that secret, being more senselessness in an age everywhere senseless. So I intimated that God already forgave him (though we were none of us forgiven — or of little concern to God at all, for all I could tell). There our conversation ended.

Some weeks later, in the bitterness of a January night, Pvt. Lorn attempted escape from Camp Ford, fared badly during a chase in the woods, and was dragged back and amputated of a leg. It was told in camp how a second man had attempted escape with him who lay dead in the woods before Lorn's capture. The dead man, I learned in time, was Pvt. Alfred Bauer.

Late in the month I found myself in audience to J.M. Lorn once more. From a spring beyond the stockade a rude sulfur stream passed through the prisonyard on one side, and it was the prisoner's daily errand to carry water from this stream. I was about that business one morning when Pvt. Lorn, now a cripple wholly dependent upon a makeshift crutch and thus naturally appearing much the worse from when last we'd spoken, limped toward me in a laborsome hurry. He had a menaced, desperate look and even before he could speak I saw that he meant to seek ministering then and there. As there was no one else nearby I indulged this urgency and stood to hear him. Directly he told me that some business had come between himself and Pvt. Bauer for which he had murdered Pvt. Bauer in the woods.

You may judge, Miss Bauer, what great wrong I have done you and your family having never till this moment repeated Pvt. Lorn's account. My silence I've kept for no Christian purpose, not to spare Lorn a lynching nor to honor an oath of confidence, but worse — because in those late days of War, and throughout the long years since, all things lay drained for me of substance, cause, or consequence. The War made nothing matter. Slayer or slain, sinner or sinned against, man was a damnable creature, unsouled and without purpose and living in a world as empty of significance as himself.

I have guessed these many years that I and no other possessed the true account of Pvt. Bauer's death in Texas (word of your inquiry at last seemed to confirm this), for having confessed himself that day, Pvt. Lorn appeared to me plainly, almost instantly relieved. He had transferred his freight, as it were. Presumably Heaven had heard him, or one of Her lesser agents, as he may have reasoned. Strange, perhaps, in one declaring himself 'no kind of believer' — but such is man in his muddle, his guilt, his murders, his wars. And what is a 'believer' after all, and what his beliefs, but hopes or opportunity leapt upon? I cannot tell whether we create beliefs or become created by them. Pvt. Lorn, to my eyes, <u>believed</u> himself confessed upon that instant. So baldly did he project this that it needed no strength of imagination to judge him, once he'd spoken, purged of the subject all his days after. Such conscience as he possessed demanded only that he shut the book and walk away — and I in my duplicitous office helped him do the very thing.

My having kept the book wholly sealed till now is Shame I cannot, nor wish to, disown. Not that I believe my word alone might have forced this matter to justice, or will do so now. I still know not what Justice is. But Shame, of little consequence in itself, may lead perchance to something at least slenderly consequential, if only in the erring and betimes malevolent human heart.

Yours in Apology and Condolence,
Horatio Webb
Ohio

Benjamin's heart was in a flurry. He lifted stinging eyes to fields going past his window — brazen summer brightness. Dead a year, his mother would never have bound him to stay had she read these words. How would she have taken them? What could she have done? And what must *he* do now?

He knew only that he would leave Perpetua. He had still to call on the Robley girl, and would, but already he was all but gone.

13.

Is his life a line, an ellipsis, a parenthesis? Outside the strutting syntax of religion you're confounded to punctuate existence, you're authored by moments you never lived. They demand you stand and answer.

But not to be authored, Benjamin chooses movement. Let the sentence run on and on — always going, purely present, blind to all preceding. Avow the line itself and no punctuation — what else but this is eternity?

He wants to *be* the humming wire, outside time. To let nothing cling to him.

Traveling is living. He cannot bear to possess a past.

How his hands had trembled as he folded those letters.

PART TWO

The electrical current stays in the wire, unless the wire touches some other conductor of electricity. All the early books on telegraphy take extreme pains to make these facts clear.

— *The ElectroMagnetic Telegraph*, J.B. Calvert

1. (1862)

Enlistment—Keokuk—A fatal accident—Sickness in
camp—Fire and a riot—Aboard to St. Louis—
A question of trust.

The war hadn't concerned itself with them but they would not be overlooked. That August they came to Camp Lincoln on the Mississippi. Stout, fresh-faced, barely twenty, they were tautly strung and pitched to a fighting key. The place swarmed already with eager hundreds.

For weeks they drilled in plainclothes under the blue-clad Major J.B. Teaz of Exline, who administered corrections with the swat of a lacquered maple staff. "Old Teaz," the murmur soon went, "doesn't tease."

Rifles were issued and compared with much scrutiny. Each was outfitted with sword bayonet. Each felt heavy as a yoke by half.

October the fourth saw muster. The drum corps, roughshod just weeks prior, was now a tight thunder of snares. In the deafening beat Lieutenant C.J. Ball, honorably retired from the regular army, paid visit to inspect the lines. They were a splendor of blue for the uniforms had come.

First November found them all waiting yet at camp, itching in flannel and wool. It was still Indian summer. Many were broken out with rashes, some with boils. They slapped at mosquitoes and watched slant sunlight sparking off the mud-dark river.

Men were getting sick. Smallpox, measles, typhoid fever. Farmboys, they'd never lived so thick. They started to die in alarming scores, bodies on stiff infirmary cots. Dead of soldiering without ever soldiering, or even leaving Iowa. The ranks grew restless. *Get us out, get us south.*

Then at target practice Jim Showkwiller's Belgian rifle exploded in his face. In the pop and burst of smoke there was a flinty noise of parts scattered and falling and Showkwiller kicked backward flat-out in the dirt, riflestock blown to chips around him. One ear, one eye, and most of his jaw were torn away, and nuggets of gunwood and metal freckled his skull and neck. He was helped to the camp surgery where it looked like he'd recover. Four days later he died there of infection. Alfred Bauer, J.M. Lorn, and Sam Needham, his compatriots from Perpetua, made a silent consensus of disbelief.

Showkwiller's head was wrapped in cottoncloth, blue forage cap laid where the face would be. They watched his pineboard coffin slide into the bed of a wagon. Alfred volunteered to take it home and explain to the boy's folks.

Watching him spur the horses through the camp gates, Alfred's friends saw a soldier in his upright form. It made them realize what was happening. Such solemnity they'd admired in men of arms before. They hadn't felt themselves becoming men in kind. They'd awaited their first fight for the purpose, with feints and parries in camp. But maybe manhood came not of battlescenes but of compatriots taken.

Returning two days later Alfred spoke nothing of Perpetua or his errand there. They did not ask. November wore on. The days cooled.

By nights the boys of C company encircled the fire. Often Captain Phillips joined them. His buttons glistened amid the rising column of sparks. The Perpetuans knew him before the war, he'd been a doctor in the town. "Might've enlisted physician," he told his company in the early weeks at camp, "but soldiering was the clearer choice. It's the Union needs healing now, lads. Fittest treatment I can prescribe is death to Rebel scamps. By my own sword or gun that's all the better."

But he proved a weak captain, flimsy of resolve. He wished jealously to make the boys love him. Consistency might have done it. Instead he demoted himself to win their comradeship. If they were ever to fight, though, they would want a decision-maker, not a ponderer.

Phillips' tongue had loosened of late. He'd heard grumblings in camp and seemed bent to endorse them for the boys. "Get us south I say, and say it daily. My lads are penned up and marched in rounds while all they crave is part of the fight. Regiment's sick, I hear it said, better to wait. I say it's waiting makes us sick. Old Lincoln best let us have at it, eh lads, and soon. Best let slip our fury, no more glumming about, or may be he reaps that fury himself. We're ready, lads. If we are not ready we are not Iowans!"

The captain's mustache, carefully waxed and twirled to the stems, by now appeared absurd to most of them. And even if his screeds by the fire accorded with the growing sentiments in camp, still few would criticize Lincoln, wary of calling down charge of treason.

"He's a fool," whispered Alfred one night, tucked under woolen and reeking of campfire. "He'll be discharged talkin that way. Not that I'd mind."

On the cot alongside, J.M. Lorn shifted, farted, grunted. "Fool for sure but he talks true. I didn't enlist to sit and watch fellows puke to death and wonder am I next, did you?"

"But John, for an officer to say—"

"Better more of em did. Shake sense into damn fool Lincoln."

Alfred had not reckoned J.M.'s agitation till now.

*

That month Colonel Kittredge commissioned the 36th to rotate as Provost Guard policing the streets of Keokuk, their town of encampment. C company soon had its turn. So Alfred, J.M., and Needham marched out behind their sergeant with Captain Phillips riding at mount beside the line. In the middle of town they broke step for patrol.

By now it was known what little welcome they could expect in this place. There were folks the nation over who'd as soon settle with a confederacy as take shares in Lincoln's war. *Divide the house* (shrug), *all the same to me.* But to find them in Iowa — and in a camp town no less. Prior companies returned from patrol outraged and muttering of Copperheads. Soldier and citizen had words in the Keokuk streets. The guards at the commissary, loath to take insult, had learned to clutch their rifles and look threatful.

On the fourteenth these tensions exploded. A fire alarm rang out late that afternoon. Cabus's Store on Johnson Street was in flames. The Provo arrived to find the Keokuk firemen at work already. The soldiers pitched in with buckets and come the hour's close they'd quashed it to smoke and steam. But someone had wet the firemen down with whiskey as they worked and soon men were bickering in the charry haze. The soldiers were "meddlers" and knew nothing of fighting fires. The firemen were "lushes" and didn't know help when they saw it.

Someone shoved. A private fell in a spray of embers. Fists flew. The fracas spilled into the street with a clumping and tumbling of silhouettes. Townfolk swarmed.

Stones were thrown, smashing windows in the Estes Hotel, lately commandeered to serve as camp hospital. A bluecoat nurse appearing on the porch suffered several concussive blows to his skull, falling atop the steps with spectacle lenses cracked and blood in zebra pattern down his face. The convalescents within leapt up, those that could, and streamed from their wards roaring murder. They flew into the street swinging crutches and canes. It would be a proper riot.

Alfred, J.M., and Needham, blacked from their work in the smoke, jostled amid drunken punches and the swirl of white infirmary gowns. J.M.'s nose was bloodied within minutes. "Sons a bitches," he snarled, teeth slathered red. Alfred watched him clubbing a man with his riflestock. Needham was in there alongside. It was a fireman bowed before them, the man's hands waving up to fend their blows. They were pummeling his shoulders. "Got us a fight," grunted J.M. fast at work. "Get in and school the fuckin Copperheads!"

Alfred drew back. Turning he saw two other soldiers kicking a plump man of middle age sprawled on the plank sidewalk. "Alf! Alf, where you going?"

Alfred swung his head to answer and an arm like a beam came wheeling at his throat to tear him backward. He fell among juttering boots, the dirt street kneaded to a clay of mud and ash. Rolling he saw his assailant and J.M. go down in a tackle. Needham was out of sight.

Alfred crawled from the crush and got up jogging. He'd come clear when he saw the coat of an officer loping out from behind the commissary atop a horse. Retired Lieutenant Ball trotted past looking stately.

At the edge of the fray the Lieutenant reined back barking orders. His horse stepped and bridled. The fight roiled on.

Lieutenant Ball dismounted shouting. He strode forth and caught a blue uniform collar and yanked. A private spun to face him, spluttering and winding up another blow — but the officer slapped him hard and proceeded to dress him down. It was vain example for at that instant the brawl distended itself, took ragged breath and closed again, and Lieutenant Ball fell in the thick of it. Limbs and heads consumed him. Alfred thought he saw him go down. But a moment later he'd squirreled free and was hastening toward his skittish horse down the block.

A voice lunged after him, a brute oath, and then a hard dark shape described a path through the shadows, faintly twirling. It struck him thumping between the shoulders. Lieutenant Ball doubled forward, wheezed, staggered faster as other objects let fly. Bricks mostly.

Alfred turned in at the camp gates and walked toward barracks. Men of the regiment were already streaming out the gates around him.

After a two-hour fight the Keokuk locals deemed themselves beat. They yielded and dispersed. They hadn't had three months of drudgery at camp to store up their fury. The soldiers returned late to barracks, almost satiated.

But J.M. wanted word with Alfred.

"You skedaddled."

"You'll pardon me, John, I was under no orders."

"Orders? They're Copperheads."

"What if they are? That was no battle, John, just a lousy street brawl."

J.M. breathed. "But a battle's different for you?"

Alfred lay on his back in his cot, J.M. crouching at his arm. He would not answer this. He scoffed instead. "You're askin if I mean to fight this war? I hear you right?"

"But don't you wanna skull the Rebel bastards? Three months we been in this damn hole."

Alfred was silent. J.M. slunk back. For some moments Alfred

could feel him watching from the dark.

"Didya see old Ball? The fogey thinks clean coat, stripes, saddle can put'm in charge of any business. Old fool's retired too. Not goin to Dixie at all, just needs some kids in uniform to slap around. Well … I got'm nice, didya see? Sent'm face first into dirt almost."

"You threw the brick?"

No answer.

"J.M.?"

By and by Alfred heard him snoring.

The night's disturbance was overlooked by the regimental command. With soldiers so inflamed, better deployment than discipline.

*

On the twenty-eighth, God be praised, the 36th Iowa departed aboard the steamers FRED LORENZE and HARRISON for Saint Louis.

The river was swift, irreversible. It seemed to suck at their very feet, though their boots remained dry on deck. The men from eastern Iowa called it the Father of Waters. It was murky all the day with mud and sulfurous foam. Treefall, trash, castoff lumber twirled in the churn. Come twilight they watched the glitter persistent in ruffled waves unfurling at stern and prow. At sun's last wink, river turned incarnadine.

But for the engine's drone and the rumble of ranks aboard, the course lay silent for stretches. At Hannibal they saw city lights, heard chug of other vessels in chorus with clatter on land, but moved past and riparian dark closed around them again. No guns yet heard, even distantly. In vastness pitch black the country absorbed the war altogether.

Few considered the strangeness of their intent. To embark in search of battle, to head it off in depths of dark land as one at home would go with packdinner and gun in carefree search of quarry.

Mosquitoes thronged the waters and hummed in droves about deck. From a sutler at Camp Lincoln some men had procured little cakes of Quassia root for protection against just such a plague. It proved little use. On the FRED LORENZE they huddled in hundreds to stern where the smokestack dispelled the swarms — but Lt. Miller came down with warning to disperse lest they hoped to sink. They sorted about deck again, slapping. Some, surrendering, lay down upon packs to rest. The lookouts, stationed to a point, suffered worst.

Huddled in the shadowy flicker of a gunwhale torch, three figures played buck euchre with a deck of cards from someone's housewife. They pulled their hands close to their noses, fairly sniffing them, squinting out clubs and spades.

"Slap down, Alf, like you mean it, man," reprimanded J.M., then leaned to murmur. "Hey Needham, oughten pay mind to our boy here. There's a lass at home, y'see."

"Mm. That'll tear your thoughts away. But I ain't seen you courtin at home, Alfred."

"No, no," corrected J.M., "she lives over to Trillium. It's all secret like."

They studied their cards, slapping at mosquitoes, trying not to.

J.M. drew up. "What's finer, boys, if wife or belle's waitin on you? See battle and come through kickin so's to give cause to wonder the soldier you made? Or get killt and leave her remember a hero?"

"There's other choices," said Needham.

"Ain't a hero she needs," said Alfred. He was still intent at his cards but listening after all.

"No? What then?"

"Husband."

"Pshaw. After two months acourting? Anyhow her folks won't nod to that, will they?"

"They dislike you, Alf?" said Needham.

Alfred shrugged. "Got someone else in mind for her."

"They're Trillium folk," said J.M. "Can't have a bluecoat for son-in-law, the Copperheads."

"She's no Rebel," said Alfred.

J.M.'s hands shot up in innocence. "I say she was?"

"No compromiser either."

"She's a Trillium girl's all I'm sayin. Can't be easy. Come on man, slap down. We'll see Saint Louis before we're played through."

They waited. Alfred set his mouth, eyeing his cards low.

"Sends'm a letter a week," murmured J.M. "Any wonder the boy holds himself apart? Can't get'm to square your eye no more, let alone play a damn hand."

Alfred's fan of cards fell closed. "I'm fixed, John."

"Fixed or not, show us a card."

"No, John. Married, I mean."

"What?"

Alfred had a faint, guilty grin.

"Oh Lord, you already done it?" J.M. looked liable to blurt something more but held his tongue, grunted instead. "Christ, man. And no one knows?"

"You know. Needham knows. We wanted it so we got over to Des Moines and settled it. Don't you boys tell."

"Well," said Needham, "congratulations Alfred. And I mean it." He put out a hand.

"Thanks, thanks."

"You couldn't tell before now?" said J.M. "I don't warrant your trust no more, what?"

Alfred looked startled. "No, John, I—" The darkness in J.M.'s eyes stopped him short.

Needham said, "C'mon now, J.M., that ain't no way."

"No, no, but we grew up together Alf and me. We're bloodbrothers goddammit Alf, and you don't trust to tell me—"

"I told you now, John."

"He just told you, J.M., c'mon."

"Just told me. Uh-huh. And didn't say the damnedest thing when we made out to join up."

"What's that meant to say, John?"

"Well, here I'm thinkin we're to fight together. Old Alf watchin my back loyal as ever."

"J.M., are we playin or what?" said Needham. "Alf's found true love. That's more reason for'm to fight true. God man, these skeeters sucked your brains out?" Needham winced and slapped his own neck. The sound rang like a shot. He held up his palm with its squash of blood and wing.

Something slackened. J.M. grinned despite himself. But it was just a reflex of humor flitting and gone. Always he'd been delicate against the smallest doubts, an oddity in one so pugnacious — or maybe it explained that fierceness. But even now after years like brothers he would search for counterfeit in Alfred. Slow, grave of aspect, he reached over to slap an arm. "Happy returns, old boy. When's it public knowledge?"

"Ain't sure yet."

They sat holding their cards having forgotten whose turn it was. The steamer heaved along.

J.M.'s eyes lay askance. "Not much of a honeymoon in camp life, huh?"

"It's what it is," shrugged Alfred.

"Best we watch this one, Needham. He's got somethin to live for."

"And don't you, John?" said Alfred.

"I do sure. To kill or be killt, that's why I'm in this. I'm no honeymooner remember."

"Let'm be," said Needham.

"I were you, I'd take care what I write to Trillium—"

"Let'm *be*, John."

They threw in their hands and shuffled and dealt anew, each wanting his game improved anyhow.

2. (AVIS — San Francisco, May 1944)

From her small desk beside the fourth-floor balustrade, Avis Kurzwald's gaze drifts upward to sunlight spangling the yellow rotunda. A masted ship ablaze above her, mainsail billowing in a sea of fleurs-de-lys. Twenty-six thousand little triangular panes to this dome of glass enclosing her: Avis could sit and count them now in the absence of customers. It would keep her mind off the troubles, maybe. Start at one on the outside edge and move in spirals toward the center. She has the exact number, 26,000, from Mr. Verdier himself, the store owner whose ancestors the Verdier brothers sailed the actual ship from France a century ago, docked in the Bay, and opened a dry goods business aboard.

"She sails above us now," Mr. Verdier had said on the day of her interview some years back. Avis stood beside him in his gleaming lobby below, following his glance as it rose to this high sun-gilded image, like a monumental Tiffany lamp. "She was called *La Ville de Paris.*" The French words fluttered magically off his lips. He opened his hands to the space about them. "And now we have the City of Paris."

Avis did her best to return his smile but his cufflinks and golden watch-chain intimidated her. The whole place intimidated her then: the magnificent store clock mounted to the third floor balcony in giant garland of bronze, crystal chandeliers constellating above marbled jewelry counters, paid pianist at the open-top Baldwin — it was more palace than department store. Avis wondered how she'd stumbled into the midst of fur-decked ladies and gentlemen on Union Square. Her awkwardness stripped away her age, made her feel a student or daughter, defenseless — not a forty-five-year-old woman and mother.

She'd worn her best gloves, she remembers, the whitest she had. Those helped her feel better. Then Mr. Kaplan and Mr. Verdier told her they loved her silhouettes. She was hired that afternoon. Avis stood in the store basement with a pristine white phone to her ear, giving Edgar the good news, dizzy with joy and apprehension.

She'd used the same phone today, on the line with Edgar her whole lunch hour, fretting and planning. They'll spend this evening, again, combing the streets of the Castro, the Mission District, the Tenderloin, Chinatown. Benny's been gone a week. So long? Hard to believe even with so much dread.

Last night while they idled at a traffic signal in the dark heart of the Mission, she watched ne'er-do-wells shuffling the littered sidewalks, bearded drunks slumped in doorways, and something unclutched inside her. Suddenly, violently, she was crying into her gloves.

"Avis," said Edgar from the driver's seat. "Avis, come now dear, we have to keep looking."

It unnerved him to see her so, she could hear it in his voice. Very unlike her to be overwhelmed that way. But she couldn't stop.

"Look at them," she groaned.

It was the most she could say of her fear. That their boy would come to that guttered disgrace.

They drove on, the street-sleepers blurring past. She'd never reckoned the number of strangers a person could see in a day. How could she and Edgar be sure they hadn't passed one who knew something of Benny? — or one who'd hurt him?

There were too many. But they couldn't all be bad, of course not. And yet she knew they couldn't all be good.

In a vacant lot beside a plumbing supply store a gang of twelve or fifteen congregated around an oildrum fire. Edgar double-parked and left the lights flashing. She waited in the pulsing car while he talked with them. He looked so misplaced with his overcoat and hat. He strode right into their midst, stepping over hubcaps and mounds of trash. Listening to him they kept their hands outheld above the fire, hooded heads down. But she could see their eyes glinting in the fire's glow as they glanced toward the car left running behind him.

Vermin, she thought. Stay where you are.

How far wrong she must have gone in mothering to be led to this dark city corner in search of her boy. And her husband putting himself so casually into danger. Hurry Edgar.

But she's never seen Edgar frightened. Always his fortitude astonishes her. Even in his younger years he was all but unshakable. With not an inkling of fright he'd gone off to hellish fighting in Europe, her betrothed at twenty-four. He'd come home seeming unchanged but that he looked somewhat older.

Not for her, that steadiness. Rigidity, unyieldingness maybe, but not that even temper. She's all opinion, conviction, loves and hates. Try as she might to alter that, to moderate, she knows it would be in vain. She's crusted into this shape and cannot be otherwise. It's more than stubbornness, it's her nature. No wonder Benny can't stand to live in her house.

Edgar returned to the car and she smelled the smoke clinging to his coat.

"I don't know how you do it," she muttered.

He checked the mirror and they pulled away. "I'm doing it for us. For Benny."

He meant no censure by it but she felt a fool. In their son's absence she's started to question for the first time ever how Edgar endures her, and why. Already loss of child estranges her from herself.

"Terribly good, aren't they?"

A voice brings her back. A lady in furs bends to examine the samples in Avis's glass-topped desk. "Warren's grandmother used to make these. Have you ever sat for one?"

"Never." A second lady also stoops.

Avis smiles but they pay no mind.

"There can't be many left still making them. So quaint."

"Why I'd thought the art was dead, what with everybody clicking Kodaks nowadays."

The ladies move on across the sun-bright atrium toward the Normandy Lane Tearoom, its Union Square dames enshrined amidst glittering silver and china. Watching them, Avis fingers the silver scissors strung to her chain necklace — and feels herself an artifact. Is she too merely a thing under glass, like her dead-art silhouettes? An artifact: is that the destiny of a mother whose child ceases needing her?

She knows her faults now, though it's too late to correct them. What if she'd listened to Edgar just once? "You needn't lean so heavy on the boy, Avis. Everything you say carries weight with him." How many times had he cautioned her? And always she disagreed, so remonstrative, so hard, for fear that Benny's flawed nature would get the better of him.

It stupefies her, the damage a mother may do in failing to credit a child's regard. Frightened in love you think yourself defenseless, and fear of defenselessness blinds you to the weapons you wield. She never believed that Benny heard every last thing she said to him.

The rotunda begins to dim. A fleet of cloud slides lidlike

over San Francisco from the Bay to make vellum of the glass. Against this moving gloom the stained glass ship seems to bob and rock. Avis looks down to steady herself, suddenly queasy, one hand braced at her desktop. Her face hovers in the glassy surface. And under the glass, modestly displayed, are her dainty black palm trees, an intricate bicycle, a few profiles, Mr. Verdier and Mr. Kaplan among them.

It was Mr. Kaplan who first encouraged her to apply. He'd stopped in her tiny booth at the San Mateo Fair. "Mister Verdier would adore these." He touched the frame of a medium harbor scene. He gave her a card. "You'd be a marvelous addition to our Normandy Lane boutique."

She looked at the card. "City of Paris?"

"*C'est vrai.* You know the place?

"Of course, but … Of course. Thank you."

She hadn't supposed she could earn a living, however modest, from this work she'd always done for pleasure — and certainly not in such a magnificent place as the store on Union Square. City of Paris was a landmark, but she'd never ventured through its jeweled doors.

Sunlight returns. The rotunda blazes. And now a kaleidoscope light enswirls her, the ship's image sweeping by at her feet. The clink of cups and saucers from the tearoom seems the sound of glassy waters and for a moment Avis is tacking forth across a sea of fleurs-de-lys. Memories …

Benny, nearly a man now, had been a brittle stem of a boy. Remember him five years old, an afternoon at home in Des Moines. The rain blowing in blankets outside, slapping the eaves. Benny lay sprawled on the carpet with crayons and colored paper. But after a few hours the rain did not quit and he tired of trying to draw a human figure to suit his own lofty standard. He came to the dining table. She was penning a letter.

"You writing to Gramma?"

"Mm-hm."

"You'll tell her I love her?"

"All right."

He stood by.

"Need something, Benny?"

He tendered crayon and paper. "Make me a man?"

"A man."

"Yes. A man for real."

"Mm. Well, *you're* a man for real, shall I make you?"

He smiled his smile so like Edgar's.

She set her letter aside. She told him to bring some black paper. She took her small cloth scissors from the table drawer, she still doesn't know why.

"Turn," she said. She framed him in profile, the rainy window behind. Her hands went to work by will of their own.

He grew very serious. Quiet.

She began at the breastbone's slope. Why? She watched the paper turning to meet the scissors at every snip. The scissors said, *Shh.* Collarbone, chin, upper lip, nose and brow. *Shh, shh, shh.*

Her small son emerged, shaped in paper. The surrounding black fell away to curl at her feet.

"There." She held the portrait up beside him. The window framed the likeness. An exact silhouette. She shivered.

And shivers now, remembering. She created then, for a second time, her only child. Did she feel the new maternity of those moments as they passed? Was that the shiver?

She laid the silhouette into his hands. He stood staring at it, seeming to read it.

"I'm like this?"

"You were, yes. But you're different already. After just a minute."

She saw this confused him. She tousled his hair.

He took the silhouette to the mirrored breakfront and did a study. She watched him. He was several minutes in thought. Finally he came back and handed her the cutting.

"It's made wrong." He tapped his upper lip. "This part."

She disagreed but made him another, again starting at the breastbone and now taking care as she neared the nose.

"There."

He looked at it momentarily, then carried it to the mirror. He was just as long if not longer in scrutiny. Coming back he said, "This one's better."

"I'm glad."

He laid it on the table before her, still pondering.

"Benny?"

"Hm?"

"What's the matter?"

"Am I different again? I mean, changed from this already?"

She drew him close and stroked his arms. "Don't worry, you'll always be Mama's Benny."

We lie, and the lies are love. Avis wonders, after seventeen years of mothering, whether this will remain her single tender memory of that child now so changed. Surely there were others once. Have the battles erased them?

Late in the afternoon Benny forgot the silhouette and steeped himself in other play. Avis laid the second profile atop the first and held them to the light. She switched them. The "better" one replicated the first exactly.

She signed the letter to her mother, folded it, and slipped the first cutting in, not bothering to explain it. Under coat and hood she galoshed down the drive to the mailbox (how different that drive with its stand of poplars from her small duplex here amid the close houses on Fourth Avenue).

Her mother's reply arrived by the following day's late post: *Who cut the picture of Benny?*

So Avis saw her sudden talent. It had come to her from nowhere at all.

She wakes in fright some nights now, certain she's lost the gift.

Avis knots kerchief at chin, pulls on her gloves, hooks handbag over sleeve. She pushes the street-door and tinkling piano gives way to whoosh and blare. A bustle of minked granddames, disheveled sidewalk wanderers, bankers, attorneys, hoteliers, dignitaries, starched cuffs and stiff-brimmed hats. Along sidestreets off the square comes a stink of urine, then the waft of coffee and cigars from open storefronts, then the chuttering exhaust of trucks, buses, honking cars.

Avis scans the faces around her. Aboard the streetcar her eyes dart out the windows, appraising figures on every corner, at crosswalks, on benches in every public square. They are too many. She's duty-bound to this, but she breathes rough, disgusted at the numbers. She'll take a bit of Edgar's brandy once she's home. And draw a bath. Supper can wait. The streetcar clatters up Market Street and crosses Van Ness toward the ocean. The car is hot and loud, a blurry press.

Her stop arrives. Alighting at the curb she halts, turns — she failed to search the faces in the packed seats around her. The bell has already chimed, the streetcar jerks into motion again, and as it rumbles ahead she stands and combs the slurring features crowded behind glass. Her own figure — dowdy in kerchief — blinks and skates across the windows. She must look half-crazed, hurling glances from the middle of Geary Street. Hope, in residue, becomes eccentricity. She fears she'll resemble, before long, those croupy fishwives who wander the wharves in oily skirts. The faces are faces only, then gone. She collects herself and starts along Fourth Avenue toward home. Not yet across Anza Street she sees the bay window faintly aglow. But Edgar is never back before six.

Dizzily the porchsteps recede below her. In the entryway she's sure. Somebody's in the house. She does not stop to slip from her coat or set down her keys.

"Hello?"

The hall unreels behind. The walls widen out and in the small living room he's rising from the armchair, turning to meet her. Benny. He's wearing one of Edgar's hats. She knows no adequate greeting. Everything within her climbs upward — and her mind does inventory of the kitchen pantry, for she'll cook him something grand, she'll send Edgar for a loaf of bread, some cut flowers to make a centerpiece — but she stops, realizing. Despite herself she says, "Benny."

"No, Avis."

Edgar comes close to take her hands. His touch brings a horrible sensation of falling.

"Why are you wearing your hat?" she snaps. "What are you doing home?"

He's still in his overcoat. It smells of outside. "Come now. Come sit down with me."

She sinks to the sofa. He holds her hands, squeezing.

"Avis, there's news today."

What an awful thing to say. It stiffens her. She shuts her eyes and blurts, "Benny—"

"No, no. Not Benny. Your father called."

"Yes?"

"Your mother, Avis. She's passed away, I'm afraid."

"What? When?"

"Today about one o'clock."

His eyes are steady. He wants to help her. But Avis looks down at her hands, still gloved. Unaccountably the white fingertips are smudged gray. What is that, grease? And clean just this morning.

"Oh my," she says, and sees now that his news almost relieves her. Unmothered, but still a mother herself. What a shameful way to think. "Goodness," she breathes. "One o'clock, you say?"

"Yes."

They sit silent. From far away something momentous creeps toward her, but right now she's alert to things up close. The carpeted floor looks very level, solid. Upon it her feet look trim and restful. From the city outside comes the opaque noise of a carhorn.

"I'm sorry, Avis. Really."

Water runs warm to fill the bath. It makes musical sounds, ludicrous. Peeled of gloves and coat, Avis unknots her kerchief. Her hands are steady. Shedding skirt, her balance is doubtless. What is this calm? And why this feeling that she can hear now, effortlessly, any little sound in its smallest reverberation? She reclines into curls of foam that fizz about her ears. She keeps her eyes open. The day, over and done, must be understood anew. She lived it ignorant of the loss.

What happens to a mother who dies? Why does death seem to lay her mother bare? Seventy-seven years old, stretching out to nap this afternoon, she slipped from life — and in the slippage a husk fell away. The woman left lying on the sofa was not just Mother or Wife. Death left the kernel of her name: Alma Adeline Robley Lorn — a newborn once, girl once, young woman. What did Avis ever know of her?

The drain gurgles softly at her heels. Slow seep down and away. She breathes, brooding, and watches one hand tracing figures through brailled steam on the tiles.

She does know *some* things: Alma Robley, born Dennis Iowa 1866; married 1889; schoolteacher for a time; daughter to a miller; member of the Dale Church, later of Perpetua United Brethren; and now: died 1944. Such rivets can hold together the frail image of a life.

Avis feels something welling now. Why would her father call Edgar? Well, that's like the old man — to step clear of raw grief or tenderness — to shape a circumstance that suits him.

Something is welling. The bathwater begins to quake as Avis weeps.

"Avis dear?" calls Edgar from the hall, concerned.

"No," she sobs. "Leave me."

She sits to supper Edgar prepared. A breakfast supper, the best of his skill in the kitchen. She's never understood why a man should deem it womanly to cook anything other than breakfast or pasta or fish and therefore excuse himself from learning.

She's dazed in bathrobe and slippers, limp wet hair, prodding a sickly cloud of eggs. Edgar talks — has been talking, she realizes, how long? In one cheek he pockets a bite of toast.

"… a good long life. We both oughta hope we live as long."

Eggs are impossible. She can't even try. Food seems sacrilege. Resentfully she watches him chewing. That he should feed himself so eagerly makes her tearful again.

He says, "Not hungry?"

"No."

"Maybe something else? Some yogurt, or rice? Something plain."

She shakes her head, grimacing.

He sets down his fork. "I'm sorry dear. It's a shock."

She permits him to stroke her fingers.

"Think you'll phone your father tonight?"

She should do this, she knows, and she likely will, but shuts her eyes and shrugs. The idea fatigues her.

"You can stay when I go," says Edgar. "Probably ought to."

He means he'll take tonight's searching drive without her. Alone in the car he'll lean from the wheel to peer senselessly down each dark street.

"It's settled. I'll go. This way if you decide to phone him … He might have called *you*, God knows. Could've done that much."

"Edgar, I'd rather not badmouth him."

"No," he presses her hand. He would comfort her. "You're right. It's just I see how it bothers you, dear, his ways. And it *should*. You've got every right to your feelings. His damn stoicism …"

She snatches her hand away. "His wife's dead, Edgar."

"Yes—"

"He doesn't … display … Stoic or not."

It's long been their custom to talk pointedly of her father and his smothered ways but she can't bear it tonight. She's accused Edgar of cold judgment where he'd only wanted closeness but she can't help that unfairness. He should have known better.

Edgar touches his milk glass. "All I meant is, he might take this chance to … to see how the loss isn't all his." He lifts his milk and gingerly drinks. "Anyway, I'm glad it was me who told you."

"When did he call?"

"Two or so. Secretary pulled me from a meeting."

"And what made you wait? To tell me?"

A clenching in her throat gives the question a bitter sound. Edgar's face falls, a look to cause her sore regret.

"Why, Avis, news like this …With what we've been through this week, I thought …" His eyes go glassy. "I suppose I was waiting — it seemed possible that before I told you …"

"You mean Benny."

Each day this week has held out chance of the boy's return, each a disappointment.

"Benny, yes. I was wrong, I see that. Should've called you right away." Edgar peels off his glasses and hides his eyes.

Avis sits still. Her husband's goodness often seems a reproach to her. She cannot treat this man with the kindness he deserves. What is it that makes her drive her hard edges into everything all the time, even at moments when being soft and passive is better? *Needn't go so heavy, Avis.* There it is: on that position her husband and boy shared a view. They know, Edgar and Benny both, why Benny could not stay. But what is it in her? A willful failing or a kind of handicap? Her mother never had this hardness. But she, Avis, stiffens to a stone even as she knows she ought better to yield, to conciliate. It comes from her father if anyone.

Something crusts over her even now. She sits and watches her husband, man of stability, crying quietly above his scrambled eggs.

3.

Still in bathrobe, she sits at the telephone table. Her bent head cradles the receiver to one shoulder, hands free for scissor and paper. She dislikes the telephone, can never sit still while talking.

Her father's voice crackles through the line, connection poor as always. Tonight that noise of distance makes her picture him reduced, a smudged figure at the far end of a tunnel swirling with snow. She could more accurately picture the burnished entryway of her girlhood home and the telephone chair she knows he's sitting in, slumped against the wooden siding of the stairwell, trousers bunched at his thighs — but no, tonight he's that blot in the static, and the conversation makes her cold.

"Bensons dropped by," he says. "Brought their respects. Said Perpetua Brethren's full up with weddings this week, might be tough getting a service. Such a quaint little churchhouse people come from all over. May hafta talk to Reverend Putnam."

"Over to Centerville?"

"Ya, may hafta."

He and Avis's mother lapsed from weekly churchgoing long ago — his decision of course.

A long silence gaps the line.

Slowly Avis turns her black paper to meet the scissor-blades. It's a full figure she's making.

"You still there, Daddy?"

"Ya, here."

But what can she say or ask to follow this? He's as much uncertain, she knows.

Now she does try to picture her father in the empty Iowa house, a man unused to the hollowness of the rooms around him. Twenty-four hours ago he and Alma Robley Lorn sat at the supper table to play their nightly cribbage.

And who is he after all — white-haired, stoop-shouldered, stocky man — sitting in his entry? Man who even at eighty can't bring himself to talk of serious matters, not on a level, not unchurlishly or at length, and so he phoned Edgar's office today.

Already Avis can hear he's reached his limit in conversation. Usually when she calls they trade a few stilted words before he hands her off to her mother. Twice a month their cursory telephone greeting, nothing more. What else should they expect tonight? But he holds to the line.

Speak Avis. Tell him nothing at all — just don't rot on the telephone.

"I'm cutting a silhouette, Daddy."

"What's that now?"

"I say I'm cutting a silhouette."

"Oh, are you."

"Yes, right here while we're on the line."

She hears a hitch in his throat like an idle chuckle. "Okay," he says.

Forever he's made her feel she speaks a tongue he's slow to interpret.

At last he asks, "What of?"

"Well, it's a person. A man. Think it might be you, Daddy."

"Oh do you." He thinks a while. "Must be right handsome then."

"Mm-hm." Empty sweetness feels permissible tonight. But her cutting clarifies by the moment and she begins to wonder if it isn't Benny.

"Your mother's got your other ones hung up around the house. You know she'd done that? They're up in frames right down this hall. Four or five I'd say. She's always sayin if you all move back here you oughta get Joe Weinburg to hire you for's drugstore."

"Yes, she told me, Daddy."

So abruptly eloquent, and just to tell her what she clearly knows already.

"But you like it out west I suppose."

"Well, there's more than like. Edgar's job and all."

"Uh-huh."

Benjamin Lorn himself had traveled the west working telegraphs for an early company. This much she's learned. A few oddments of his antique life survive: a telegrapher's desk slotted and cubbied, an operator's visor, blank reels of tape paper, a slim box or two of company stationery. Unexplained artifacts, they populated the out-of-the-way places of the house in her youth. Even still they live with the silent old man in those rooms. An old signal key numbered among Avis's toys. She has it in a box or closet somewhere — years since she last gave it a thought. She would never have known what that toy was had her mother not explained. *A person could tap it and make a message. Like this. See?* So despite her father's silence Avis got to know a few little things — for instance, that he traveled in those years without his father's blessing. This gray grandfather to her own missing boy was himself a runaway of kinds. No, but he returned to Iowa in the end — and then lost everything when his father's store, the Lorn inheritance, burned to the ground. Was it that fire that first fueled his bitterness?

"Did you eat supper, Daddy?"

"Well, it's late here, I got two hours on you." This in his surly, condescending way. "Ate fine, ya. Your mother kept some leftovers."

Avis could ask what plans he's made to feed himself once the last of his wife's dishes is gone, but she lets it be.

"You all'll come out on Friday then," he says.

"That's right."

Plans and distractions. Busy yourself in your loss.

She has yet to inform her father of Benny, but now she knows she won't mention it tonight. Edgar's gone out with the car as agreed. Useless to search this way — but what alternatives have they? Edgar phoned the police the night the boy vanished only to hang up after five minutes, told in so many words they should not expect police assistance, not for a boy a whisker shy of his eighteenth birthday. So having felt that her staunch honesty about his age would save Benny from the war he so wanted to join, Avis saw this honesty could not save him from the streets.

"All you gotta do is vouch for me, Ma," the boy had pleaded. "If you'll just walk in and vouch for me. They'll take anyone eligible."

Alone he'd gone begging to the recruitment office and come home spurned and angry. He was six months from his birthday and believed himself entitled to adulthood. An Allied invasion of Europe is imminent. He's sure that in the melee he should find out or prove what kind of man he is.

She and Edgar will go to Iowa without him. This is dreadfully certain now. And it means she will be forced to explain to her father.

The last of the surrounding paper falls away at Avis's feet and she holds her finished cutting between the knuckles of two fingers. She still isn't sure just who she's rendered, as sometimes happens when she cuts without a model. She'd folded the paper for twinning. Now she slides the two images apart. They separate with a whisper. She sits holding one to each hand, silhouettes of a man or men unknown to her.

4.

Never has a person pledged allegiance to cause or campaign and survived in full possession of himself. Avis senses this, and feels proof for it in the warped figure of her grandfather, her father's father. She never knew this man. He died before she was born, but she keeps an old photograph. He sits stiffly in a chair, one leg cut off to a stump, and glares. That wound disfigured him inside as much as out. In privacy her mother had once or twice declared this, meaning to help the child Avis understand Benjamin Lorn's frequent coldness. *His father was like that, I'm afraid.* So always Avis saw in the grandfather's unsmiling face, in the way those spectacles hid his eyes, a man's lifelong anger. Was it Andersonville where they'd imprisoned him? She dimly recalls a family rumor of that.

Yes, in swearing allegiance you make a fateful sacrifice — an intuition Avis never doubts, but she's never formulated it altogether till now and could not make it clear to Benny, so how could he ever understand her disapproval?

Six feet tall he'd lumbered through their small Victorian rooms. Making way for him in the hall, Avis was unnerved. Had she been blind to his dramatic changes? — their little Benny translated to this creature of lean solidity. One day she realized she could hear the thump of his steps from clear across the house. At the kitchen sink or at the icebox he towered, exuding manhood. His muscled arms, even at rest, flared away from his body.

Soon he seemed to flaunt that presence as if he wanted to overbear her — and defy the more subtle manfulness Edgar had modeled. Together they'd made known to Benny their feelings on the war. Edgar had served in the trench-gashed country of the Somme and deserved the boy's deference if she did not. But Benny would martialize despite them. Three of his schoolmates had joined up already, all seniors. They'd be shipped to the Pacific or North Africa before graduation. Benny wanted to fight in Europe. Avis saw his anticipation simmering, his fear lest the noble invasion occur before he'd come of age — and seeing this she began to wonder whether young men of his kind would exist forever everywhere. They must, or wouldn't wars have met extinction long ago? Young men, baited by glory or righteousness, unknowingly harbored longings for their own destruction — primed for the orders of generals who sat at polished desks, tea and biscuits at hand, plotting devastation.

It unsettled Avis, troubled her, finally maddened her to wonder why *her* boy, her Benny, whom she and Edgar had raised to such different values, should choose to join the dumb elect in that horrendous game. It made her judge him. She wanted to shake him, unglove his conscience, but he was too big for her now, so she gave him her violent reproach. That she was too hard on him, too relentlessly cold and dismissive — she sees this now. It was beyond her though, how to deal rightly with a son who'd become something she despised.

She believed it rebellion for rebellion's sake. He clearly didn't realize what violence he nurtured wishing for war. A few months ago during a momentary truce she bought him a copy of *The Red Badge of Courage*, hoping it would mature him. She can't be sure he ever read it — anyway he was past repair by then. If he would not read her gift he would memorize ranks, jargon, tactical trivia, worst of all varieties of weapon.

Lately he'd broken his reticence toward them only to declare news from the fronts. Otherwise he was silent, surly, locked in his room with the radio squawking of victories, casualties. Covertly he went out and got his thick hair barbered down to the hideous style of an infantryman. Avis raged. Somewhere he obtained a military ring, a garnet stone. That made her embarrassed on his behalf, it looked so gaudy, so unintentionally feminine on his pale hand. It was as though, failing to locate an actual person within, Benny had selected a stock persona without. What had she done or failed to do that left him so lacking a sense of self?

Daily the papers and magazines and radio tout the prospective landing in Europe as the essential move toward victory and the close of war, but it wrings Avis with fear to see that this disaster will drag on — in Europe or Asia — till Benny turns eighteen. And she dreads most horribly that he'll find a way to enlist before then. She's heard of recruitment officers turning blind eyes. Might have happened already, how could she know? A fibbed age and their boy is off to the bloodbath. What would be worse, Benny bedding down on filthy city streets or Benny shipping overseas? Impossible to pretend a preference.

She was ashamed that the boy failed to understand his heritage. He would not see that his roots lay in Europe. Edgar in his own time at war had suffered torments of the mind over this thing mainly — laying siege to his ancestry. The Kurzwalds had come to San Francisco from Hamburg at the start of the century — he had shoals of aunts, uncles, cousins over there still. At his rifle's every shot he'd bruised with knowing that had his parents never emigrated it would likely be *him* ducking fire on the other side. Little as he talks of his war, that much Edgar has told her. And the Versailles Treaty, as they both saw it, was an outrage. Benny, in his fervor, will not see the unknown numbers bound to be left dead or displaced in the raiding and burning of German cities. Avis despises Adolf and his minions, but this all-consuming war — where can it end? She flinched to hear Benny refer to the Germans as "Krauts." The word came out at dinner one night and she swiftly cut him down.

His fork clattered. "You and your cockeyed heritage, Ma! You think they're not all bad? Hitler and his thugs shove half the people in ghettos or prisons and leave em to rot and what does the other half do? Nothing. Or they cheer it on. If that's what a German is, I'm no goddamn German!"

She would have clarified her point — of course she could see that the Nazis and their collaborators were no true Germans — but instead she leapt on him for cursing at her table. He shot to his feet and stalked away and slammed himself shut in his bedroom.

She shouldn't have expected, she knows now, that he honor vague ancestry over his sense of the injustices in Europe. How could that have been anything but hypocrisy to him? He'd never met his distant Hamburg relations, didn't know half their names. And he saw how seldom she spoke to her own father, how little she really grasped of her lineage. It does seem absurd to her now that she claimed so fervently her Old World heritage. As if this were her best stance against the boy's warring wish. As if she could reach behind the shadows obscuring her father's and grandfather's lives to some better lit, more stable, more interpretable history supporting her and her kin. She might grasp something in that backlight for Benny, to make him stay at home, to bring them closer.

She would never have guessed, when he was small, that a world war would come between them. That Benny would claim so surely his right to die.

5. (1862)

Putting ashore at Saint Louis they marched to Benton Barracks, a vast hundred-acre encampment suited for twenty thousand. They were but six thousand in residence in the new infantry quarters all commodious with piped water and stoves.

On the third day it sprinkled snow. After that the regiment began to feel winter.

On December the fourth came orders to stack arms at the arsenal for repair. Soft tumblers made the rifle locks defective. Deeply reluctant to part with their guns, the more mistrustful among the men feared a scheme to keep them even longer from the fighting they felt owed after four months of army.

They were unarmed till the ninth, unnerved by their lightness, resisting the creep of unsoldierly thoughts. There was drilling and fatigue duty but these were now a kind of playacting.

December the eleventh brought word of the Union bombardment of Fredericksburg, a hopeful sally. The guns were back by then and every man remembered himself battlebound.

On the twelfth a soldier in F Company died of measles. He'd

first been sick at Keokuk, rallied for a time, but had lain in the camp hospital since arrival. Neatly boxed he now went down to a numbered grave. As they lowered him a second soldier of the same company was busy dying of lung fever. Come dusk that was done and he made a second box heavy.

News of Fredericksburg arrived: a vicious defeat, more than ten thousand killed. The young recruits from Perpetua repeated the figure but could not be helped to fathom it.

Capt. Phillips called at the camp surgery seeking a certificate of disability. A young orderly overheard the captain's plea in the ward. His account traveled back to C company. Patrolling the edges of camp at guard duty one night, J.M. related the news to Alfred.

"What disability? they ask him. Blisters of feet and neck our brave Cap'n answers. Also toothache and digestive concerns. And these, they say, prevent your serving? And Phillips tells em, Each complaint alone is small but together I fear they impair my powers of judgment. Which they all know is fresh hot horseshit, but Phillips the priss expects himself favors being their chum at medicine. Well, they are just not havin it and he's toddled off to barracks advised — *advised* — to heal himself if doctor he is and do his duty if he's at all American. We're to follow this turnspit into cannonfire? He came to service to duck the draft. Now, no draft, and he'll do his all to get out."

"Well, but he'll be captain till then."

J.M. stopped in his paces. "What's this? You said yourself he's a fool."

"Like him or not, it's a fact of rank, John." Alfred feared he'd been too vocal at Keokuk. He judged fit to censor himself for counterweight to J.M.'s rashness.

"He ain't *my* Cap'n. And what cap'ning he do in the fight the night of the fire? Where was the Cap'n then? Round the block watering his horse. Oh, but where were *you*, come to think of it?"

"God John, leave that be."

Their footfalls clattered again in the cold packed dirt.

"This army's all flimflam, may come the day I draw pay and go home. Won't be the only one to do it."

They spoke little the rest of the night. Relieved at dawn they hurried to thaw hands and feet at the fire. Lieutenant Miller was there with the company mail calling out names. Alfred had two new letters from Trillium.

J.M. was filling a coffee cup from the campstove. The pot clanked down. "She feelin twice as lonesome this week, what?"

Returning later from mess to barracks Alfred found J.M. lounged out on his cot reading the two letters. He came and stood at J.M.'s boots.

"Might've unshod yourself."

J.M. didn't flinch or move to rise. He held a letter unfolded above his face as if searching for watermark. "Writes pretty, don't she?"

"Hand em over John."

J.M. read aloud: "I fold my heart herein and send you all my Christmas love."

Alfred skirted the cot and plucked the letters away and folded them. J.M. stayed reclining. "Now don't chafe on me. Just needed to see she ain't treatin my boy to Rebel sympathies."

"Outa my bed John."

J.M. swung down his boots. "Who's lookin after you if it ain't me? Pretty letters though, like I said."

He left Alfred to brush at clods of mud dotting the blanket.

✳

Late December the 36th received orders to fall in. Aboard the steamboats JENNIE DEANS and WARSAW they set out for Helena Arkansas on the nineteenth.

The ranks swelled with rumors regarding Major General Grant. He'd set sights on Vicksburg. Many believed the 36th would join that campaign. On the JENNIE DEANS J.M., Alfred, and Needham huddled together enshrouded in clouds of their own breathing.

The steamers landed their first night above Cape Girardeau. The companies slept aboard. Next day they saw Cairo at the mouth of the Ohio, a bustling supply station. Gunboats and captured cotton steamers clogged the waters.

Late day they were put ashore at Columbus Kentucky. Great stone bluffs fronted the river here, dwarfing the boats. The Rebels for a time had commanded those heights — Gibraltar of the West it was called. The men's feet alighted on land dark in the shadow of the prominence.

They poured into a stand of sycamores. There had come murmurs of impending action, then the order to prepare for battle. The Rebel General Forrest was approaching from the south.

The way was scattered with deadfall, eaved with moss. They broke step and climbed along with guns gripped, awake to ensnaring woods. They saw for the first how the river had lulled them. The world was not theirs. They'd not allowed how separable they were. The earth could shed them.

The wood fell away to a clearing, winter fog breathing fat above the grasses. They formed lines and received issue of forty rounds.

Would the Rebels come quietly? They stood and felt the meadow's exposure. Officers conferred and studied maps.

"You keep my back I keep yours, you hear me Alf?"

There was a shiver in the voice.

"Of course John."

The fog pulsed before them. Beneath it, indecisive, the future crouched in abeyance. They waited. The longer exposed the more they accepted exposure.

At length it was concluded Forrest would stay truant, so the 36th turned ranks and re-entered the wood, marching by torchlight to the boats.

They were delivered next day to Memphis.

Christmas night they slept at their guns in cold rain on a Memphis city square. A bust of Andrew Jackson watched over them from a plinth. The words "THE FEDERAL UNION MUST BE PRESERVED" were etched in marble but someone had gouged them half away.

The Rebels lay in strength beyond the city. From the dark came noise of guns all night long. In the deepest hours the regimental guard shot down two Memphis citizens who'd pressed too near the billet. Daylight revealed the body of an aged man with ear trumpet in his coat pocket. The other was a boy of school age in plainclothes.

That morning the regiment marched to Fort Pickering on the Mississippi where fifty siege guns stood at the ready. Three companies would sleep in the parapets with pickets stationed, two companies at sally ports. So J.M., Alfred, and Needham lay on a tarred jetty just above the river's stink and were pummeled all night with rain. The Rebels did not appear.

Dawn arrived brown, absent the sun. Day followed day.

One dun noonday J.M. Lorn and friends were detailed to Provost Guard along the river streets, ordered to clear and fire every house and building for seven blocks.

Officers rode at mount overseeing the operation. The blocks

had been largely vacated in the earlier fighting but still the Provo flushed holdouts by the score. Some of these were dragged protesting into the streets, others came slinking from their doors. A sorry sight every one.

An old woman, panic-stricken, caught J.M.'s sleeve and tugging it wouldn't let go. "Son you mustn't you mustn't I beg you don't burn it that's my house it's all I got."

He'd torched the curtains already, the windowglass smashed out long before. He was about to call the wagon for straw. He turned and met her ancient face, grooved features contorted with her plea.

"Let go my coat."

"Son, son I lived here all my life don't burn it son."

"It's burnin already woman. Let go my coat."

Alfred came and pried loose her grip. He pulled her away and stayed her flailing arms while the flames gained strength. When the fire had grown to the second floor he felt her sink.

They left her humpbacked on her knees in the street, weeping. J.M. clapped Alfred's shoulder and smiled as they walked. "Done good Alf."

"What?"

"Nothin, nothin, you held her is all. Eases my mind."
"She's old. Frail as a bird."

"Didn't pity her though."

Alfred grimaced at the ground.

New Year's Eve the regiment formed lines again and marched to meet their boats. They slept in port then steamed by daylight south to Helena.

6.

Benjamin Lorn stands before her in double-breasted jacket, composed. His shoulders bulge in tweed, left one slanting off as always — some old injury from his youth. His grizzled throat chafes in starched collar.

Old man, thinks Avis. Old but never shrunken. Still a stone.

They're in the hall of her childhood home in Perpetua. Avis holds a putty-gray shoebox girded with a single rubberband. A pair of her mother's glossy overstraps once came new in it — black or brown or beige, the kind she always wore.

"You know what this is, don't you?" says her father. With one finger he taps at the lid. His hand lies atop it while he awaits answer.

The box has a slight weight as though it may hold shoes even yet. At first Avis thought he was giving her a pair from her mother's closet. This morning she saw the sets lined neatly along the closet floor — dresses and blouses hangered above, arranged fastidiously by color. She stood sobbing into her hands, her mother's scent coming off the clothes.

Now she's just outside that room her parents shared for decades. Past the doorway at her father's back stands their high, broad four-poster bed. No doubt they conceived her right there — Alma Robley Lorn thirty-two years old, Benjamin thirty-five. Ten years they'd been trying, before their only child finally took seed. Did something in the Lorn line prevent fruitfulness? Avis and Edgar, too, were allowed only Benny. And Benjamin Lorn had been the only child to her grandparents. The bed's covers, as always, are crisply tucked to enfold the pillows. She cannot picture her father doing so neat and womanish a job as that. Behind Avis, at the other end of the hall, mourners mill about the living room.

"Letters," grunts her father. His hand slides off the box. "Don't know how many, but you have your mother to thank for em. She insisted we keep em."

His eyes are cool and clear and tearless. Icy, Avis might say. And she knows what Edgar would say just now. Damn old stoic.

"You mean *your* letters?" Her mother mentioned once or twice the "courtship record" she'd kept all these years.

"Ours once. Not now." Her father pockets his hands.

"Well, I'll keep them for you Daddy, and if you want them back—"

"Just take em," he gripes. "Ain't mine anymore. Don't want em and can't well throw em out, can I?"

He brushes past her with a level gaze, starting to walk out of the hall, but pauses in the doorway and puts one hand to the jamb where over the years her mother set the nicks denoting Avis's growth. There's a whistling in his throat. "Some while now I've been standing ... a bit on the outside of things. ...The day and such."

It's the only confidence she's ever had from him. Having said it he waits. Avis can't be sure he meant his words for her. Does he even know he said them aloud?

"Daddy?"

"You oughta read all of those. If you mean to read any."

She looks at the box in her hands.

"Sort em by date. Don't read em less it's all of em."

"Okay."

He watches her a moment, as though she must see beyond

doubt the importance of his instruction.

"I'll read them, Daddy."

His hand drops from the jamb and he moves out across the groaning panels of the parlor floor, slowly.

Later, Avis stands by the buffet. She's spread the polished cherry wood with her mother's doilies, brought out the dulled silver wedding platters from the breakfront and arranged them with ham, ementhal, rye. Now she watches her father across the room. He sits knees crossed in the wingback chair by the hearth. He looks a man taking his ease of an evening. Friends and relatives file before him.

She does not pity him. She resents him. His stern deflective ways, his oppressive reserve. She always has.

Bequeathal is defeat. Come the close of life you dispense the things you've kept. They move outside of your control, tell your secrets large and small, and you accept this humility — to do so makes you lighter for the journey ahead. So, defeated, her father gives up these letters. Yet he might have kept them — or burned them. Why didn't he? Why did he seem unable to do either thing? Has Alma Lorn's withdrawal stripped old Benjamin of a lifelong protection?

He looked very old, Avis thought, soon as they stepped off the airplane to find him waiting in the drab lobby of the Des Moines airport. She'd seen him just last year but what changes already. Hard private grief — and then his stunned outrage at their news of Benny. Kissing his cold cheek she told him forthrightly. He stuffed his hands into his jacket pockets and stood back from them, reproachful.

"Missing?" he said, the word an angry slash. It would slander him deeply to bury his wife without his grandson present.

Since then he's been quiet and cross, unapproachable on the matter, avoiding it entirely. And yet suddenly out of that taciturnity comes this afternoon's bequeathal.

The last of the funeral guests gone, plates and cups collected, cleaned, stacked in the cupboards again. Crumbs swept into the sink, rinsed away. Night falls on Appanoose County nostalgic as ever, but for the estranging fact of Alma Robley Lorn now boxed in the cooling earth of Perpetua's Hillcrest Cemetery. Window by window the lights of the Lorn house go out, but by the bedside lamp in her girlhood room Avis sits awake.

The bedside table is the same, skirted in the green ruffled cotton her mother sewed. The sashed window drafty as always. Thirty years gone and the room is unchanged. She remembers what it meant to shut her door, to breathe at last the uneasy relief of bedtime. How many nights did she go to sleep in this room upset by things she couldn't understand?

It was never tyranny. Her parents rarely squabbled — and discreetly when they did — but something brooded in her father, and her mother bowed to its power. Avis, too, learned to make her breath shallow so the thing might breathe.

Benjamin Lorn sold insurance in those years. He was often called to Des Moines or Omaha, less often to Chicago or New York, and how different the house became in his absence — how the walls widened out and the rooms yielded to noise of play. Avis stomped freely on the stairs. She hung on the banister. Her mother's clear voice would ring from the kitchen calling her to supper or snack. In her father's presence such noise was forbidden. "Is this a fish market?" he would growl.

The old floorboards creak familiarly as Edgar crosses to the bed in pajamas. Marmish Avis in nightgown and cap perches on the mattress edge with the box upon her knees. Just so she used to sit with her mother behind, Mother braiding her hair before sleep. Back then it was a dolly sprawled across Avis's thin knees. Black button eyes stared past her to the ceiling, blindly intent.

The letters are brittle, cracking along the folds. They smell of ghostliness. Tucked amidst them are crumbling newsprint clippings, a few photographs. She withdraws one small photo and turns it right side up. In the faint brown surface floats a woman's pale form, frocked. The lady holds a swaddled bundle in her arms. No background, the figures just floating in the fog of the tarnished photoplate.

Edgar looks on. "Who is it?"

Avis turns the plate over, unsure. Then she finds a small cardboard frame tilted in with the letters, and the picture fits exactly. There are some words in pencil along the bottom edge. She reads aloud: "Harriet Bauer Lorn and baby Benjamin. Oh, it's my grandmother."

"Didn't recognize her?"

"I never knew her. She died when Daddy was young."

"Mm. And there's stoic old Benjamin before stoicism flowered."

They stare at the image. And though the son in the picture still lives — he lies in bed behind a door downstairs — Avis knows she's staring at ghosts. Impossible to imagine her father and this infant a person one in the same. She feels a sudden urge to get up and look for herself in the mirror. But she stays regarding the photo.

That's what life does to you.

"Hm?"

Did she say it aloud? "Oh, nothing."

Edgar deflates on his pillow with characteristic end-of-day sigh. She feels his fingers tracing circles on her back. "Turning in soon? Don't mean to read those tonight, do you?"

"Maybe a few, yes. And I want to get them in order."

"Suit yourself." He sidles over and to save himself rising pecks her elbow. "Night."

Avis thumbs through the folded letters, seeking dates, shuffling the marked ones in amid those still in envelopes, ordering the envelopes by postmark as she goes. A hundred prior lives loiter in her head. Hers, her mother's, her father's, earlier Lorns.

Scattered throughout the box are several letters lacking dates. She glances them over. Oddly, there's one addressed to her grandmother.

> *Miss Harriet Bauer*
> *Albia, Iowa*
> *Dear Madam —*
> *I beg pardon for so long delaying answering*
> *of your letter of February, the moreso*
> *because of the nature of your queries. I fear I*
> *must disappoint in telling you that I was not*
> *acquainted with your brother Alfred*
> *Bauer...*

She folds this page away, to begin instead with the earliest dated letter. It's written by Benjamin Lorn in his twenty-fourth year.

. . .

July 5, 1887

Perpetua, IA

Dear Alma Robley,

No doubt it will surprise you to get this. Truth be told I surprise myself writing it. That you kept memory of me at all, let alone from many years ago, seems a wonder. But I'd flatter myself to think you may recall our meeting at the Fourth Festival beyond a day or two. This is why I write today and do not wait.

I must send apologies because appearances to the contrary it's not lost upon me what an ill-mannered fool I seem. Also I send Sincere Regards to assure you I do think of you highly and all shortcoming is on my part, including failure to recall your person from those years ago.

What I mean to say is I wish I'd been more sociable last night. Plainly you are a kind hearted person and should have been let to enjoy the Fourth in better company than what I supplied. I think I offended you. If so I beg forgiveness.

I might tell you Alma Robley that you brightened my mood not a little, for all my awkwardness showing it. I don't just mean I was pleased you should clearly remember me, I mean you had the very certain effect of lifting my spirits.

No doubt there's many a thing to account for my own oddities. One would be my mother's death last year which was unpleasant schooling. But I don't wish to bore you or make excuse.

I know I'm writing this badly. Let me move to the point.

I see much to admire in you though I've had the pleasure of your company but briefly. Maybe this won't mean an awful lot coming from one such as me but it's the truth. And now I must ask, Would you allow me to call on you?

I do not write letters of this kind. You can see that plain enough. I shall hope but by no means expect to receive your answer soon.

I send my high regards

Benjamin Lorn

P.S. Excuse pencil here. I would have done better to write this in ink for ink is like my memory for you. Indelible.

July 7, 1887

Dennis, IA

Dear Benjamin,

Your letter received and much appreciated. You say I would forget you but this is mistaken. And also you're mistaken to say you are "ill-mannered," &c. Is this what happens every time a girl treats you decently? You must get tired. Now let me tell you something and I want you to remember it. You are not a "fool," only a little bit shy. Any sensible person can see this. And I'm awfully sorry to hear of your mother's passing. My father noted it in the paper when it happened. The Lorn family is a name we always recognize on account of my grandfather's friendship with your own grandpa Thornton. And though being all Dennis folk over here we don't see much of your people, we've always kept apprised of old Appanoose families yours no exception. I would be pleased to visit with you at better length than allowed on the Fourth (and with much less noise about!). I hope you come to see us in Dennis. Please bring your own pleasant self and no more apologies. You might come next Sunday if it suits you. You could come on the cars. Our house is a little tucked away so I'll write out the route from the Dennis stop below.

From

Alma Robley

July 14, 1887

Perpetua, IA

Friend Alma,

Reading this, don't fear I mean to put apologies into every letter I write you.

That I owe apology this time you must agree. Isn't it ungentlemanly to start off on distant travels so soon after my first pleasant Sunday in your company? That it was pleasant for you too I will endeavor to believe.

I dread my long absence shall now make you forget me after all. For that I shall strive to stay in your memory by writing. I hope you won't habituate yourself to shredding these letters for batting! I shall do my all to make them interesting. In any case they'll show I was sincere asking your permission to write. I trust you to say if you wish me to quit.

To my view letters are shoddy substitute for what visits I would happily pay could I remain in Appanoose. Forgive me I cannot, and believe me how greatly I regret this. Though I couldn't explain it any too well last Sunday I have sound reasons that prevent me staying at home. To write them would take a very long letter.

As it happens I had hopes of going more than a year ago but these I gave up for what I thought good reason — to do what my mother wished. In fact on the Fourth when we made our reacquaintance I was still of a mind to stay at home. I'm sorry how matters have changed.

What I may tell in brief is this. It seems to me that my father's life should remain his and not become mine. I daresay if you knew my father you would think this not an unreasonable idea. Indeed my own mother once thought so and kept faith with me though it cost her pains with her husband. At any rate this has proved a sore point between Father and me for years.

News came to me very lately by which I am given a fuller picture of things I thought I'd understood, and see how wholly I was in the dark. This makes it impossible to honor my mother's request and stay at home. Strangely, having once long <u>wished</u> to go I now find myself <u>driven</u> away. There is simply no staying you can be sure, else I would gladly take remaining as your neighbor to the prospect before me of scratching down poor letters.

But I confess: Were I to stay at home I'm frightened to think what would become of me.

Alma, know that I am my own severest judge. Consider how the affairs of family escape the understanding of lookers-on. What I mean to say is that you would not hold my actions against me, breaking a vow to my mother &c, were I able to lay before you everything accounting for them. I know this letter does a poor job. But maybe one day I will tell the rest, who knows? At present I would not overburden our young friendship.

I cannot say when I might return again to Appanoose nor in truth whether I could settle in Iowa at all. I tell you this and the rest to release you from the chore of writing me if it should seem aimless now. But I hope you will send me letters all the same. Your word is the single one I wish to hear amid what lonesomeness I face in going. Save your kindness Alma Robley I lack any reason to consider a return home sometime. That's to say that without it I would hereafter be gone from Appanoose forever. I do believe that.

Now we see what a fine job I make of writing pleasant letters! Trust me to write more nicely in my next and not so long either, if you will receive another. I sign myself

Your True Friend
Benjamin Lorn

7.

A vis wakes to darkness, a muted clatter of cupboards. Not yet daybreak, but her father stirs downstairs. Edgar snores quietly into the sheets.

She slips from the bed into morning chill. Briskly she dresses.

In half darkness at the kitchen table her father sits hunched before the gray pane of the back window, dawn beginning out there. Curled over his coffee with elbows propped on his wife's knitted placemat, he looks gentled somehow. Momentarily he seems to give shape to the dim quiet of the house, the hollows of stairwell and hallway, the long years unreeled, all but played out now.

"Morning Daddy."

He turns, face shadowed. "You're up, huh."

He's dressed in Oxford grays, Madras short-sleeve, suspenders — and he's his steely, tack-like self after all. Nothing yielding. He was never a father to slouch about in pajamas. Lazy Sundays did not exist to him. And he'd never been ill that she could remember. Never the robed and slipper-shod invalid. He'd forcefully expected, all but required, the same diligence in wife and daughter. In youth Avis saw nightgown as nakedness, took pains to keep her shoes on whenever he was about.

Always Benjamin Lorn had seemed to fight in himself and his household the glacial process by which habits were formed. It was tiny things in ever-present thousands that eroded a person's character. Loving one's rest became laziness, idleness, indolence. Begging favors softened the soul and tainted regard for others. Ask your wife or mother to bring you pencil or cup and you've made her handmaiden to your sloth.

Avis rubs her arms. "Should we light a fire?"

Now as in her childhood half the house's warmth must come from the kitchen stove. Her father gets up and sets about the task of kindling.

"Hall closet's got your mother's mackinaw in it."

She finds the coat. Caped in her mother's scent she sits at the table watching her father on his hard knees before the stovedoor reaching for tinder and wadding up newspaper.

"Did you rest last night, Daddy?"

"Uh? Oh, slept most the night, ya."

He fans a paper. Smoke puffs. Matchflame blooms and catches.

His chore done, he hoists himself to his feet and swipes palm against palm, then stands at the stove with a sideways gaze like he's straining to recall something. It seems to escape him. He lets it go and turns to the counter. "You drink coffee?"

"Take a little, sure."

Bathed in incremental morning light, she waits while her father lifts down cup, saucer, napkin. Here and there about the cupboards Alma Robley Lorn's adornments give a homespun softness. In a frame there's a silhouette scene Avis made her some years ago. A crowned kitchen queen waves a scepter at three footmen bearing platters. Underneath, in Avis's hand, a doggerel dug from an old book of verse: *Little kitchen you're my throne / For 'tis here and here alone / That I ply my queenly art / Each dish to win king hubby's heart.*

Her father brings the coffee but he's awkward with avoidance. He goes back to the sink to rinse a spoon.

Avis waits.

He dries his hands on a yellow cloth. Refolds the cloth and drapes it neatly across its dowel. Finally he comes to sit again.

"Was a fine ceremony," says Avis.

"Mm."

They share the silence.

Benjamin Lorn's eyes stay low. He stares down the length of his arms to the cup between his spotted hands. Beneath his jaw the skin sags in rumpled layers. His question, when ventured, is gruff.

"Will he come back, you think?"

"Hm? Benny?"

"The boy, ya."

"We hope he will."

"Of course. But *will* he is the question."

"We hope, Daddy. We can't know."

"Can't you."

"It's San Francisco, Daddy. A big place, not like here. We're looking for him. We'll keep looking."

"Huhn."

His gaze roves out the glass over the garden bed. Her mother tended it every morning. Her watering can sits as she left it, fuzzed with dew.

Every surrounding betokens loss. House and town drone daily absence to the old man now. Avis was shocked to see so few remembered folk at the funeral. "Not many left," said old Benjamin, unwincing as ever. "Gone away or dead most of em." And that seemed more insult than sorrow to him. And Benny's absence, a sort of extra death, can only insult him further.

"I want to ask you, Daddy ..."

Avis waits, seeing how he's removed himself beyond the window. Sunlight pricks the stringy whiteness of his hair.

"Yesterday, Daddy, you said ..." She waits again, breathes. "You said you were standing ... that you've been standing outside of life."

His profile hangs motionless.

"Dad?"

She could reach to touch his hands — they're there on the table palms down, big-boned fingers asleep to sense. But beyond the daughterly kiss twice a year, she's never touched the man.

"Daddy, we need to know ... Edgar and I. Would you ever come to San Francisco?"

"Uh?" He awakens, though still he won't turn. "When would I? How long?"

"To stay I mean. Would you come to stay?"

"With you all?"

"Yes. In our house."

He makes a noise, not quite a word, some thought or retort buried in his throat. How to force upon him this thing so alien to him, this talk? His eyes are hard and bright and dry.

"Don't expect him back, huh?" he says. "There's room with the boy gone."

"No, Daddy. You'd share a bedroom we thought."

Now the blue metal of his gaze straight at her. "You can't say why he'd just go off like that." It's not question but statement, flat and accusatory.

Beneath the tatty linoleum the kitchen floorboards creak and groan, stove heat seeping through. They sit.

"Dad, what was it about Grampa? What got between you two?"

Questions to crack the fisted father. She expects no answer.

He pushes out his chair. "Can keep that mackinaw. Might as well."

She touches the rough collar. "Will the letters say? Is that why you gave me them?"

"Seems to fit you anyhow," murmurs Benjamin Lorn, and he's gone.

PART THREE

The West is less a place than a process.

— Wallace Stegner

He consented to go out there, content to orphan himself to the moment as he might encounter it or it accrue to him, such being the myth or metaphor he had read about, or perhaps — as he sometimes believed — he had dreamt it.

— Bruce Olds, *Bucking the Tiger*

1.

July 15, 1887

Dennis, IA

Dear Benjamin,

Your latest is at hand. You forgot to tell where to address you. Consequently I am sending this over to Perpetua knowing it needs forwarding to wherever you may be and hopefully won't take long to get there.

Much thanks for forthright remarks. Some of it was surprising to tell the honest truth, but you knew it would be so. Of course I can't imagine what trouble besets you and your people to send you off so suddenly, therefore it would be very petty to "think less of you" on grounds of what I'm unable to imagine. I trust in time you will tell me what things you may, and trust they are not so shocking as you think. Anyhow, you don't frighten me as you worry you might. And you mustn't be afraid to write as you please.

From the start I could see you were no stranger to sadness. Now don't take that wrong. I only mean you have a sort of bruised quality, and as I see it this is no shameful thing for it has made you gentle, I can tell. It brings to mind those Christian converts come from hard living into salvation who are some of the kindest folk you'll ever meet. I suppose misfortune now and then grants us gifts of kinds. Is that an awfully unfeeling thing to say?

As for me I am a strong and sensible girl and will be very pleased to have word of your adventuring in the Far West. I'm a little jealous all told. Dennis and Centerville can be horrifically dull. But I too will get away, or so it appears. I have an uncle over in Oconee, Nebraska *whose town is getting up a school and they need lady teachers. I suppose I wouldn't mind edifying a few young scholars. But maybe nothing will come of it. I'm raising no hopes.*

Now let's the two of us agree we won't talk anymore of keeping up or stopping these letters. Wouldn't you rather write other things?

You say you cannot know if you'll ever return to Iowa for good. Well, though I do not doubt the need for your journeys I do think this would be a shame. Maybe the life of the road will instruct you to reconsider? But you are a bright fellow and I suppose this is your thinking already.

Come what may we human beings have only got the one day at a time we are given. For now let's not look too far out ahead of each, and just mark the time with pleasant and friendly letters. Agreed?

I enjoyed our visit too on Sunday last. Thank you for a fine time.

Yours

Alma

P.S. Do you mean to visit for Christmas at least?

July 28, 1887

HANNIBAL & ST. JOSEPH RAILROAD COMPANY

Salvage, MO

Friend Alma,

If it happens that you did reply to my last letter you could not know to address me in Missouri of all places. I must be a fool for I left Appanoose Co. intending travel West but by some blunder consented to go South instead. As they needed a man at this office and as I am the more easily hoodwinked than others I am down here at Salvage. My position here is called Expensing Clerk for I sell tickets, send messages, expense bills. I am really an ordinary operator besides.

The Hannibal & St. Jo you may notice is something less than my ideal employer. But this was to be just a meantime arrangement. I do not know yet exactly how long they shall need me, it is day by day, but that it is not permanent is consoling. The managers know I am bound West. I won't let them forget it in fact for I ache to go.

To illustrate what an awful heathendom I am in I will give you the happenings of one night. A gentleman by the name J.S. Shanks was in town. Much in Salvage spirit Mr. Shanks washed a late evening away in drink and then, starting home along the RR, was run down by the mail express. This man left his family over to Kansas City some days before and never telling them where he was bound, and until they read news of his sudden death they'd had no clue to his whereabouts. The papers say he was a postal agent of decent character whose conduct had lately taken a turn for the worse. Good Lord it troubles me to hear of such men. Salvage seems to draw them. One must ask of oneself, Were I a Mr. Shanks would I have the sight to see how lost I'd got? Or does a soul stray blind over some toeline and never notice? Does it not haunt you to think of it Alma, what senseless wanderings can overtake us, or how small an accident can kill a body. Is there not some hand that authors us? Do you not sometimes feel it is so?

And Mr. Shanks's ignominious end was but one event. Same evening: an elder of the Christian church shot twice at his daughter crippling the girl for life. Same evening: two men at drinking got up a rumpus that spilled from a saloon into one of the main streets here in town. It was all fisticuffs till one was knocked thoughtless. But the winner of this brawl, wanting better bloodshed, ran back inside to fetch an iron poker and none in the crowd made to stop him as he laid in with it on the felled man. That man is not expected to live. Same evening: had three different fires in town.

If I had not written this letter I would hardly believe its reports. This is my dwelling place at the start of my journey. Does it hang an ill star above my going away, you think? I try to believe not. But that

I blundered coming here is certain. Can the Wild West be wilder than this? I do wonder at times now why I am going. Why I left, I mean. But then I remember Perpetua and my life there and all is clear again.

I'm afraid this shapes up to be another letter with "Disagreeable" writ large all over it. And what temerity from one whose correspondence you may have declined to welcome by now (in your last letter I mean, which I have not rec'd).

I might as well say it. One wants to speak rightly to a soul like you. Some moments I think this must be one reason I saw fit to leave — in order to talk to you in letters as I likely wouldn't in person. Has the Authoring Hand made this so? Maybe so, in which case I cannot judge the Hand ill as I've been tempted to. I do want to be clear and well in my letters so as to provide you reason to await instead of dread them. Would that this imperfect science of word, comma, and period had something pure and singing in it like the Electrical Energy of the telegraph wires. I think if the wire signal were itself the message not just the means, or if we mortals needed nothing but currents to link up each to each and be understood, we would likely become more perfect creatures and this world a kinder place. After the natural murderers had all murdered each other that is.

I will tell you (though you'll think me a fool) that this is my second try at this letter today. Quitting work for the evening I went around to the rear of the Depot house to sit upon a freight truck and pencil my thoughts to you. My hotel I've discovered is much too noisy and disorders my brain (I do not sleep at all here despite exhaustion but that is a different affair). A wind had come up, it was roaring along the station platform. Just as I finished a page my paper was snatched away. It flew so quick I didn't bother to scramble after it. I just watched it flap West along the tracks and I suppose it is to St. Jo by now if somebody in a passing train didn't reach out a window and catch it. Why do I tell you this besides to make you smile at my expense? Because as I watched the letter fly I began to think it was best, maybe meant to be, if you see my meaning. Oh what can anybody do whether writing a letter or trying to speak to another to make oneself understood? Some wind takes our words Alma and flings them. We cannot say how they go or how unscathed our fragile thoughts will be once heard or read. I suppose it must happen that words messages letters bring one soul closer to another and not infrequently either. But to me it's a mystery.

Anyhow, I now write this sitting up in the stablehouse behind the Depot. It is windy yet and warm though nearly midnight. Knowing how fires like this town I guess I'd better put out my lamp for thought of the straw around me and get back to my hotel. I tell you I almost fear to walk so late through the Salvage MO darkness. As a price for writing to you however that is nothing to pay. If you only knew what a relief it is to me after answering questions at the office all day to sit down in this strange place and think on the goodness of a soul like yours you would excuse the disagreeable illegible and uninteresting parts in this.

Very Respt'
Benjamin
I will await reply to this if one is coming before hectoring you with another. Never fear.

2.

He shuts the stable door and starts back through darkness with his letter in its envelope and the envelope in a coat breast pocket. The byway between the Depot and the first shoddy outbuildings of town is a slough of black mud. It gums his shoes and slows his going. He can't figure why it's so thick in dead of summer. Stinks of rot. He breathes through his mouth. Never been in a place so reeking with curses.

The wind is dead. All asleep.

Smacking forth he feels shadows pressing closer around him. He's amid the buildings now. Off to either side weeds are hissing. Otherwise, deathly silence. Seems impossible. His first sleepless nights here accustomed him to stopping his ears with candlewax when he goes to bed.

He rounds a black bulwark — the cobblery? — and comes into Main Street and stops at what he sees. In the building at the street's end every window writhes with yellow flame. His hotel!

And there's no one about. The fire burns, no alarm. He stands appalled in lashing light and momentarily, as if coagulated from that flurry, a small bony figure grows taller and lumbers toward him.

Gaunt face. Dented top hat. The man draws up and Benjamin stares into shut lids recessed behind the bony nose, skin slack and bluish as dead hatchlings. The blind man still carries his limp duffel slung at one shoulder. His knobby chin tips upward and Benjamin watches the red-pocked Adam's apple bobbing.

"Sickness touched ye, has it?"

"Sickness? No."

"Oh but ye mean to take the traveling cure, yea ye've drunk a draught already and find it bitter tincture."

Save for guttural fire the night is soundless yet. The blind man's head ticks here to there but the bulbous lids do not move.

"Each season issues serum to stop thy throat and yea ye grimace it down all the same and never cease walking but know this, yea, and mud may cake to firmness for thy passage, that it is Hacklebarney ye wander toward. Hear me boy? Hacklebarney say I and signify the vast horizon's house whereunto none may trod for natural decree but whereunto many assay to go all the same."

"I'm going West."

"Ye go to Hacklebarney first and last and nothing West is yers for West is even farther on, yea, there is no West for even Geronimo once of warrior stock is bowed and made to dance bear-wise in those vacancies where men will seek swim dig scrape make haste till thoughts of pearls pull thee under. Look!"

At once the duffel is unslung and two black snakes lie loosed and scribbling in the mud at Benjamin's feet. They hiss and spit, winding, clotting, winding — till stillness overcomes them. They've clutched each other mouth to tail, tail to mouth: a perfect ring that edges Benjamin's boot toes, pulsing.

"These asps would show thee symbol of thy better desire, though ye be a man and man knows it be impossible."

"I'm dreaming."

"Nevermind now. Infinity's of greatest moment."

"I should wake. I'm traveling."

"Infinity you hear? Let ye parse it from its falser reflections."

"I should wake."

"Who is thy father?"

"My father?"

"The man you would fly. Think hard on him for he traveled like thyself he did."

"My father's a cripple."

"What's in thy pocket?"

"What?" Benjamin's hand rises to guard the letter.

"The paper in thy breast pocket. Bring forth and read."

Helpless, he obeys, unfolding the paper to find it enlarged, tribune-size and boldly headlined.

"This isn't ... Why, it's changed."

"Read!"

Benjamin, stuttering, begins. "One morning he made him a slender wire, he drew from heaven the strange fierce fire—"

"Hogwash."

"He carried it over the mountain's crest—"

"Rubbish."

"—and dropped it into the ocean's breast."

"And time and space ruled man no more — is that how ye'd close this dross?"

"But that's how it's written."

"Burn it!" A shank of finger stabs the air. "It shant withstand true fire believe me — and dare ye travel by so papery a creed?"

"Creed? Why, I ..." Benjamin stops short as the paper crumbles to flakes between his hands, flutters from his fingertips.

And now the blind man stoops and his knobby claws sprawl in the mud, collecting the snakes like lengths of rope.

"Think on thy father first. Infinity follows."

He folds the rubbery bodies and stows them in the pocket of his coat and his gaunt gullet shakes as he chutters, "Wake, wake, wake ..."

3.

Old Benjamin Lorn stands fists at hips, white head bowed to eye the worn boards underfoot.

"Never much cared to live in this town. Not till I met your mother anyhow. Still didn't much after that."

Behind him the stairs climb in cascading sunlight to the landing window. To Avis there is something sorrowful in that brightness exposing each step, each edge once sharp but long since rounded smooth — and the flayed paths their feet have made in the middle of each riser, and the scuffmarks at each panel, and the many nicks and soiled places along the dowels of the banister.

She once knew every dusty joint of baseboard and floor in this house. Spiderlike her imagination crawled and hid in those spaces with their fertile smells: under the breakfront, behind the wingback chair, on the landing with her dolls. It was never perfect, never serene, but the house meant something like safety then. She knows the greased bronze scent that would greet her if she knelt to the casters on the tasseled ottoman. Furniture, floorboard, doorframe persist — and human beings file past, convocation of ghosts. It's all to be left. In leaden farewell her father has walked the rooms.

He bought the place the month he married Avis's mother. His old schoolmate Will Cummins built it in 1888, let him pay a pittance those first years. In time, thanks to Benjamin's insurance salary, the Lorns were able to buy it outright. All this Avis learned from the title records, helping her father settle the papers. He and her mother never lived anyplace else.

He seems to see the necessity of going, she's had no need to campaign the matter. Still, though he won't admit — and with all his power avoids showing — he's plainly oppressed. Needful or not it's unpleasant business this wrapping up of a life. Nothing left for him here of course, with his wife dead and buried. Town's changed. The old house had gaped around the aging Lorns. In Benjamin's solitude it's cavernous.

He was quick forbidding a sale, insisting the furniture stay. Will Cummins's young grandson is to marry one of the Turner granddaughters within the month and they'll need a place. They'll have the house complete for a pittance. To Benjamin it's only fitting, and Avis saw his mind was set. Didn't question.

He stands fixed in the center of the parlor. Sunlight wastes itself around him. The air of finality in the room makes her feel obtrusive, so she steps out on the porch to wait.

There in the shaded scent of honeysuckle rising from the lattice, Charlie Cummins stands looking like a man, fencepost-thin in checked flannel shirt with sleeves rolled. Beside him waits his bride-to-be, Wilmina Turner. Both barely twenty.

"He wants a minute, you understand," Avis tells them.

They understand of course, oh certainly they do. Bright-eyed children, they know little yet.

"Your father's doing us such a kindness, Mrs. Kurzwald. Charlie and me, we can't hardly express."

"Thank you dear, I know. Take these now."

Handing them the keys, she hands them the house — and suddenly remembers this porch as it looked after a spring rain, how the sun would break the clouds to fall upon rail and slanted deck panel and start the drenched wood steaming. Mornings this time of year bluejays took stalwart stance upon the handrail and shrieked at the world. None today. She hadn't looked for them yesterday or before. Strange to be the guest here, hatted and gloved with purse looped over one wrist, waiting to go.

"You all leave for San Francisco today, Mrs. Kurzwald?"

"This evening, yes, Charlie. Everything's hurried some, I'm afraid."

Edgar left two days ago, as agreed best, Benny on their minds. She stayed to settle affairs and see her father home with her.

"Wilmina dear," she rests a hand on the girl's arm, narrow bone beneath the printed sleeve. "I'd like to keep a few household things, maybe. We've packed as time allowed, pictures and such, but I'd be grateful now and then to have you send some things."

"Of course, ma'am, anything you like."

"Anything, Mrs. Kurzwald, least we can do."

Then Benjamin is ready and down the porchstairs she goes beside her stiff-gaited father, the young couple atop the stairs behind bidding thanks and goodbye, front door open beside them, keys glinting in Charlie's hand. They'll stay there waving till the Lorns pull away, then their young lives begin.

In the car Benjamin keeps his head down, hunched on the benchseat, eyes on the dash. The back seat and trunk carry two suitcases and sundry boxes.

At King Street he says, "Turn right."

"To the square?"

"Mm."

She idles past the vacant lot on the square's west side where Lorn & Son stood, nothing but gravel and weeds there since it burned — and that was before she was born. On summer weeks in her schooldays the Rotary set out chairs and put on entertainments with the neighboring brick wall for backdrop, old Major Farrows's cabinet shop. Because she was a Lorn they let her in free. The Farrows store still stands, complete with painted signboard, but for years the building has been a shell, windowglass dust-dark, dim interior strewn with nails and cobwebs. Most the old storefronts look the same now.

Her father points her south along Henry Street. Within a block the low hill of the Old Burying Ground slopes into view, grass summer-yellow already. Avis slows along the pebbled drive between headstones and stops, he needn't say where. He gets out and lumbers off up the slope, soft wind tousling his hair, dry lawn crunching.

She watches him stop at the weathered marble stones. His trousers flutter. Would make a fine silhouette, his form against that hill with the stones about his knees and, behind, a single high cypress stretching into the sky. She shuts off the motor and gets out.

Coming up alongside she finds him pondering his father's marker.

> J.M. LORN
> 1843 - 1889
> 36TH I.V.I., CO. C

Staked in the grass before it stands the small wrought-iron star of the Grand Army of the Republic.

"Boy from the G.A.R. phoned me," he says. "Said he heard I was going. Told me not to worry, they'll put a flag at the stone every year." He tosses a hand, grunts. "Hell ..."

He turns to the neighboring tablet, the inscription badly worn.

> HARRIET LORN
> 1846 – 1886

He stoops to touch the rounded top. To stone he says, "Well, darlin. I'm goin."

For a moment his hand remains upon the grave, then as if from ice recoils to his pocket.

"She'll be here. Huh?"

Avis is startled to see his bunched face turned her way. Hard eyes pink and wet. "She'll be right here. Like us someday."

The newer cemetery, Hillcrest, is off the highway a mile west of the Old Burying Ground. They stop on their way out of town. Stand silent at Alma Lorn's tender grave.

4. (1863)

Helena—Rumors of Vicksburg—A fusillade—
A reprimand—A quarrel.

Helena was a scatter hardly deserving the name of city. It looked a battlesite pummeled to bits and hastily reassembled, so cackhanded were the streets and jumbled structures flung across a knobby hillock. But by all accounts the Rebel army had never given a fight here and deserted it but recently.

The 36th took up garrison duty at Fort Curtis, a ridgetop bulwark established the prior summer. Tent encampments aproned the town, nearer the river.

It was forbiddingly cold, persistently wet. The aspect in all directions but void and mud. Winter cloud scarved atop trees bare of leaf, branches clawing out strands like yarn. The dribble of water could be heard in every corner. Helena drained and the Mississippi swelled, licking inchwise uphill to lap at the first stilted houses cantilevered off swampy slopes.

Upwater from Vicksburg, this was a crucial stronghold, or so the soldiery heard. Being primed to fight they thought it no place to stay. But they did not fear a lengthy posting, for the first days in Helena hummed with promise. One morning fast upon arrival came word of Sherman's victory downriver: Vicksburg was theirs! The news flew through the ranks and all were soon jubilant. To command Vicksburg was to command the Father of Waters at last. Wily Sherman had seen them through.

The line officers permitted a salvo of muskets from the Fort Curtis guard tower. Soldiers cheered and slapped backs, smoked and laughed, picturing their progress farther south. They would move in merry quickstep through the conquered city.

Late afternoon Alfred was straddling a stool amid Sibley tents at the far edge of camp. He was whittling with jackknife to keep warm, rifle leaning at one knee.

"Hey Alf, you heard yet?"

Knifeblade scraped to a halt and Alfred lifted eyes to J.M. slouching in bunched field jacket, boots and trouser shins mud-caked, one arm akimbo. "Another win?" said Alfred.

But J.M. was frowning. "Come see."

Outside camp they stood looking down upon the wharf. A steamer had docked and bluecoats were bustling. Litters of wounded juddered to shore. On deck under small awnings of canvas several officers parlayed, sabers glimmering at their belts.

"What regiment?" said Alfred.

"Illinois boys. Comin back from Chickasaw Bluffs. Their colonel's dead on that boat. And they say Vicksburg's not won at all."

"What? Sherman didn't—"

"Not won at all. How bout that? And they say very heavy losses these boys. Say that's the real truth. Say they don't know how we got the word we got. See, they were dyin down there all this time. And here we are just sittin watchin the river run by. Celebratin even."

J.M. spat and walked away.

The smaller boats skidded and rocked in their moorings below. The wounded continued coming forth. Behind them the brown soundless sweep of the Mississippi, vision of dread.

*

In following days Helena swarmed. A fleet of steamers crowded the riverbank, decks abuzz and pilothouses donning armored panels all round. Gunboats assembled amid them, sulking under humped casemates like mean turtles. From upriver great mortars floated in. Taller than the raftsmen, they tilted skyward in their mounts, black craws yawning at the rain.

The force in garrison was said to number twenty-one-thousand now. J.M., Alfred, and Needham bent brows to daily fatigue duty, waiting. They supped on stringy beef, chicory coffee, hardtack. Potatoes a dollar-eighty a pound here. No choice but basic rations.

There came no straight notice what lay in store but Vicksburg branded the brain of every man.

Then, come week's end, the fleets had gone to fight but the 36th remained, one of but several regiments left in garrison, ten thousand soldiers all told. Rebel guerrillas scrabbled at the fringes, emboldened. The chain guard saw its men snatched prisoner by the score each week. Damn graybacks would torment but never treat them to a proper fight.

One day the Perpetua boys stood twenty-four hour guard under Capt. Phillips, posted to a muddy back lane lined on one side with lean-to's and tin huts, brush and tall timothy grass along the other. Beyond the field a rim of dark trees.

Nightfall brought drizzle persistent for hours. The road in short time was a standing sluice. In the dark they felt exposure and did best to keep quiet and let the grasses hide them. J.M. however seemed all nervous joy.

"Johnny Reb wanna run at me I say, Have at it son." He leveled his rifle and made a concussive noise, bucking the barrel. With gun at support and cap tipped high he paced his piece of road and did nothing to quiet his plashing boots. Rods away on one side Needham smiled and shook his head while Alfred on the other sent up a shush. J.M. stopped to glare. Then boots slapped water again and Alfred heard him muttering.

An hour before first light there was commotion in the grass, an encroaching rustle, and before any in line could interpret J.M. gave a shriek and dropped his barrel and fired.

Immediately the trees across the field exploded in crackling retort. Bullets hissed in grass and the guard squatted to every man with shots papping in mud and humming overhead to perforate wood and tin siding.

"Hold!" called Capt. Phillips. "Hold fire!"

J.M. smothered a squawk. "Hold fire? I dropped one already!"

His shot had laid the body out, grass flattened in its fall, most had seen that.

"Hold!"

The powder smell had reached them. Smoke drifting over in the gray dark. But now the fusillade ceased. They listened to voices in the wood — snort of horses and snapping of twigs.

"They're going," muttered J.M. "Turnin tail and the damn cap'n wants to let'm. Hold, he says. Good God."

Alfred hissed. "Shut it, John!" Then saw J.M.'s shadow springing off its haunches to clobber sideward in the stream of mud.

"You ever mean to fight you ninny shit?" He fell upon Alfred in fury, rifles clattering, head and heel thudding in the wet.

"John!" On his back Alfred was grunting short of wind with J.M.'s knee in his gut, and at his cheek a mudslick palm shoved vicewise till slime wormed cold in his ear, grit in his teeth, then he was snorting mud. Still J.M. bore down.

"Shut your own yellow fuck trap why don't you!"

"J.M., get off him." Needham was trying to pull him back. "Goddamn man, he ain't done nothin."

"You men there," called Phillips. "Straighten up!"

A bitter snuffle, a final push, and J.M. let off. Alfred, coughing, blinked away mud to see J.M. standing over him, tall above the grass, a clear shot for the wooded guns and not caring if he was. He would not glance down, but his eyes were gray with rage. He spat and leaned away, gone.

Needham offered a hand. "Jesus Alf, can't say what he's thinkin."

*

The body felled in the field was a goat. J.M.'s shot had pierced its gullet. The company named it Contraband and cooked it on a spit that afternoon. Seeing mockery in the meal, J.M. refused. He kept to himself most the day. By evening he was tensely contrite.

"Hey Alf, I oughten done you that way, huh?"

"Forget it John."

But J.M. sidled in. "Truth is I'd a whipped that prissy cap'n if I could. You took his treat looks like, and hey I'm sorry for that. That was no good and I know it."

Alfred whiffed insincerity, but let it go. "All right John."

*

At morning the company was paraded before the fort with Lieutenant-Colonel Drake in attendance and made witness to Capt. Phillips' formal reprimand of Private John Lorn on cause of reckless conduct under fire.

"Had we met with ambush then and there the disturbance provoked by Private Lorn may have imperiled us considerably. It is fitting that stern example be made…"

Phillips declaimed from his saddle with spurs sparkling despite the mud. His horse in polished bridle brayed as if in emphasis. Lieutenant-Colonel Drake looked on from his own mount.

Before the fort wall J.M. stood alone, unrifled. Men peered down at him from the towers. Alfred could all but read his thoughts, how his mind glared sideward at the captain, jaw clenched in loathing. He'd fixed eyes so hard upon the middle distance that the company arrayed in front of him could only be a blur.

He was turned to the wall, unjacketed, and whipped with horse reins.

The penalty complete, J.M. returned to ranks. The company was busy at fatigue duty all the day. But that night the three sat back from the fire with J.M. talking low.

"He took me aside before it and says how he wishes he needn't shame me this way. Given a choice he surely wouldn't he says, but the staff officers have been *exerting certain pressures*. Told me I could *surely understand* his position. Says the penalty's mostly show, speech and parade and dozen lashes, I oughten take it for any *great significance.*"

They had their guns across their knees all three, running kerchiefs up and down, metal dark in the fire's play.

"Granted he had *every cause* to discipline me, *surely* I could see that. But he'd as soon let it pass were it his choice. Sadly it wasn't, he says. Drake and Hamilton preferred more stringent action. I could trust him in this *as I surely knew.* Surely I knew *how Captain Phillips looked after his men.* Well, he was right, damn sod. Penalty was no great significance. Worst of it was the fucker schoolin me how he does me favors."

"He's havin his day is all," said Needham. "Dogs always do."

"And hypocrite shiteaters, them too?" said J.M.

"He's liable to get demoted before we see a fight. Or finagle his damn divorce and do everybody a favor. Said yourself he's a coward. Prob'ly won't have to fight under him at all."

"See, that's why I like you, Needham. You got an eye sees a brighter side. And maybe you're right. But what's sure, I ain't takin no damn fall for no yellow fuck cap'n if he's to lead us into Reb guns. Course I can't claim to put much stock in the other officers."

J.M. stayed his kerchief and looked up past Needham.

"Say Alf. You're awful quiet."

Alfred spat to wet his cloth. Firelight gilded a solemn face. "Ain't much to say, John."

J.M. grinned to Needham. "Boy's takin lessons over there, Sam."

"Huh?"

"Listenin to you talk sense. Shuttin his trap and listenin. Damn sight better'n playin highhorse soldier."

Alfred raised his head. "John, what's gnawing on you? Thought we made square last night."

"Last night," J.M. grunted. "Maybe so. Then I stand your punishment by mornin and you've nothin to say."

"*My* punishment? Dammit John, talk sense yourself for once."

"Alfred Bauer shall have it be known he took no part in Private Lorn's recent *disturbance*." The last word chunked off hard as jerky. "You provoked me, Alf."

"Man, I did no such thing."

"No? So who gives you rank to shut me up?"

Alfred was silent. He pursed his mouth and moved his head side to side.

"Provocation, Alf. Provocation's grounds for this shitbag war we're waitin to fight. You gonna tell me the Rebs ain't provoked us? Say *they* ain't to blame?"

"You're talking two different matters, John, you know it."

"Do I now? See Alf, first I judged you were guardin your ass for your Reb lady back home. Now — well, now I've cause to wonder if you ain't a damn Rebel yourself."

Alfred's campstool wheeled and rifle dropped as he jacked to his feet. He lunged but found himself blocked in Needham's arms — Needham already pushing him back. "Whoa, whoa, come on boys." And behind Needham J.M. up in planted stance with shoulders squared, a bitter grin.

By the fire some heads turned and laughed. A voice whooped. "Fight it out, sons!"

"We will," said Alfred. "Hear me, John? We'll settle this."

But he was moving backward at the press of Needham's hands. He turned in the shadows of the tents as J.M. nodded and tipped finger to cap.

5.

Aug 3, 1887
Salvage, MO
Friend,
Rain today of the hot summer kind as we've had here the last three or four days with no relief. It is properly a State of Mud and Misery suiting its name — and to Heathendom you can add Pestilence for there is sickness here to boot.

Do you know there are four separate RR lines running through this place? Our best (worst?) days see no less than 60 trains coming and going. Who in Perpetua or Dennis could imagine? And since it's the RR that built Salvage the town has never known anything but bustle and hurry and strangers and "drifters" of every type. To be frank I suppose I am one though I hope not of any breed common here. I treat myself to daily reminding that my escape from Salvage is set but I've heard nothing promising from the managers. Any-day-with-not-much-notice seems apt description of when and how I'm to be delivered.

Did I tell in my last how I've not had a Sunday since I've been here? Yes it is a grinding work. If you're an agent or operator you're at the mercy of those above you turning the crank without cease. Unless you care to set off and make yourself a "boomer" that is, in which case you can't rightly tell day to day where your supper or room will come from. In such circumstances it will be a wonder if I avoid getting sick myself with the illness hereabout which seems to worsen and spread daily. At least two who work in the Depot have fallen ill that I know of. But our trains those "beasts of steel" charge on and we are but their servants.

Bone weary as I am, still I ask myself looking back at my last days in Perpetua, Did I not know that my going would prove rough and unpleasant as often as not? And I see I did know. This puts me at peace with circumstance though it be trying. So far anyhow I am well despite the hours. My only complaint constitutionally speaking is a bleeding of the nose which comes on me unawares and for no reason I can say. It happened three times this week, luckily away from the office each time. Once while sleeping once upon waking and once climbing stairs to my room. A woeful mess when it happens but as I am otherwise hale I must take this bleeding for nuisance and little worse, brought about by the climate here maybe or possibly the smoke in the station yards.

My ceaseless labors have had the peculiar effect to put me in mind of religious concerns. A part of the Bible I always esteemed was where it says "He that breaketh my Sabbath day shall not enter into the kingdom of Heaven." That has long seemed to me one of the Lord's more sensible conditions, a rare place where Man did not muddle the Creator's word taking it down. And yet here I am a Sabbath-breaker by no choice of my own. Fearing what may become of me if there is a Lord and he keeps a Heaven as reported, I seize upon another Bible page where it is said "He that has work to do let him do it with all his might not regarding the day, that it may bring honor and glory unto my name." What can a man do in a dilemma like mine but tell himself it's the latter passage he tries to follow? Still I must wonder am I becoming one of the tomfool Christians who do not fear their Lord enough to live in any way besides what suits them for most convenient? — the very sort of Christian who keeps me loath to name that faith my own? Wouldn't you agree that the better part of the Christian flock is made up of these kind if we're to look honestly at it? In face of this fact I'd prefer to stick to Atheism. Better isn't it than to join that creed of Excuse-Making?

Well, now I'm started on this I guess I'd better ask you, Are you a practicing kind of Christian? That is, Do you believe Church-house to be as important to faith as Change-of-Heart? After much delay I received your last letter from Perpetua. I reckon it is not too late to remark upon some things you said in it one being your comment on how I resemble a "Christian convert." To speak frankly I once attended Perpetua's United Brethren but have not been for some years. The Rev's long discourses tire me. I don't believe half he says and doubt the other half. What would you say to that? As you see from my line of thinking above sometimes for days at a spell I fear I'm getting into a bad fix Spiritually. I have been reading much strange literature in recent years from authors such as R.W. Emerson and Carlyle. I study these books and they tell me there is no Heaven and Hell. Then Pascal says there is and refers me to the Bible to prove it. But I can also prove there is not on the basis of the same strange and incomprehensible book. Oh it makes me tired.

You say you took me from the start to be "no stranger to sadness." Now that was a remarkable thing to observe. You were I think correct which I fear my few letters have already shown too plainly. As for you, you are no stranger to Kindness and Insight.

You made mention of my "adventuring in the Far West" and said you are jealous. Well, now you've heard how little enviable this journey is. I reflect that even if my lot should by some measure improve once I'm Westward bound, still what might for any other be called Adventuring can in my case be naught but Escape. Did you know that in telegraphy we use that word "Escape" when the voltage in a wire weakens and the connection drops? Well, so it is with me. My energy, my Willpower, abandoned me almost completely while I was at home — and you might say my "connections" there became disrupted.

You asked for "pleasant and friendly letters." Again I am not sure I'm the best source for those. You may find worrisome how I unguard myself in letting my pen go this way. Well, it is only because I have

*been betrayed in my time by those who would dissemble. Better to be
an open book I say, as far as that is possible.*

> *I am your Friend*
> *B. Lorn*

*P.S. Mr. Blaine the Chief Agent here tells me a tale. He was at his
post when the funeral cortege of Jesse James stopped here a night on
its way east from St. Jo a few years back. He says two KC policemen
near got up a gunfight in the waiting room at the issue of which man
could best be trusted to guard the outlaw's coffin till morning. Each
feared the other would steal the body away and sell it to a sideshow
— and they might have come to shooting if Blaine had not warned
them against drawing pistols in his depot. Good old Salvage!*

Aug 10, 1887
Dennis, IA
Dear Friend,
*Rec'd yours some time since but haven't had time to answer and have
only a little now so please excuse brevity. I'm half wild with packing
and preparing for I'm to teach at a school in Glenwood Iowa. So I
will go West as I told you — only not even so far as Nebraska. It is
the same institution where Anna Miller is teaching (she says you know
her from a sack supper at Centerville, and though I've not chanced yet
to quiz her on your character, do not doubt I intend to do just that).
After so much waiting and silence I hadn't the least idea I'd be
wanted at any school — but a week ago rec'd the letter telling me to
come along very soon, &c. Pa doesn't like to have me go at all, says
I'll surely get sick come winter, but then he always objects when I'm to
go anywhere be it only so far as Forbush. For all my wishing to see
something more of the world than the villages of Appanoose, it does
seem awfully hard to leave now that leaving is upon me. I find I must
make myself go and that's curious.*

My mother you might like to know came in last night and asked me "Does Mr. Lorn know you are leaving?" She smiles to see your letters arrive. Though she knows you are traveling far away she counts herself your ally I believe.

Must close now for I'm to go to Mr. Wales in Centerville and be photographed. This was my father's idea. I suppose he wants something to remember me by in the event that I die of frostbite in Glenwood.

Yours Very Truly

Alma

P.S. Sorry to hear of you stuck in that bad place. It must be unpleasant, yet I wonder if it might by some mystery prove a blessing to have gone there? I will hope I am an accurate prophetess.

Aug 21, 1887

Salvage, MO

Dear Alma,

I meant and hoped to write sooner but have found my best intentions bushwhacked by the sickness in this place which got ahold of me a week ago. I have tried to keep working despite it but that was not to be so I've laid up these two long days. It is a strange thing to turn sick in a strange place. For my part I cannot entertain the thought of going home so I tell myself I will get better. In truth I am quite weak and fear I'm worsening. I think the closest thing to my cure will be to leave here and continue West but it's no choice of mine and I will go wherever they can send me so long as it's away from Salvage.

It made me very glad for you, hearing of your teaching post. Do keep yourself well for not only your Pa's sake but for me, a friend who counts you dear.

You said you were to have your picture taken. Why you don't know how well it would please me to exchange Photos with you if this

*strikes you favorably. You will send me one won't you? Say so and I
will reciprocate with a piece of Pasteboard with a spot on one side
supposed to be a representation of me. An inequable trade but it can't
be helped. If I may anticipate your Photo I feel certain it shall put me
on the mend. Sorry to close so quickly.*

Benjamin

*P.S. If your mother is on my side as you say it must be that I am
blessed for reasons I know not. Perhaps it's the blessing you
prophesied?*

*P.P.S. Would say give my regards to Anna Miller but they are now
reserved entirely for you.*

Aug 25, 1887

Salvage, MO

Dear Alma,

*This fragment to inform you I am leaving Salvage tomorrow for
Oregon. Stars be praised. Health remains poor but I must go, chance
is now. They say it's the dry part of Oregon and I hope the climate
repairs me. Who can know? I do what feels necessary at present —
and necessary for more reasons than one.*

*Send any letters to Postmaster, Pendleton OR. I will await your
Photo.*

Benjamin

Sept 14, 1887

Glenwood, IA

Dear Benjamin,

*During my first day or two here I thought I would turn right about
and start back to Appanoose, and so might I if I didn't know they
would laugh at me in Dennis as to say I proved all their presumptions*

true concerning me. So I managed to stay, part in dread of that humiliation — but in larger part by saying to myself, Think of Benjamin. All alone he is, out there in the world, and sick as a hound too, but he is undaunted, and here you are silly girl not even out of Iowa and in fine health and availing the comforts of a friend who's here beside you through it all. Well, that humbled me, and now I have caught my breath and looked about and learned to like this place somewhat better.

It is not so good a town, there is no doubt. I shouldn't have come if I had known. But here I am. I find to add to my dissatisfaction that I haven't much to do or haven't had so far. The Matron or Boss Teacher or Principal, whatever she calls herself, just hates me I guess. At first acquaintance she remarked how she found my stature disappointing for she'd saved me a mean grade but now thought I could not manage them. I think the Superintendent thinks slightly better of me. He is not so horribly particular as she is and does most of the real managing by his visits to the grades every few days.

Some of the children here stammer and some are hard of hearing so you must yell at them, and in this way making a likable impression among them is not so easy. As I am already very blue from this place it looks to be a long autumn.

Are you in Oregon now and what is it like? I hope your condition has changed and you did not trail noseblood the whole way West.

Anna just got off duty and we have had quite a talk. She has a fellow who writes to her from business college at Omaha. His letters are such that she usually lets me read them (they come just about daily). Each one is written up along the same design (viz.) "I take my pen in hand to let you know I am well and that I hope you are too" &c. He makes no mistakes in grammar or composition but must claim he does so he can apologize and that way have something to write. Poor fellow. Anna finds him an awful nuisance but she is also glad of his attention and makes it a game with herself to imagine the letters

much more interesting than they are. Glenwood being what it is, such
fancies are necessary to keep from running mad. Though I laugh
about those letters (and Anna doesn't mind that I do), I must admit
it's frightful to see what girls have to put up with. It makes me the
more thankful for the letters you write, and makes me wish the more to
prove a good correspondent though letter writing is the least of my
strengths if it can be said to count as strength at all.

Really, having just looked this letter over I feel certain it offers
nothing worthwhile but only goes to show how ego-centric I can be.
Well, this one can't be rescued, but let me finish with a promise to try
and get better on paper and with a few pertinent questions.

1. *Are you well again?*
2. *Whatever is Oregon like?*
3. *Will you come home for Christmas?*

On the topic of the last, I mean to do so and already I'm counting the
days.

Hope you will write instantly. Don't forget to put the county on
the address. And tell me how you are faring out West.

From

Alma

P.S. I am having the folks at home forward my Photo to you. Will
expect yours as promised.

Oct 20, 1887
Pendleton, OR
Dear Friend,
Imagine my joy upon receiving your last away out here in this country
where the eye roves on and on finding nothing it may stick upon. This
West or what I've seen of it is all empty distance scarcely more than
Rock or Sand most parts — stretches of these as you cannot imagine.
Other parts, wild wicked-looking grasses or desert bushels sprung

from the stoniest, forbiddingest soil. Amid such an emptiness under these most uncaring skies, your letter was a liferope. It gave companionship for I saw something more of yourself there than you shared in any previous. After my several tell-alls to you I took that for comfort, for all I'd started to fear the scale of disclosure tipping too steep to the Lorn side. The last thing I ever wish is to crowd myself upon you.

Goodness, I pity that poor suitor of Anna's and shudder to think he should ever discover how she shows his letters around! I see the humor of course but sharing somewhat his position I cannot fend off natural horror. Alma please say you do not show Anna what I write. If you have ever wondered whether I show yours the answer is No. How could I? They are, I might tell you frankly, essentially sacred to me in a world where little else is. They shall become the moreso as long as I'm privileged to receive them and the more you entrust me with your true and living character as in your last. I will strive to remain worthy of this trust. Anyhow who would I show them to, alone as I am out here? Or, a better question: Who could possibly warrant a glimpse of them?

I mustn't forget to honor your three principal questions with answers, so to your first: Am I well again? I wish I could give happier reply. You remember prophesying to me how my going to Missouri might prove a blessing? As yet I've had some trouble finding the blessing unless it be that for some reason still unclear it wears the guise of misfortune, for when I first went to Missouri I looked myself, enjoyed strength of a kind, and could manage a day's work. Now I am altered. I do about 10 min. work before it seems a lot. I regret to tell you that you are a failure as a prophetess. Still I do best to appear fitter than I am for there are prospects here.

How are your Blues in that little schooltown? You are not alone in suffering them rest assured, for you've seen the Benjamin Blues of my Missouri purgatory. Quick departure West has in some measure helped shed me of them but I see they will not go completely now I am here. And it was no help how I had no chance to see you on my passage north from Salvage to the U.P.R.R., knowing you'd gone for Glenwood. At that place where the rails drew nearest to old Appanoose Co., even though a rain was starting I stood out on the platform of the train with the wind whistling at my ears and looked across the flying country toward Dennis and your family home and wished — oh but nevermind what I wished!

Now I will try to describe for you the Pendleton country which is like none I've seen. This will answer Question number 2. You see I am a dependable answerer.

There is a little township above us called Milton. Were I a wagon wheel you could set me rolling at the high grasslands south of that place and I'd keep going (it's wide sea of a country and stuff of a wheel's dreams) till I dropped unexpectedly over a ledge to land in Pendleton. This township is a crouching place, huddling below the rest of the land and all boxed in with bluffs. You'd think it wanted to stay a secret from the wider world and maybe it does.

I hope to leave here soon and continue West. You asked how I was "faring" but you will see from this that "wayfaring" is more like it. You know that old song about the Stranger? But I hope to remedy this. There's a man I shall try to meet regarding a Steamboat position. I also know an acquaintance in Portland who works Cabin Man on an Ocean Steamer and told me he could get me a good position. I may take such employment if offered but must tell you that should I do so I cannot be sure when if ever I'll have opportunity to receive word from you — and that fact alone makes the whole notion very disagreeable, even so that I can hardly imagine accepting after all.

Your third question I liked best for its suggestion (or do I imagine it?) that you hope to see me at Christmas. Regrettably I must hold off

answering till my winter circumstances come clear. Maybe after I
reach Portland I shall be able to say.

    What kind of school are you at in Glenwood? What do they
teach? Is it a County, State, or Private institution? I am enclosing
with this a little slip of stamps which I hope you will use to send me
some fine and enjoyable letters like your last. You don't know how
your words tumble down from the angels' dominion upon my
unangelic West.

    I also enclose my Photo, not at all proudly you can be sure, but in
good faith that you will hold to your promise and send me your own
portrait. I have every belief in the solvency of a promise from one such
as you.

       Your Friend,
       Benjamin

Nov 2, 1887
Glenwood, IA
Dear Benjamin,
Your last is at hand.

    First you really must excuse me for I do not want those stamps. If
this is a customary thing for a boy to do, it needn't be our custom, for
we will suppose your letters are worth the postage it takes to answer
them and say no more about it. Stamps therefore enclosed.

    Second, I am sure you shouldn't be standing in the wind and rain
on the outside of a moving train. Whatever wish you wanted to make
would have been better made in warmth and safety behind a shut
window. I've made my own share of wishes and can say quite certain
they go through walls floorboards ceilings glass brick, &c. The point
mainly is you should never go and degrade your health on my account.
This I say in full seriousness for here just yesterday death came and
called a child out of my grade. After breakfast today I helped make the

girl's shroud. A pretty chore, wasn't it? Before the material was cut the head teacher wanted me to go and take measure of the child. I knew at once I could not. I suppose I have a godless fear about corpses — the moreso when the corpse was at play with stick and hoop on my Recess just last week. I told the head teacher I didn't know how to take measures and this way escaped the errand. She sent someone else. But I think she looked at me in a manner as to see I'd made false excuse. I am no practiced fibber. All the same I don't think it was altogether a lie, for I know I haven't the strength or composure to go and do a thing like that.

The school since you ask is one supported by the state for weak minded children. That's got an awful sound about it, but the place isn't so bad as you'd suppose. Many of the children are not even cursed in the head but only lack folks or homes so they're sent here to live. The ones that don't know anything at all are in another building set apart from mine. A force of men over there looks after those boys, who are all in such a state that no attempt is made to teach them anything.

The measles are what killed the little girl. They came on fast and awful bad. She was first to be sick and naturally it has got everybody worried. She was an affectionate creature. It's bitter to see no relations about who would mourn her, they say she had none in the world. How is it a child of ten comes to such abandonment? It almost comforts to think her misfortunes now ended.

I'm told it is not irregular for children to die in this place. There were two deaths last year and Anna counsels me to "brace" myself.

I was pleased to know my last letter was a triumph. You mustn't fear a breach of trust on my part. I would not show Anna anything you write, on the basis of feelings much like those you describe. She is not the inquisitive kind anyway. Odd, I grant, how she should tell me every little thing and yet I don't bother her at all with my affairs.

Anna's fellow is coming up from Omaha next Sunday. She says she's going to let me "pass judgment on him" before she answers the dreaded question (for she's certain he means to ask it). But since the things you said concerning him I think I'm likely to be the most gentle judge on earth — and as that cannot be any help to Anna I believe I will just try to stay out of the matter. Your point was well taken is what I mean.

As for your absent blessings after Missouri, have you forgotten the one that you yourself recognized a while ago? I will provide hint: She wrote me from home just yesterday to say she had mailed my Photo to your Pendleton, Oregon address. She vies for you yet.

Your Photo came all right, thank you. It looks just like you. Although you say you are somewhat altered now after your bad spell, I hope you may see this man in your mirror again before long.

It's time to go on duty so I will close.

As Ever,

Alma

How long do you mean to stay in Oregon?

6.

The stenciled door at the head of the stairs reads:
T. WREN, ESQ., NEW CRONUS CO.

Benjamin pauses on the landing to catch breath. A scent of vanilla pipesmoke creeps in the stairwell. He looks to his boots and frowns, lifts one to his trouser heel and hastily buffs. Shifting weight he buffs the other and looks again: improved, but nothing to do for the blacking, too far gone. *Well, worn shoes show a workman, let them speak for themselves. Do bend to dust your cuffs though.* Bending brings the blood and phlegm to his face, dizzying. He steadies himself at the wall.

Look fit. Do not cough.

He knocks. The door swings before his knuckles come away. A gentleman looms in stout waistcoat of paisleyed satin, Meerschaum pipe grimaced in his jaw. Muttonchops, a bullfrog chin charcoaled with stubble, bassooning voice. "Thaddeus Wren." Words clench the pipestem. And teeth flicker unearthly whiteness. Wooden? Walrus tusk?

Benjamin meets the proffered hand, praying his own palm is dry, gripping firm. "Good afternoon, Mister Wren. Benjamin Lorn."

"Lorn indeed. Come amigo. Sit."

Benjamin's boots crush a carpet of figured red and gold as he trudges to a highbacked chair before the man's desk. Hidden springs make a bellows-like wheeze as he settles. The armrests are done over in glove leather, the wood where it curves carved in lion paws. His hat slips when he tries to place it there. He holds it on his knee.

Thaddeus Wren rounds the desk, one thumb hitched at waistcoat pocket. "Well, Mister Lorn." His pipebowl has a coppery luster where his fingers polish it. "I've high report of you from Mister Blaine. You worked under him at — where was it?"

"Salvage Missouri, sir, on the Hannibal and Saint Jo."

"Mm. And prior to your employ there?"

"Prior I was on the Keokuk and Western, sir, under Edwin Mueller."

"What line, you say?"

"Keokuk and Western. Off the Wabash in south Iowa."

"Iowa, Missouri, mm, capisco. Well, as I say, I've high report of you."

"Thank you, sir."

In the corner by the window stands a pedestal of blue ceramic silvered over with a delicate webwork pattern. It looks a thing brought from overseas. Mr. Wren steps to it and begins to pet a dwarfish tree growing in a tureen of porcelain. Little arthritic branches sprout florets of green fur. The man's pipesmoke plumes to mimic those shapes. "I take it Mister Lorn that you are thoroughly and dependably a railroad man."

"Beg pardon, sir?"

"Unattached, I mean. That's to say, you have no special or particular, ah, entanglements out West here?"

"Oh. Indeed I don't, sir. But it's your steamships I wished to see you about, sir."

"Steamships, what? The railroad does not suit you, mein Freund? You mean to quit it?"

"Well …"

"You won't take me amiss Mister Lorn, will you, if I tell you that you belong — man like yourself belongs — on land?"

Benjamin clears his throat. *Do not cough.* "Amiss, sir? No. Only I —"

"Who was it gave you ideas to go asea?" Wren squints, studious cant of the head. "Couldn't be your own notion — you'll forgive the observation."

"Well ..." Benjamin bounces his knees. *Quit it!* "Matter of fact, sir, it was one of your boatmen Mister Austin. I knew him under Mister Blaine. You're right it wasn't my notion at first, but Mister Austin thought me suited so I've come."

Mr. Wren stoops, seeming to sniff his queer tree as if nosing a rosebud. "Do you know bonsai Mister Lorn?" He's produced a monocle, the lensed eye leering down at each green tuft, fingers in tickling motions.

"Pardon sir?"

"Bonsai, mon ami. A species of the Far East. I have a specimen just here. An ancient husbandry, bonsai. The name denotes the tree but also the art. They're extremely delicate organisms yet they've longevity of an awesome kind. You see it interests me, Mister Lorn — questions of time, timelessness, seemingly neverending things. To wit: in bonsai one is tasked to know one's specimen well, to anticipate its unique nature, pre-vision its growth, observe its hunger, its special leanings, know where to indulge and where to prune. I've had this one some years now. It lives yet, you see. And you, Mister Lorn, belong in telegraphy. In its service I mean. On land that is, railroads or not."

Mr. Wren straightens and moves to the window. His sumptuous carpet, Benjamin observes, runs short of the walls, giving over to raw pine flooring, hardworn and bespattered. Along the baseboards lie lumps of sawdust, sand, trickles of dirt. But this office seems a place where studious hours accumulate, thought upon smoldering thought metered to the stately metronome of a clock. Yet there is no clock here. And save a single lithograph — a framed landscape hung behind the desk — the room is unadorned. Bare stucco walls whitewashed but soiled and smokestained. Window shutters but no curtains. A cracked wooden doorknob, not brass. There's something, then, in this figure of Thaddeus Wren esquire. Yes, he seems to exude philosophy — a quality attributable to men of property or power in this West — or so Benjamin has gathered in his brief time out here, noting men of the kind in stations, in restaurant windows, in haberdashers and tobacco shops. Mr. Wren pauses at a sideward angle to the window. Meerschaum in hand he peers down slantwise upon the street like somebody spying on a neighbor. "Mister Blaine reports you to have a most thorough apprehension of the trade, Mister Lorn. You are no mere operator he says. You can survey?"

"Yessir."

"Set poles?"

"Yes."

"Hang wire?"

"Yes indeed."

"Mm. You see, these are no Job-Chaser's skills, mi amigo. You, Mister Lorn, are no journeyman, and better than a boomer. A Servant of the Telegraph Entire. Yes, like myself. I need your boots on land. Do you smoke, Mister Lorn?"

"Uh, no sir, thank you." *Must not cough.*

"Tell me, were you a native of Iowa?"

"I am sir, yes."

"*Are* or *were*, Mister Lorn?"

"A native, sir? Well, I was born there."

"Naturellement my friend, but every man is many men, as

you surely know. Life sees to it, does she not? We meet with some seven rebirths before our denouement. I forget who it was first set the figure at seven. A Persian philosopher I should think — the desert honed those men. At any rate, this West, this majesterium of wind and waste, renders us natives of no place, men like you and me — for we've no real home to start from at the first, have we? We've no destiny but that which demands we get up and leave. You notice I did not ask what entanglements you have *in Iowa*. Had you any you would never have left. You see, Mister Lorn, something makes us servants, something greater than ourselves, something large as these wilds out here. Ah, but forgive me. I wax eremitic." Mr. Wren lifts the sash. *Tap tap tap:* dead embers tumble from his pipe. "A foible of mine I fear, the bent of the philosophe. Gets the better of me when I sense a kindred soul." He brushes the sill with the edge of his palm, head turned back to purse a grin, then leaves the sash to fall with a thump as he crosses back behind his desk.

A drawer squeaks. Wren's fingers rustle in papers. "You know the names Holladay, Hunt, Villard."

"Of course, sir."

"Claro, for these are demigods, n'est pas? Si, si, titans of ingenuity and imagination, figures not unlike those other greats: Stanford and Hopkins, Crocker, Huntington, Judah. Yes, and our special demigods Mister Villard and peers have brought a naissance to this far country. With every stretch of rail they draw the boldest lines against these wastes. Lines, Mister Lorn, in which we read like scripture all that the railroad, the telegraph, have done for mankind everywhere. How these twin advancements shatter, wholly shatter, our tidy conceptions of time. To wit, the locomotive has carried us in a few short decades from life by crop to life by clock. Can we yet comprehend the implications of such a shift Mister Lorn? —

the immense consequences in our history, the very consciousness of our race? We have learned irreverence toward sun and
season. And the telegraph Mister Lorn, the telegraph is …
preternatural. Come, mio fratello, look close."

Mr. Wren's hands sweep the desk and a great map
unscrolls with a whisper. Benjamin stands in the wind of the
parchment.

"Maps, ah, maps are man's longing made manifest. What
soul has ever looked upon a map unmoved?"

Pale reaches of blue and pink depict the far western
territories from San Diego to the 49th Parallel. Mr. Wren's
pipestem drills the paper.

"But *these* territories Mister Lorn, this West, ah, no
cartographer can capture the longing *here*. And what is that?
Tell me Mister Lorn, what longing is here?"

Benjamin looks up. The question is not rhetorical. He
crosses his arms and hums his contemplation. But Mr. Wren is
in form and does not wait.

"I think of it Mister Lorn as a special longing endemic to
immensities like these. What are we in such wastes? Where can
we be bound? We creep small and wayward like flies on a
billiard table. God's sun breathes hot upon us. His waters soak
us to the bone. And all the while we stand isolate in time,
Mister Lorn. Our loneliness adheres us to the earth. We crawl.
Can this be the promised freedom of the West — this crawling,
this desolation, these barrens of the soul? No! And thus we *long*,
Mister Lorn, to allay the immensity, to ease the ravages of
time, to unstick ourselves and crawl no more. Ah, and
telegraphy, mi hombre — *telegraphy* answers these longings as
nothing else can!"

There comes a crisp little noise and a flash of white as Mr.
Wren tenders a slip of cardstock. "You will keep this upon your

person, Mister Lorn. It is your amulet in those wilds."

Benjamin studies the card.

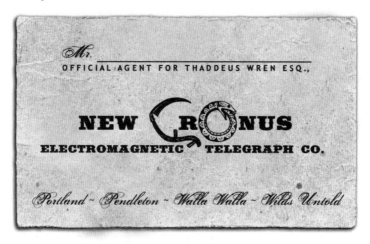

"With this card, mi bueno hombre, your boots are winged."

"I see, sir."

"Mercury, my friend. Hermes if you will. The upshot Mister Lorn is that telegraphy … telegraphy lifts us out of time. Ah, but you have the look of a man who knows this already. Do I misjudge you?"

"I think I do know it sir, yes."

"I'd venture it was this that brought you West."

"You may be right, sir." *Do not cough.*

With clean white index nail Mr. Wren taps the edge of the card. "Cronus, you remember, castrated his father and escaped the netherworld. Cronus was *Time* — Saturn to the Greeks. Our father out here, our overlord, is Time. It would bind us. It would have us be bound. But with the telegraph we wield a new sickle. We are a new Cronus, you see?"

"Ah, I see, sir."

"Break the circuit Mister Lorn and you've broken the flow of time. Every dash, every dot transcends the natural law. This country's immensities reduce us no more. Think of it mein

Freund, for the man awake in India, this very moment is a different day. It is tomorrow. Yet we may touch him by wire in matter of moments. We may reach from *this* day to *that* futurity. What have we done then but overthrow time? — and geography, time's confederate. Even mountains needn't encumber us. That's where a man of your experience comes in, Mister Lorn. You will carry our strange, fierce fire through those wilds."

"I know those words."

"Of course amigo, and well you ought."

"He drew from heaven the strange fierce fire and he carried it over the mountain's crest."

"Indeed Mister Lorn. And such words are no mere fancy. They're a commission."

"Commission?"

"The very thing, my friend. Don't you see? These words, Mister Lorn, are for you."

The newest agent to Mr. Thaddeus Wren esquire descends from the Pendleton office of the New Cronus Company, his company card snug in jacket pocket, duly certified with signature. It will serve for railroad pass, Mr. Wren assured him. It sidles against Edwin Mueller's transcription of "The Victory" on its faded scrap of paper, paper depleted these years to a flower-petal softness that does not rustle, paper airy and doubtless and humeral as faith.

Since boyhood Benjamin has known the credo bespoken today. Moving pole to pole with lightning speed, electromagnetism transubstantiates all things into Now. And from here on out, if he can keep moving, keep booming, he will stay spliced into that current — a person all energy, outside time, not subject to the claims of change and instability. He's becoming a modern man through and through. The West will make a man so.

For the whole of the lovely moment coming down the stairs Benjamin feels no need to cough, not a tickle. Then, stepping into dizzying fall sunlight, he stops at the realization — complete and instantaneous — that Thaddeus Wren is mad.

And he understood the madman's every word.

7. (1863)

His sight is beveled glass — each fist flies at him twinned. And the men cheering, jeering, they stand a circle in boots and caps, smoking some, guns at shoulder some. They move in carousel as he sprawls and dodges, goes down, gets up — but their feet stick fast like the tents pitched taut behind.

Cheering, jeering — and now he's flung out again ass-flat and they've scattered to let fall.

There looms Alfred ruddy-cheeked with fists held high on chance he'll get up.

And does he rise — or is it someone propels him up the sloping dirt? … back on his feet anyhow and swinging. Lurch ahead. And slash with lurching arms. Cheer and jeer. Alfred the bastard a sideways grimace his eyes seedy and sharp as darts. *What love we lost between us Alf once bloodbrothers what are we now?* — Alf's knuckles barbed and every day this war a choosing of sides not to be undone.

Then ass over elbow and down amid boots in frozen runnels of mud.

I'm down again. Even struck that time? …blood in my beard…

Nearby a horse is bridling — jibbing at the hitch. Smell the dung smell even through nose all broke the hoofing snort and square teeth chomping.

Where's Alfred now?

where you gone my brother once? And how long we been at this and how'll it end? ... the girl over to Trillium sends letters by the bookful and married in secret which only shows we come apart — brothers like but oh we changed somethin changed us.

Stay down, says Alfred — words ice-clear in ice-crust noon. Alf's fists crosshatched and bleeding — *my blood or his? how long we been at this?*

and ya I read her letters — why? cause I wanted part of it is all cause I someway got shed from you ...

Blood comes masking, blood warm in the eyes and stinging — *how's it to end Alf you do me like this on the ground for all to see? and this girl over to Trillium and like brothers once and this war—*

Stay down.

stay down stay down he'll boss me to the goddamn grave the shit — look at us this mud...

The men turn quiet cheering no more they only watch now — *all hoping I don't get up ... ready to help once I'm down to stay ...but I see you Alfred what you become and how you'd leave me lay here ...love shed us someway but mostly it's that damn cap'n come between us ain't it? ya yellow turnspit's to blame, oh but see you turnin your back and means it's over ...*

over and you done me like this front of all — over!

The men lean close.

I'm to take their help I knew it they hoped I'd fall just lay down not get up — slap em off. Off! Bat at the whirling faces—

No no. Leave me …

no goddammit …

leave me fuckin be.

8.

Benjamin Lorn has hardly left the house since he arrived. Each morning he sits to breakfast with *The Examiner* or *Chronicle*, big pages crackling above his plate. He folds them back to sip coffee or spoon his cereal. Darkrimmed reading glasses tilt to the tip of his nose.

"Mother of Two Throws Children from Golden Gate," he reads aloud. "City Selectman Resigns Amid Extramarital Scandal. ... O'Farrell Street Murder Victim Identified as Prostitute. ... Cable Car Kills Pedestrian, Injures Second."

He's taken to clipping stories in the afternoon. He keeps them stacked atop Benny's dresser, beneath the boy's U.S. Army paperweight. Does he catalog his own grief this way — borrowing upon griefs of others?

In Benny's room he sleeps beneath the boy's pennants, heels overhanging the mattress. The hairs snagged in the old man's comb are white, the stubble he straightrazors each morning is white, he suspenders his trousers, tucks arch supports into his shoes — but Benny's room fits around him like a glove, for old soul and young are confederate. They stand at the twin gates, entrance and exit, close to the edges. And then there's middle-aged Avis, marooned at the bulge of life, out in the open. This is the trouble between parents and children.

Avis feels him observing her. It galls her to sense his judgment, the opponency of his silences, as his sheaf of news clippings thickens. He will brood, and make her feel obtrusive in her own house.

Evenings she spends at the telephone, ringing enlistment centers in Lafayette, Walnut Creek, Concord, Antioch, as far away as Stockton. Edgar tried the local recruiters while she helped her father settle affairs in Iowa — nothing of it. But at the end of a schoolday last week she stopped one of Benny's friends outside Lowell High, a lanky, curly-headed boy named Shreve. Shreve said Benny dropped hints of bussing to an enlistment office outside the county. Where? Shreve thought a minute, shrugged. "Past Berkeley maybe, out east."

Avis pleads into the receiver, pen and notepad ready. The officers and their clerks listen and apologize. In their tones she hears the shaken head, waved hand, the shrug that means it's likely hopeless. And in the rooms about her lurks Benjamin Lorn like a figure come to play her conscience. He plods in hallway, kitchen, coffee cup in hand, evening paper in hand. He sits with scissors at the dinette, his shirt buttons done to the top and suspenders snug, shoes double-knotted. Buttoned old man even after nine o'clock.

She hears him hearing her futility. He casts no glances, makes no comment. He sits. Passes in the hall. Retires to Benny's room with no Goodnight.

Absences amplify.

Edgar is out with the car. She'll sit up till he's home, and strive to expect nothing.

—*Make me a man?*

What softness there was to him then, fair hair and the bright whites of his eyes, and earlier his wet gums before teeth cut through. She'd given her pinky when he was restless and wouldn't nurse, finger's pad pressed to warm dome of mouth. They were each but substances she and the boy, not yet molded and shelled, hardly people, hardly even bodies.

—*A man?*

—*Yes. A man for real.*

—*Well, you're a man for real. Shall I make you?*

Her boy emerged shaped in paper. And that first small silhouette, like each one after, had seemed to cease the world's turning, briefly.

She thought then — with what looks like blindness now — that she would always remain a mother.

Avis speaks by telephone with an enlistment officer in Livermore.

... entirely sympathetic ma'am, believe me ... done a tour myself and I thank my stars that I get to look at the inside of this office every day ...

But he tells her in well-meaning bluntness she's wasting her time. Almost certainly her boy's enlisted and shipped off to training someplace.

"The man's right," she tells Edgar at supper. "It's time we admit it."

Across the table Benjamin Lorn saws his roast. "Is it so bad the boy wants to fight?"

Edgar sits back. "He's not eighteen yet, Benjamin — and could be on the street somewhere."

The old man shrugs, cheeks dark with anger. "Won't let you find him less he wants you to." Snaps meat from fork and irritably chews.

Avis watches Edgar frown, his eyes drifting gray in thought. They both know it's no use contradicting the old man.

Anyhow he's made his point. Benny does not *want* to be found. Only she or Edgar can be at fault for that — and she knows, as Edgar does, just where her father lays the blame.

Avis leafs through his baby book, scouring each pasted page, rummaging the paper pouches fat with congratulatory cards and locks of babyhair and first drawings.

    She searches her drawers, files, keepsakes, picture frames. She checks Benny's room, dresser drawers, desk, under the bed, between the pages of magazines. She tips books from shelves and thumbs them back and forth. No use. No idea where it could be. She's lost his silhouette.

9.

Nov 13, 1887
En route, Umatilla Oregon to Portland
Dear Friend,
You see I am moving again. I expect it will dizzy you to read these shaky lines but as you are much in my thoughts and this train ride is to last a whole long day I will make the best of conditions and write. Your sorrowful last arrived at Pendleton as designed — but now it appears that your Photo will have to pursue me (the PM will forward my mail to Portland so you can trust what my first stop in that city will be). The Photo till I retrieve it shall haunt my thoughts every bit the way the flesh-and-blood original does. Do I shock you to say so?
    Was saddened to learn the fate of your little orphan charge. Look here, if that place proves too dismal whyever shouldn't you go back

home? I see no shame admitting dissatisfaction. Of course that's a pretty bit of counsel from one stubborn as me, so far from home myself and still traveling farther.

Well, there is something awful hollow and lifeless about this West. We were kept waiting in the station at Umatilla for near two hours. Nothing but Sandhills there far as you can see. Should somebody deed me that whole territory and even grant me the PO on their RR I'm sure it could not make me stay.

Pendleton being not far from Umatilla was little (or maybe _a little_) better. And the skance-looking Pendletonians put me ill at ease. They've seen a great many railroaders free agents boomers and rodeo kinds which accounts for their cautiousness. At least that's what I surmised, but they made a body eager to get moving again.

My health keeps on getting better. The West has helped in that respect as hoped. But it's prospect of movement that's best for me. Thank Heaven for travel resumed. I cannot be wholly well till I have got away from this horrendous Sand. Everywhere about you this Sand drifts ceaselessly, much like the snow in Iowa — but Sand is worse for it will scrape down and soften your better sense till you're left only madness. It is a torment to reason.

You ask how long I mean to stay in Oregon. I have as yet no proper calendar in the work before me so do not know though I suppose I'm to remain this side of the Rocky Mountains no less than one year but likely many more. Truth be told Alma, I will stay unless a certain person tells me in no uncertain terms and gestures "Come back." Can say no more of such a circumstance now. We shall not mistake it however if it should arrive. Do I dwell too much in fancies thinking so?

We are traveling alongside the Columbia River. It is every bit the rival to our Missouri and Mississippi and looks to be fairly a torrent in places. The far shore stands off a very great distance all wilderness, cliffs and trees. This side is little more civilized. There is Sand blowing everywhere. It swirls off the dunes along the RR. There's enough to make you think it would bar up a lesser river. We cannot raise the windows on account of this Sand though the sun through the glass makes an oven of the cars. This closeness in the car was I think the cause of another bloody nose come to nettle me about an hour ago, my first such onset since Salvage — but what an awkward chore on board a train. It has stopped and I am better now.

The track we travel over is a wonder of engineering considering the wildness of this country. But I hear told that just last winter a horrendous blizzard stranded the Pacific Express several days. No fewer than eleven Relief Engines were bogged down in snow while coming to its aid.

There are now to be seen in the waters just offshore ranks and ranks of white stumps sticking through the surface. A sight most peculiar and haunting in how it calls to mind jagged bones. They stick up very still and numerous amid the foam and blowing Sand. I heard somebody in the car tell how these are trees from a forest drowned and petrified long ago. Said Lewis & Clark saw the very sight in passing here a near century back. There seems no end to these stumps, their numbers stretch on and on. Around them a wicked wind kicks the water into sprays that flash little rainbows.

I have not said my business in going to Portland. I have taken a position with a new telegraph company ...   [letter breaks off]

Nov 19, 1887
Vernal, CA
Dear Friend,
My destiny such as it is has led me to California. As you are not likely to have predicted this turn I think it good to tell you my whereabouts and the poor circumstances that led me here.

I have been sick again. Whatever my benefits in health when last I wrote you they were appallingly brief. I reached Portland underwater or so it felt, for there was little light in that city the sky fully closed up in clouds and the ground boggy and slick and rain beating down without mercy. It was no place to go though it took so long to get there and though having come through wild country a body wished keenly for a finer friendlier destination. A city is wild in its own way and Portland is a city in every respect with shipyards stone storefronts and hotels. There is even a Chinese quarter that swarms with those little folk. Down in the close streets fronting its river the traveler finds much noise but little rest. It was there I lodged and there I wondered tossing in my blankets at the strangeness of so gray and miserable a city sprung up at the limits of the earth. Whatever was it led me through the Sandy wastes to such a place?

My health did not falter right off, but after two days spent in the weather there wasn't much to spare body and spirit sinking. My third morning in Portland I woke early suffering a new attack worse than any before. A doctor looked me over at my hotel and brought me to understand how far gone I'd become. I had no idea. He asked where I came from and hearing Iowa replied "Oh an Easterner. You people are awful hearty or awful foolhardy I can never tell which." Sternly he told me to go away to a dryer place before I worsened past help. I cannot express how blue this made me. I felt no special fondness for Portland but where to go? I could not turn back for Pendleton, that would be defeat and my spirits would not take it. The doctor then told me of this place called Vernal which lies in the foothills of the California Sierra Range. The weather while cold this time of year is dry and often clear like east Oregon — and as Vernal sits in a valley below the snow there's little danger of freezing.

I arrived here day before last seeing no choice but to make the journey though I can't say my health profited along the way. Rather — I would tell you the truth — I wonder if I had better give up hope of improving. A doctor here will see me tomorrow and yet I am so low

I doubt that whatever he says be it good or ill can seem of much importance. It is no help how I'm forced to forfeit my work for the New Cronus Company. I wrote to tell my employer my condition and was ashamed. The man had judged me something better than I am. But really who am I and what do I matter blown about this West lacking plan or promise of any kind?

Write me one of your nice letters, Alma. Heaven knows I need cheering up. A soul remembers itself in these Wilds, it sees how shrunken small inconsequent it is.

Next day. Well a Doctor Meadows has seen me with the result that I'm commanded to ride the stage to Oswald first thing tomorrow no matter condition or discomfort. Oswald they say is a pretty village situated between two mountains. There are several soda springs noted for medicinal powers. I hardly care to go but arrangements are made.

Three days later. In my hurry to get to Oswald Springs I never finished nor posted this letter. I'm now back from two days at that place. I cared not at all for their treatment so got myself free soon enough. They wanted to keep me buried in mud made from the waters of the springs but I objected to this early interment. It must be that there is life in me yet, agree? Oh but sometimes Alma I fear what sickness I have is of spirit as much as body.

Maybe these words will surprise you and cause you pains to read, but I wonder should we forfeit these letters? Do I not treat you dishonestly making myself "known to you" only on paper? If instead I were before you in person I could not disguise my true spirit from your clear sense and sight. It is a diseased spirit Alma. What I feel always is hunger and it is hunger not of belly but of breast. My heart near starved at home now sups on Sandy rainy dusty dry air and is no better fed. My grandfather's people had a word for sickness like this. Wanderlust they called it. Everywhere here you see its sufferers, all these Placeless kind. In churchyards the young stones stand alone without relations, cut off by how many miles from their begetters down the generations? For me these stones mark lives and deaths lonelier than any I'd imagined. Is such a stone my destiny?

It seems to me the more I study my fellow "Westerners" that we are most of us but doing paces in a wild sanatorium. We are not all sick in body though I'd wager better than half are sick in spirit. That is we haven't arrived here so much as fled someplace else. Somewhere back along the way we left our point of birth, our heritage hateful shameful or just unsatisfactory to ambition. To live without a history looked desirable to the lot of us. But here's the conundrum: Probably the farther you get from your history the more this sickness festers. The more gnawing your hunger. You want to shake history right off your shoulder and brook no ghost or shadow — and yet man needs community after all, and what is community but a kind of history? Do I write at all sensibly?

I cannot go back to Perpetua, not as I am and not as matters stand there. This far country is too empty open and that place too crowded shut. The bolt dropped fast back there to lock away a man I never knew in whole — nor chanced to know for something broke him before I was born. This man as you see already is my father.

It was in order to save being broken that I went away, though it's plain now, is it not, how those hopes may fail me. It may be I'm to break much the same as him no matter what.

I am sorry for the spirit of this letter but maybe it's the first honest letter I've sent you. We ought anyhow to quit and save ourselves greater pains of doing so later. These lines though wild will perhaps help you see the sincerity in my reasons. Though I don't want to quit I do desire Alma what is best for <u>you</u>. Knowing myself and all that made me I would be wrong to conceal longer that quitting is in your best interest.

I close knowing I may expect one more letter at least bearing your

answer. And though I am rather beyond caring for my life I hope I
may live to receive that letter.

Your Friend
Benjamin

Dec 2, 1887
Glenwood, IA
Dear Benjamin,
Your latest came this evening and you don't know how sorry it makes
me. Do you think you write to someone who cares nothing what
unpleasant things you propose? I wish you were right here so I could
tell you how I do care ever so much, and that I needn't write it, for I
don't like this sort of thing on paper do you?

Your "truest spirit"? I can't see how you fail to reveal it, it speaks
through your letters in every line, how could it not? To write is to set
a thing loose that won't be reined back, though at times we could wish
it to be. So if I was slow and guarded in my own first letters — as I
believe I was — in truth my slowness and shyness revealed me the
same.

I mean to say: I see you and know you better than you think.

Now as to the unwelcome subject of quitting this correspondence
that you may draw your head back again and ignore the world
rapping on your shell, I have a plan. Come home this Christmas, I will
too, and then let us see. Delay decision until you've spent yuletide in
Appanoose and benefited from the counsel of this letter-writing school
marm. I daresay I can school you for the better still.

I know that generally speaking you would rather stay away, but
you won't deny a friend's request, will you? I have here a recent letter
where you write: "I will stay unless a certain person tells me in no
uncertain terms and gestures Come Back." As to traveling in your

condition, can you get a sleeper car? Once in Appanoose stay at a
Centerville inn if you must, only come.

Of course the first thing you must do just now is get well. You
must get well. I could never bear to think of that. Please try. I know
this life is worth living even though it doesn't seem sometimes.

As Ever

Alma

10.

Arriving in California Benjamin had a wire from Thaddeus
Wren:

> *Your communiqué at hand and situation*
> *noted. Keep fast the card and let it clear your*
> *way. I shall hold your post till spring. I*
> *admire and trust the wandering soul.*
> *Godspeed and good mending. –T. Wren*

And now he is going: eastward by rail across country fit to pry
the soul agape, along brindled deserts and on against long
horizon seas of sage star thistle soapbrush fireweed — volcanic
cinder piled up in cones to block the sun. Elsewhere along
morainal slopes the queer red pumice reposes in fingerlike
crags, a sort of petrified desert Christmas tree — mantled,
these scenes, with dusting of snow.

A body goes with senses armed. A body misses nothing for
everything leaps. Finding you sick or tired the country insists
no less. In shuddering seat, in heat and torpor, Benjamin tries
to dim his eyes. No use. He is a flexing eyeball. Ringing
eardrum. The country stands in a shout. All emptiness yet no

oblivion. It throws you back on yourself.

He's got sickness of inward kind. This thing snagged within him tight as twisted thorn — affection increasingly acute. It must battle his many loathsome qualities. It wants to improve and reform him but his organism revolts.

Late-November laid him low, health and spirit weakening, no saying which quailed first. Propped in blankets with board and paper upon his knees he watched his inked pen scrawling:

> *We ought anyhow to quit and save ourselves*
> *greater pains of doing so later....*

To open, to disclose, was the purpose to this journeying, true as the pull of wires.

> *... In order to talk to you in letters as I likely*
> *wouldn't in person ...*

Still, though he's been faithful, even incessant in letters, they've not come easy. How many times in weighing a thought or reading a line he's had the sinking fright and wondered alarmed where these letters are leading them. He would spare her his lowness.

So reading the letter over he questioned its effect. She could be spared but that was for her to say, the letter her chance. He sealed and sent it.

He malingered alone on the duckfeather pallet in his Vernal room. He drank the rancid broth pressed upon him by the hotelier's wife. Days oozed, his window dim with frost. He thought of Alma constantly.

Her reply found him in lowest sprawl, clammy, scummed throat to toe under the blanket. But he lay with her two pages fanned upon his chest and words seeped off the paper through nightshirt, breast-flesh, heart, into the permeable core.

Stay at a Centerville inn if you must, only come.

At once he knew he would go.

Benjamin drifts and dreams and in dream the blind speech-maker takes seat beside him, corrugated face bold in profile before the windowglass, lids as ever shut, black lashes long as tassels of honeysuckle but clotted with rheumy discharge.

—*Now ye travel back and tis well ye do. Aye infinity moves aft as much as ahead and ye draw no nearer being tempted toward the flood but ought take pains to trace the leeward tide. To lapse no more from what commands him a body must know first himself complexion defect or fault.*

Scenes beyond the glass are like reflections in a lake: snowy cathedral range capsized and wavering. Dimpling of the visible world as though a hand reached down to tremble the waters, colors running.

—*The gods are just and of our pleasant vices make instruments to plague us and what is a wire but one of these? Yea and heresy makes us heedful till blood and judgment swim at odds, but think on thy father first. He awaits and don't forget it.*

The top hat swells and slips to cover the blind man's face, swells again entubing shoulders and arms — then blackness obliterates like a bellsnuffer as Benjamin sleeps.

He wakes to a dark car, wheels screaming, world atremble.

His father, a murderer. And what is the son to do?

Outside above black desert someone has hosed the heavens with stars...

PART FOUR

Memories move in our brains like small fires,
electricity that in fact flows through us, like
blood. We are inescapably part of every
lightning storm....

— William Kittredge

Why, look you there! look, how it steals away!
My father, in his habit as he liv'd!
Look, where he goes, even now, out at the portal.

— *Hamlet,* III:4

1.

The winter solstice, Benjamin arrives in Appanoose County. He convalesces in the upstairs room. Realm of boyhood nights.

His father regards him askance and it shames Benjamin to suffer this homecoming, to lie down an invalid in the forsworn house, to shuffle in its guilty rooms. He knows what J.M. Lorn surmises. Scampered home at first need of mending. In a way it's true, only Benjamin will not tell how he's been summoned. How a pretty young girl has told him in so many words, Return and I shall mend thee. He tells no one. But in his grandfather he sees a glint of knowing.

The old man embraced him at the door. His white head shivered more than Benjamin remembered but his watery eyes shone warm.

"Well, well."

"Hello Grampa."

"Look at you."

"Changed for worse, I know."

"Pshaw. It's nothing, boy. Get in."

That welcome seemed to say that all had come to pass as expected. Now the old man brings him towels and tea and changes his basin water and asks how he sleeps. Though the grandfather's own constitution quavers of late, he's an eager housemaid. And in a day or two Benjamin feels improved some. So was he never as ill as he'd supposed? Old Thornton seems certain he wasn't. Hunched with heavy basin in his hands, shuffling to the bedroom door, he seems practically to wink. Heartsick, is all. Does Thornton hear rumors from old Gavin Robley?

"Grampa, should you carry that basin?"

The old man makes a phlegmy throat-clearing noise, as if the question merits no further answer.

The day before Christmas Eve Alma Robley calls at the Lorn home. Benjamin's breath snags at the sound of her clear voice from downstairs, his father's affected gentlemanly reply. Then up the stairs J.M. Lorn comes kloking in measured creak as of old, body slung banister to crutch. A tap at the bedroom door.

"Benjamin, uh, Miss Robley's come over from Dennis."

Voice mannered as Benjamin has never heard it. Play a man of decency as long as she's in the house. They both feel her listening from the parlor below.

"Be right down."

He rolls from bed. Ducks to check himself in the shaving glass: dull jaw mottled with whiskers, hair askew and jug ears jugging, a prodigal picture. He hurries to dress. Stocking-footed on squeaking floor he feels very timid and rough. Rough-traveled, rough-mannered, bred to roughness he conspires with his father to disguise — laborsome effort, for the house expresses them. Any who step inside must read the Lorn men plain. In entryway the hard years make an unmistakable whiff. In parlor where embittered silences have baked for decades, you must all but breathe through a cloth. But now he's keeping her waiting in that staleness.

Out the door and starting downstairs he suddenly knows he's written his letters wrong — and with irksome frequency too. At the foot of the stairs he pauses, damning his fretful waffling ways, the imps that hounded his pen to tell him at every line that no matter what pains he took his words were clumsy, cluttered, inscrutable. He's feared nothing so much, he sees, as making waste of their delicate beginning.

He breathes and crosses to the parlor. He will go trustingly into her graces, let her see that. And here she is, she's rising, and in every way she is the vision he's nurtured for thousands of miles and months on end. The parlor seems small. The ceiling very low. How is it she's standing here?

"What a surprise," he says.

"Benjamin. I guess maybe you were resting? Didn't mean to get you up."

"No, no." He's pressing her hand. "I've stared holes in those walls. You're a better picture."

She smiles. "Oh, my picture — did it ever reach you?"

He shrugs, no. "No need of it now though."

For a minute they stand looking at each other, silent, yet sure in their silence, strangely natural. She wears a long mackinaw, her hair a bit hazy from the hood. Her cheeks and nose are still colored with cold and that ruddiness heightens the bright green opacity of her eyes. Benjamin realizes suddenly how well he really knows her. A marvel, a thing that happened while his thoughts lay elsewhere. Can she know him anywhere near as well?

Empty-handed, he remembers and begs pardon and returns upstairs. The paper box awaits him atop the bureau drawers, no larger than a pocketwatch and tied in a thin ribbon of satin. The bow, done prettily by the shop-woman in Calaveras, is crinkled. His coat pocket kept it through the journey east. With finger and thumb he tries to fluff it. And then bearing it downstairs, its meager contents so light in hand, he blushes to feel himself a stupid King of Orient. But now she's seen it and there's no choice.

"This ain't much, I'm afraid. But it's for you."

"Oh goodness."

"Ain't much."

She holds it now. "Shall I open it?"

He couldn't have known the feeling it would bring to give this in person — the difference compared to mail or telegraph. She undoes the ribbon and as the lid comes away so does the shell that shielded him till now. It dismays him to see the oblong chip of stone and tuft of reddish brown. Not at all the mystic articles they seemed before. The tuft has dried out, and beside it the stone looks very rude, a thing fetched from a scullery.

Alma glances up.

He clears his throat and plucks the withered tuft. "It's moss," he interprets. But how scatlike it looks. *Toss it away and wipe your hands!* "Grew on the trunk of the largest tree in the world. A California redwood, Calaveras. They say this tree's old as Jesus. Takes forty men joined by hand to surround it. You wouldn't believe the size, the height."

His foolishness must beget foolish explanation. It feels rote, of course, and devoid of spirit. That place so far away as he stands here. Other world altogether.

"This was green as a jewel when I got it. Course was months ago. Well, I guess I said it wasn't much. Wish you'd seen the green of it."

She holds out her hand. Her other still cradles the box nestled in its lid. He drops the pitiful moss into her palm, watches her study it.

"A redwood. My."

She means to give him the gratification of an effect.

"Pretty worthless now, I guess."

"But wait, what's this?"

"That, that's cave stone," he says. "Calaveras caverns. Old as earth probably. Thought you could make an interesting talk to your school, tell em how a rock like that gets formed."

A small smile. "Thank you, Benjamin. How kind to bring these back."

"Oh. Makes a poor gift the moss all dried that way. I just ..."

He trails off. But she's listening.

"I just ... I suppose those very, very ancient things — they put you in mind, don't they, of ..." His grasp in trying to say the thought slips from it. "Sorry. Don't know what I meant."

They stand.

And what if instead he could tell her plain how he's pledged himself to entrust her a share of his loneliness? how his gawkiness in letters has been just an effort to unguard himself and honor her interest? or tell how faithfully he's preserved her letters, keeping them on his person weeks at a time, folded into a trousers pocket or swaddled in a kerchief inside his shirt so he could draw them forth and reread at whim? Could he tell how her letters have lifted him? how after falling clothes and all into a spring at Oswald he painstakingly dried and restored a sheaf, like some desperate, ill-equipped curator?

"May we sit awhile?" says Alma.

He kindles the fire and soon she doffs the mackinaw. Her shoulders in the minor ruffles of her dress look very narrow against his father's stern hearthside chair.

She's gentle with him, light of voice. It makes him see how altered he must look. She asks about his health and yet he feels finer than he has for weeks. No doubt his rumpled blouse, hastily tucked and puffing between his braces, adds estrangement, but she looks past the dishevelment.

He sees, blindingly, that she's come because she cares for him, because she knows she will help him. She's fulfilling the promise of her last letter. Soon they both understand: a courtship is happening.

The fire glows in the winter-dim house. Above the mantelpiece the Confederate cutlass flickers, a modest crescent moon.

2.

Benjamin remains abed through Christmas, cautiously improving. Two days later he ventures out, going by cars to call at the Robley home. He will visit each Monday after. He loves the scent of her family's parlor.

There is no Christmas tree in his father's house. Admiring the Robley tree one day he mentions this and Alma says, "But how can that be?" It's in such moments, awakened anew to Alma's innocence, that he most believes himself unworthy. Sometimes in her company he suffers surges of self-disgust. Beside that trim perfection he loathes the shape and bearing of his body, the way his trousers puff at thigh and hip, most his mass lumped there even after thinning down in illness. Something in his bones — Lorn bones, not Bauer. I'm a woman, he thinks. A proper *Hausfrau*. And when this self-reproach becomes its worst he mistrusts his own attraction. Interrogates himself. What really draws him to Alma Robley? Is he a sick man yet and she but an antidote? He vows to deny himself the happiness of her friendship should he ever conclude he seeks it as a palliative. Then, realizing his ardent wish to protect her he starts to wonder if he's fallen in love.

They welcome the New Year dancing with Gracie Carmichael and Will Cummins at the Grand Masquerade Ball in Centerville's Armory Hall. Benjamin's mask, procured at the door for a nickel, gives him the ringed eyes and blunt snout of a raccoon. Skulking night-creature, shadow-retreater, the mask lets him lope foolishly about the floor amid the natural dancers. Will Cummins is a peacock, Gracie a goldfinch and Alma a brown sparrow, as if each part has been knowingly cast. Half past midnight Benjamin, overheated, begins to nosebleed into the mask. Alma sits aside with him, lends her kerchief once he's soaked his own. He stains it wholly red, and somehow drizzles blood on her yellow skirts too. She's valiant. Blots the poplin with water from the dipper. Finally the bleeding passes, but he's done for dancing.

"Why don't we go now," she says.

"No, no, it's early."

"You're sure you oughten get home?"

"I'm dandy right here. And there's a girl whose dancing I'd care to watch."

Her hand comes up to touch his wrist, fingers hot as life. She's smiling. "You'll say when you're ready and we'll go, yes?"

"Okay."

He sits on the margin, sweat-soaked shirt drying inside his coat. Watches her turn about the dancefloor. Not once does she want for a partner. He's at pains to believe that's his blood upon her dress.

Next day he consents to go with her to the Dale Church for New Year service. Little white prairie chapel by the highway.

He stands beside her in a narrow row amid the pews and from the stained glass up front an angular Christ with saints and benefactors stares down on him. Jesus makes better sense if you've been to the desert. God is love only once we've loved each other.

Alma has a little book called The Fortune Teller's Almanac. In the early year they play at deciphering the future. You snip a tiny lock of hair and count out filaments one by one, or drink down a cup of water and turn twice round and tally up your heartbeats over a minute, or cut a deck of cards in some precise style a few times over, and with the values obtained by each process consult an index of minutely printed fortunes. The game needs two or more persons. Can't tell your own fortune, only that of another, and suspension of disbelief is crucial — doubt invalidates clairvoyance.

"Have I told you," says Benjamin, "about the blind man?" Their prophecies have brought the figure to mind, and as he relates the memory he's surprised to realize he met the man but once. There's a shorn swale of pasture inside him, gloaming aflicker with fireflies, where that soothsayer has stood all these years.

"He told the future?"

"In a way, I guess. Don't remember too well. And that's strange cause I see him so clear. One of the first faces I really looked at maybe."

"And he was old?"

"Uh-huh. Must be dead now, the codger. He's in there forever though." With middle finger Benjamin touches between his eyes. Tap tap tap. "Even dream about him sometimes. Like he's talking to me."

"Saying what?"

"Oh, dunno. Can it matter much? Just my mind nattering."

But he could easily tell her: *Think on thy father* and *Don't go West* and *Stay at home* and *Believe in something*. Instead he falls silent, closing up.

So Alma's little book brings them just shy of intimacy. In the hairbreadth Benjamin sees how he stalls them. Rues his resistance. What's it take at last to give up your secrets, to stand in passing day with all your doubts? — pledge yourself to time that way, creature with a past, mortal and muddled but willing to be known just so for as barters go this one above all may warrant faith?

Watching Alma read his fortune Benjamin first understands her stake in his future. She's all her own — but bonded to him too. How did that happen? It floods him with joy — and fright.

For her he's prolonged his stay. Even sat before his father in the parlor choking back pride to ask may he return to employ at the store. J.M. Lorn lounged in his cowhide chair, waistcoat undone and leg unspooled on the ottoman, gaze flat behind lenses. Those eyes these days show no paternity — but Benjamin has nullified the son in himself, and J.M.'s coldness matters little. Here then was a merchant loath of waste appraising a specimen of labor, and the merchant could not deny he needed help.

Benjamin hates reverting to the dim interior of *Lorn & Son* but there's no telegraph in Perpetua anymore — nearest office at Centerville now. He's heard told how Edwin Mueller died of electrocution. Struck down in a summer lightning storm. His horse was found standing in the tracks — wouldn't budge at the whistle of a passing engine and forced the cars to stop. Like the horse would point them out what happened. They found

Mueller crumpled at the base of a scorched pole, end of the broken wire still in his clutch. His sons arranged a service in Buxton, buried him up there among the miners. The Perpetua depot stands shut, just a platform now, and the desk in the Pabst Hotel serves for post office. The wire company at Centerville sees no cause to put a new agent in Perpetua.

So Benjamin, absent other means, dons waistapron and garters and stands in the store's dusted aisles staring mindlessly at his hands stacking tins of talc or turning brands of rope onto spindles. But he finds that the klok-klok-klok of the passing crutch signifies almost nothing — none of what his crippled elder once called forth. A girl's love helps him obliterate his father.

Late January, frost crusts the fences of Appanoose. Noon suns are gray cavities gouged in skies of ice, remote as moons. And one midday old Thornton Lorn is driving back from Forbush when his mare's crownpiece snaps apart and the wagon rides against her croup and scares her into a bolt. A minute later the wagon is cheekwise in a farmer's ditch with top wheels spinning, the mare off circling in the farmrows, and the grandfather sprawled aground with shattered hip and scalding cold ditchwater flooding overshoes and boots.

It's more than an hour before somebody passes that way — a man schoolteacher from Walnut City riding horseback. He helps Thornton from the wet and leaving him his saddleblanket hurries to the nearest house.

Ashen dusk is falling when the grandfather comes home laid out in borrowed clothes in the bed of the Lorn wagon with Mr. Hixson, a Forbush farmer, at the reins. "Could as soon get him home I figured as take him to my place and fetch the doctor from there." What he means to say is, Poor old fellow was good as gone already when the schoolteacher found him.

In the wagonbed piled in blankets the old man is gnawing hard at woolen hems, his face a stiff crumple of agony.

Benjamin with Hixson's help drags him from the buckboard in a sling of wool and bears him up the porchsteps into the house. White hair hangs limp, ears bloodless blue as fisheyes. The farmer is right. This day will slip him his death. A man lives the better part of a century but ice and time undo him of an afternoon.

Doctor Whitlow comes along within the quarter hour. Seeing the heap in the parlor he sets his satchel by. Leans above the sofa, frowning, hands coupled at his coattails. His voice booms with volume to break a stupor. "What say, Thornton? A little spill today I hear."

Grampa blinks. Stertorous throat falls quiet, clicks a moment, rattles again.

The doctor nods and reaches to pat the blanket where the old man's hand is buried. "Keep warm old friend. Hear?"

In the entryway Whitlow murmurs, "He'll go I'm afraid."

"We feared as much," says Benjamin.

"He's had the farmer's lung for years," Whitlow tells the father. "Some months now he's been pleuritic too. Matter of time or accident was all, wouldn't have been long either way. My condolences, J.M."

J.M. does not answer but holds the door as the doctor takes leave.

The doctor did not say how long.

They keep old Thornton bundled on the sofa, neighbor the hearth. They warm his feet and brow and listen to the sticky heaving breath. Faithless father and son wordless in vigil about the dying man. He's a kind of god, nearest they've known if only for his constancy — impartial joiner of worlds. He labors for air, his very dying a gripping fast to life. The broken hip seems past bothering him, hung halfway out of himself as he is.

He holds on through the night, a guttural bellows but otherwise unstirring. Death will play him like a hurdy-gurdy. The crank will stop.

Next afternoon he's still breathing. Every few hours his hands stir the blankets, dumb puplike things moving to no purpose.

Benjamin writes to Alma.

> *My Own Dear Friend,*
> *Have sat up the night with my Grandfather*
> *who is dangerously Sick. He is I'm afraid*
> *unlikely to live out this day.*
> *Whenever any trouble comes on me I*
> *cannot help turning my thoughts to you and*
> *wishing you beside me where I may hear*
> *your voice.*
> *May I come see you tomorrow?*
> *I have a wire from Washington T'y*
> *telling me I will have to report to a meeting*
> *place in California by the fifteenth of Feb,*
> *and sooner if possible, or lose the position.*
> *Benjamin*

Come evening the grandfather's loose gaze draws tight. He fixes Benjamin's eyes and says, "Bed!"

Benjamin moves close. "Your bed? Upstairs?"

The eyes are furring again but he answers, "Not. Here." And jerks his head seeming to intend a nod.

Not here? Does he mean he's going now only doesn't wish to go from the sofa?

"Wait," Benjamin tells him.

He coats, scarfs, and mittens himself and hurries out into evening freeze. Brings back Will Cummins twenty minutes later, fully dreading to walk in on parlored death. But no, the old man did wait. So they gather him into a hammock of blankets and fret the burden off the sofa up the stairs into the grandfather's bedroom and Will gets a good fire going in the little hearth while Benjamin smoothes and snugs the bedclothes. Then, standing back to see Thornton Hanson Lorn gape-mouthed atop his pillow and sucking as if to draw the very ceiling dust down into his trembling frame, Benjamin knows they've fixed him his deathbed. He won't greet the morning.

But by morning he has not gone. And breathes better. Eyes are even tracking now, as if he'll watch and wait turn to speak. Does he forbear to go till he can make a farewell of sorts?

First of February. It snowed heavily all night, the Appanoose winter very cold but dry and light of snow till now. In the afternoon the grandfather takes soup and sleeps almost peaceably, breathing deep, the rattle mostly gone.

Benjamin received an answer from Alma after breakfast:

Poor Dear. Yes. Come today.

So he leaves the old man to the father's care. Drives heartsore by sleigh to Dennis. Arm in arm he and Alma walk out in rising drifts.

"Haven't you missed it?" she says. "That whisper sound?"

Behind them stands the blue Robley house shawled white. The gravel drive has disappeared. World's edges all soft.

"Wouldn't have thought to miss it," he says, "but yes."

The printless snow makes everything a oneness. Benjamin hardly believes how beautiful he finds it. Knows the long Iowa winters too well — how the snowfall, after its first weeks, imprisons. He watches drifting divots alight soundless on

Alma's woolen hood. Her profile retreating in the hood looks younger, more delicate. Wouldn't have thought it possible. She's twenty-one and makes him feel his years at twenty-four.

"I'm sorry for your grandfather. Did you get to make a peace?"

"Well, he's breathing anyhow. Or was when I left."

"Then he may come through?"

"Don't think so, no. Think he's apt to go before I'm back."

"Oh, but shouldn't you be there? To say goodbye?"

He hunches, purses his mouth. "Guess I've said goodbye these three days."

Their feet as they walk say *hush, hush.*

"My grampa's been griefstruck since I told him. He counts your grandfather such a friend. Hard to see old men these ways."

They stroll further into whiteness. Benjamin feels the plant of his feet in the snow. And in his ears the rich susurrus sound, and sees how this courtship defies his own intentions to withdraw. Pulls him down and makes something come alert inside. So noise of birds warbling in trees is less an impression received from the outer world than a sensation originating within.

Still, he's leaving — within the week or not much later. And for how long? Standing beside her in the snowfall he wants to beg a kiss, but at her cloudless look damns the wish.

"I've decided," she says. "I won't go back to Glenwood."

"No?"

She shakes her head. "They keep saying they'll take me late or not. And Anna coaxes me. But she'll marry that Omaha boy before summer I'm sure, then I'm abandoned. Anyhow, I don't want to go."

"Well, you weren't so happy there. Seems right you should stay."

Snowflakes drift sideward to perch upon the red strands collected in her hood. Her face amid the glistening.

"Have you thought of that, Benjamin? To stay yourself?"

He makes a sore smile. He'll have no grandfather now. And cannot share the house alone with his blameful, broken father.

"Couldn't," he says.

Under a bright moon he sleighs back, breath in strands of steam behind. Topsnow icing to crystal in the lunatic light.

He finds a wakeful house, Grampa propped on pillows alert. But that's no living alertness. Palled haggard white and harrowed to the bone, Thornton Lorn is turning a minute at the charnel house door. He wants to make ready.

J.M. clumps about as if harried by mosquitoes, crutch beating time. His eyes behind the lenses are ghastly, sunken, mouths of eels. Benjamin would see teeth in that stare but turns away.

"Been waitin on you. Refuses to die damn fool till he sees you. Go in goddammit."

So Benjamin shuts the door. And stands at the foot of the bed appraised by his grandfather and half as much by waxing death.

"Closer boy."

Benjamin bows and steps nearer the pillow.

From the blankets a knotty finger strays to wave at the door. Voice a valvular whisper. "Man out there. Hates what I'm to say ... to tell you ... and you'll hafta forgive'm that. He'd as soon what's past be killt all in all. ... His son's the same, uh?"

Benjamin doesn't understand. Voice is wet but the deathly

mouth is dry. The cheek turns full to the pillow, eyes sideward in the sockets, fixed.

"Tell me boy. You mean to stay at home?"

"No sir, I do not. How can I?"

"Well, the Robley girl."

"No. Just told her I'm goin."

"What do you disdain in your Pa, Benjamin?"

"Disdain? No, it's more … It's knowing things."

"You think you know the truth do you?"

"Yessir."

"I may say a fuller truth. Would you believe me?"

Cracked lips meet and part with rasping noise, hustle of shells.

"Tell me these things you know boy."

But Benjamin hesitates.

"Don't fear to say. I'm goin before the night's through. Who'll I tell?"

Benjamin looks to the door. Strives to even his breath. Then, leaning, breathes into the coil of the old man's ear: "He killt … In the war. My father … killt my mother's brother."

"Ah. Think it so plain do you?"

"I know it, sir. Mother saw I should know before she died. But even she didn't know all of it. I have word since she died of those that were there."

"No."

"But it's true."

Bony finger sways. "Truth of a kind. Not complete. One truth's seldom complete all itself, they live…in webs. Member the story I used to tell, the rainbow ring?"

"Of course."

"Thought I'd live forever. Or could. Thought that the

meaning of it. Well, today we see different. But that ring's still true see? Partly anyhow."

Benjamin does not see — but in blindness he lies. "Yes, yes."

"I'm dyin boy so let me tell you now ... let me say ..."

Oh the things the grandfather has known all along. With all his body Benjamin listens. The very fiber in his clothing warps tight to hear.

3.

Again he is going. He arranges to meet Alma on the cars and they ride together to Centerville. She brings a buffalo blanket to share across their knees. Wonderful warmth. Out the windows the country dead white with branches everywhere barren gray, the sky itself of granite. But in that still-frame a raven flies to leave a top limb bobbing weirdly.

At the Centerville station she waits with him for the 9:00 a.m. Des Moines and when they see it coming he takes her hands, pledging to write as faithfully this time out.

"I still need to tell you," he says. "I owe you a kind of biography."

And then his hands are rising to her face. Her startled eyes in the shell of his palms, and rushing he stoops and kisses her, feeling her flinch, a tiny jolt in her shoulders and neck. He's treading wholly blind.

He makes it a short kiss. Coming away, she's colored to her curls. Having scared her he realizes he's scared himself. Feels the heat behind his eyes and knows the dumb blushing look on his face. Embarrassed she stares, but he drops his glance to their hands still joined.

"Badly done?" he says.

And feels the warm squeeze of her fingers.

"Guard your health this time."

"I will."

The train chugs him toward Omaha. From there it's on through Platte country, Colorado, Utah, Nevada, to Sacramento where his party awaits. Two thousand miles laddered with rails, strung with humming wires.

In his watchpocket he carries the old poem put down in Edwin Mueller's hand.

... He drew from heaven the strange, fierce fire.

And yet, poor Mueller, lightning was his slaughter. They said it charred his hands black, scorched his bootsoles.

Already this looks to be a journey to the earth's far rim. But he has to go. In J.M.'s presence, after all his grampa has told him, he fears himself, his own vengeful intent.

4. (May 24, 1944)

Dear Mrs. Kurzwald,

I'm sending those things as requested. I hope they are all here and each is the one you had in mind. I found them just where you said, but with one or two items guessed between things that looked alike. There was two of your mother's scarves in the attic to match your description so I enclose both. The clock is a beauty and we had it carefully wrapped but if it gets damaged just tell us and we'll pay repairs. Also enclosing here this page found in the old cubby desk. I was changing drawer linings and one of the top ones had this pasted under. It is badly torn for that reason. I for one don't know if this paper will interest you at all, but Charlie insisted it go along in the package. You can of course trust us both we did not look past the salutation.

Tell me as you please anything else I may send and you may have it. Size or weight are no concern. I say this in case you wish for any of the furniture. Charlie and I are ever so happy in this fine old home. We both hope that you, your father, and your family is well in S.F.

Wilmina Turner Cummins

The page as Avis holds it is gapped with ragged holes and tacky with adhesive but otherwise crisp and bright. Its woven paper never yellowed like the other letters long folded in the shoebox, the ink is still undimmed. She sits at the dining room table in light of the amber-glass chandelier, the page tilted before her.

Dearest Friend,
— written in the same tight-looping hand as all his letters.

That history, or rather
biography, that I said I ought
to tell you I will relate here
and now. I don't think you
have any idea ... would to
God I had a better st— ...
could not blame you ...
concluded, all is over between
us.

"Avis, you say this takes a signal?"

In the living room Benjamin Lorn is down on his knees at the radio set. Trouser cuffs flop large around stringy ankles, black socks.

"Yes Daddy. Keep trying."

Benjamin adjusts his glasses and twists the radio knobs. Vacuum tubes chirrup and squeak. Dipping his neck to read the needle up close, mouth ajar, he bosses the antenna here to there. The shoulders in his shirt are the sinewy, horselike bones of old age. Left one slants as ever.

Avis reads:

... things which are always too
much in my mind to let me stay
at home. ... wish to keep them
no longer. ... letters, a packet of
them ... hoped I think that these
would help me understand his
bitter— ... done so for her at
least before she died ... further
letters arrived ... blackness.

Her father keeps fiddling with the radio. There's to be a special broadcast from Washington. Benjamin kept it noted on the calendar. May the twenty-fourth, Mother weeks dead, almost a month since Benny left. Edgar's out with the car, still searching. Avis for her part has quit those nighttime rides. What use?

Now a squelch, a hiccup, and the radio delivers a bold round voice.

... unveiling today on this centennial a plaque in honor of Samuel Morse's historic achievement.

"There it is." One knee at a time Benjamin hoists himself up. "Got the broadcast Avis. They're starting." He settles attentively into the cane-braided chair beside the speaker.

... much more than a milestone in the technology of American or for that matter world-wide communication, but a revolution in our understanding of the physical world. And now ladies and gentlemen they're pulling down the curtain and the applause you hear is in reaction to the plaque, a very fine rather large plaque with a striking bas-relief portrait of Morse. And Mister Lawrie it appears will read out the inscription.

In the crackle a new voice faintly echoes, small in a great marbled chamber:

What Hath God Wrought! Samuel F.B. Morse the inventor on May twenty-fourth eighteen-forty-four in the old supreme court room in the capitol sent the above message to Baltimore Maryland by the first electromagnetic telegraph instrument.

"They're in that room now," says Benjamin. "Same place."

"Yes Daddy."

So strangely ceremonious, sitting up alert in his chair with hands on knees and gaze set fast on the wall before him. Nearest ear tuned to the gold-threaded mesh of the speaker, he does not turn his head. Proud, pugnacious message-sender — letter writer and wire operator — in what way, really, has Benjamin Lorn ever made contact? To Avis he's as good as a ghost. And what use eavesdropping on this father's youth, decoding her parents' crumbling letters. They're gone to her now, all. Boy, husband, father, old man; girl, wife, mother, old woman — each life has its own generations: they move in sequence, only forward. You can't trace them backward, not from outside. We are each and every one born alone amid strangers. It begins this way, how could it not? Early as the cradle, even with mother come to comfort, you drill at darkness with your cries.

... memorial to the humility and vision which enabled this inventor to be the conveyor of this universal blessing to mankind.

The voice concludes to further applause. The announcer cuts in again.

And now ladies and gentlemen it appears the telegraph is ready. And I should note that this is the very same telegraph instrument, preserved in good working order, upon which Samuel Morse himself transmitted those famous words one hundred years ago. Today's telegram will travel the same distance of forty-four miles to Baltimore, and there in the old Pratt Street station, if all goes according to plan, a second machine will register Morse's motto. ... There is, one must say, something magical in these proceedings — ah, the operator is now at the key ladies and gentlemen. ...As I say, one marvels to consider how this evening's ceremony should summon up those particular moments a century behind us now. We may pause to contemplate the wonder this technology first represented. And now ladies and gentlemen let us listen as the operator transmits.

The faraway chamber falls hushed. Silence, snowy radio noise. Somebody coughs a thin cough. Then comes a momentary clicking and ticking like the noise of a clock picked up and shaken. The announcer lowers his voice:

The telegram has been sent ladies and gentlemen. The message What Hath God Wrought is off to Baltimore at the speed of a wire. And now we will await reply from the operator in that city...

· · ·

… Benjamin hangs forward. Hands fumble to the chair arms and squeeze. Radio says, "…something magical in these proceedings…"

Yes, thinks Benjamin. *… From heaven the strange fierce fire. Carried the poem in my watch pocket. Ed Mueller wrote it out — and what all else he tell me? Strange fellow Mueller, but my I revered him. Oh. We tune ourselves, tells me, break the signal and listen to it like music all of a piece. Wire's nothing but noise without we interrupt the signal. Odd old fellow — but wait, was never much older than Avis now.*

The message What Hath God Wrought is off to Baltimore …

And then the crackpot Wren out West, New Cronus man, what'd he say? We have learned irreverence toward sun and season. Talked of magnets in the earth. Said … said, Even mountains need not encumber us. Hunh. And later, They dine on dog you know. Goodness was I half as mad as him? Wren it was who told me of old Copernicus …

"Copernicus," blurts her father from his chair, trance suddenly broken. "May the twenty-fourth, Avis. Same day Copernicus died, you know that?"

"I didn't Daddy, no."

"Uh-huh, and same day he published his book sayin as how the planets go round the sun. Morse sent the wire three hundred years after. To the very day."

And now ladies and gentlemen we have our reply from Baltimore. What Hath God Wrought, receipt confirmed!

The radio gives out the stately, full-bodied applause.

Samuel Morse's achievement one hundred years later remains
undimmed. . . .

Again her father's head hangs forward, chin suspended by
an invisible cord. Avis returns to the page in hand.

> *Would to God I had a better*
> *st—*

What to make of a gaping letter? How draw out what it
refuses to tell?

The broadcast ends in a tinny fanfare of brass, then a
different announcer begins an inventory of the day's war
events. A guard shot a Japanese man at the internment camp at
Tule Lake, American pilots bombed an aircraft factory called
Wiener-Neustadt, at least one B-25 went down over Arezzo
Italy, other bombs are dropping on—

"Used to be no news of the day," says her father, interject-
ing, his gray gaze unbroken. "Before the telegraph, was news of
the week maybe. Of the season. Moved real slow."

It's as if he's talking to the wall. And what can Avis make of
this news? Where is Benny in this? News quaking deep in the
silence of a day. *Will you hold your ears, Benny? Will you hunker
down, squeeze shut your eyes, pray?* News unknown till evening —
and then just a voice reporting to silent rooms. *Are you to fight
soon, Benny? Will you march or make thunder while scissors go Shh
Shh at midday, while the store pianist plays, while your grampa clips
the Chronicle or sits with coffee in your empty bedroom?*

To Avis it's long been somebody else's war. Now it insists
on being hers. And hasn't she, haven't they all — Benny,
Benjamin — kind of stumbled around in each other's lives, lost?

She calls softly. "Daddy."

He doesn't hear, still adrift in the radio. She calls louder and
he stirs.

"Uh?"

"Daddy, I'd like to cut your silhouette. Do you mind?"

"Uh? Right now? Here?"

"Would you mind?"

He seems to consider, then shrugs self-consciously. "Okay."

"Good. Wait here." Rising, she folds the tattered letter back into Wilmina's envelope. Old Benjamin in his chair waits still as a bust as she goes down the hall for paper.

Hands clasped in his lap and a table lamp lit behind, strands of thin white hair fall slant across his brow. Thick-rimmed reading glasses bulge his shirtpocket, folded there. The radio chatters on but Avis isn't listening. She turns black paper between scissorblades, chin ticking up and down to study his profile.

"Daddy, will you tell me about Grandfather?"

"Uh?" He doesn't move. "What about him?"

"Well, I've got an old picture is all. I never knew him. Was he a cruel father?"

All your life you never ask anything, then comes the time. His hands don't twitch, eyes don't flutter.

Avis scissors down the point of nose to upper lip — then sees it isn't right. She holds up the cutting to compare, one hand curling back the scrap. No. Swift shears send canceled paper dropping in halves to the carpet. She takes a fresh sheet in hand.

Benjamin looks down. "Make that poor a profile, do I?"

"Don't be silly."

Again he's motionless.

"Say something, though, won't you, Daddy?"

"Was the only picture he ever took, that one. Makes'm look cruel, don't it."

"Mm. And Mama said he was once."

"Well. Mother never said a false word in her life. You oughta know that already."

"I know it Daddy. I just wish you could tell—"

"Wasn't your grandfather."

The scissors stop. "What?"

He speaks low, eyes ahead. "Man in the picture. Wasn't your grandfather."

"J.M. Lorn? He wasn't — what do you mean Daddy?"

She's at the edges, blocked out of his gaze, blades and paper poised. "Daddy?" She's like someone calling through a shut door.

But finally, slowly, her father starts to talk.

Deep in deathbed old Thornton Lorn admonished the grandson.

—*Truth of a kind. Not complete. Here's another piece of it, so you see my meaning* ...

Benjamin leaned beside the pillow.

—*Alfred Bauer wasn't brother to your Ma.*

—*Sir?*

White hair shook.

—*Was my nephew. J.M.'s cousin. Grew up together in my house.*

—*But ... But Mother was Bauer. She was Bauer before she married Father.*

—*Ya, and before that she was Taylor.*

—*Harriet Taylor?*

—*Her maiden name.*

That was the night Benjamin swore he would go forever.

· · ·

—She wasn't from here. Came from Trillium, Wayne County. Her folks were over there but they gave her up soon's she told them she'd married Alfred. They was confederates at heart, Copperheads, lots up there like that. Disowned her, moved south after the war, couldn't abide a bluecoat in the family. She never heard of em again. J.M. brought her here after that. Told it around that they'd been married in secret all the time.

Later, in blackest hour, Benjamin crept through the house in nightshirt and mended stockings. Heels on cool hearthstones he reached and with quiet scraping brought down the tasseled cutlass. Heavier than reckoned. He'd never held it before. He gripped the hilt downward. Bladetip hissed at the runner as he eased upstairs in darkness.

—Why'd she call Alfred her brother? Why'd she pretend Bauer was her maiden name?

—Easier I suppose. Not so many questions for J.M. once he'd married her. Or herself either. You know how a town'll talk.

—She never told me.

—I know it.

—Even when she was dying.

—Ya, never understood that myself. 'Cept to think she had some shame of her family. Wanted to wish all that away.

—Why'd she marry J.M.? She knew all he'd done.

—Not then she didn't. She never did know what happened in Texas. And her folks didn't want her, Trillium didn't, what else could she do? She had a boy who needed a Pa.

—What?

—You needed a Pa, Benjamin.

He went slow to see the floor didn't creak. The cutlass winked and darkened along his side. In the drafty upstairs hall with white shift skirting out at every pace he felt himself a ghost or weaponed angel passing the dead grandfather's door. He felt the sword's tassel soft as rabbitfur at the heel of his palm. The blade's weight curving down from the pommel. The weight of a duty befalling him now. A son's righteous duty.

Something in the flooring, or foundation, or earth itself, tugged. In his loins, chilled and surprised beneath the shift, something stirred.

—He's damned himself for what he did in Texas — all these years, can see that. To me he talked of it only once, never again. Was clear that didn't do him no good. Told your mother nothin far as I know.

—But she knew. He was bad to her and she knew. That's why she wrote those letters, to have it proven. She died thinking she was wrong but she was right all the time.

—Well. J.M.'d say the same. To his own mind he murdered your Pa. But don't let that taint your thoughts. It wasn't that way. Not so simple.

—How do you know?

—I listened to him.

Thornton Lorn talked on for some moments, but his eyes were heavy.

—Need to sleep now boy. I'm to die tonight and hour's almost come, need my rest.

A sickly smile.

—You're son to him all the same.

—Don't say that.

—Well. Grandson to me anyhow.

He stopped at the hall's end before the shut door. He listened past it. He turned the knob and nudged and the door swung slow on its hinges with a faroff creak. Upon that threshold his figure spilt no shadow. He stood and felt the doorposts and lintel ensquaring him. Felt the dark of his palm curled at the sword's hilt. His footsoles gripped the floor.

J.M. Lorn's snore hitched and steadied.

Benjamin shifted stance to step and the man's breathing snarled. In sleep he slurred, "What? Who is it?"

Benjamin waited. The blade's edge winked in the dark, at the ready. The sleeper did not awake.

The young man stood and thought upon the things a man will do.

5.

"You about done there?"

"Wait Daddy, let me understand. You thought great-grampa was wrong. To you the truth was clear. No accident, no confusion, J.M. did murder your father."

"Well. I had a letter said so. And J.M.'d lied to me all my life." A stern surety in his eyes. "Just reasoned the man'd lie to his pa the same."

"And *was* it murder? Did you find out?"

He stares away, silent again. But she's seeing now. "The whole thing was worse than you'd ever thought. Wasn't it?"

The scissors on their chain lie shut against her breast.

"I mean they deceived you all that time — your grampa, J.M., your mother too."

"You never knew her, remember. Don't you blame her."

She sees his shame — to talk of these matters, to have been raised under such deception, to have no means to fix the wrongs, unable to speak of this all his days, let alone make it right. What can it mean to talk of it now — what but to dredge the muck of years? And yet he gave Avis the letters.

"I told your mother all of it," he murmurs. "Before she married me. She oughta know who I was and what I come from, seemed like."

Would to God I had a better st—

"She never told me," says Avis.

"No. She promised me that."

It's plain he's weary now, done with talking. So she sets her cutting aside and lets him go. He moves noiseless down the hall and then Benny's door clicks shut.

6. (1863)

A letter before battle—Hell in Arkansas—
The commandant's "negro position"—A rebel north—
A resolution—A new command—A floodplain—Into the
narrows—Attempting the Yazoo Pass—Pillaging—
Blood brothers.

Fort Curtis
Helena, Ark
My Own Dear Wife,

*The sun comes up cold. A man's whiskers grow little icicles that
will not melt through the day. Our sole convenience is mud freezing
over to aid movement of wagons, supplies, &c. You tend to wonder
though if mud-trough streets are not better than bones of ice clattering
under your clothes.*

*The reason there's such great movement around here for a change
is we've got orders to steam lower into Dixie by route of lesser water-
ways. Maj. Gen. Grant with one division passed through here on the
22nd inst. Did I write of it?*

*There is as much relief and excitement in the regt as you'd think
after our gloomy months here, and yet we bear in mind our purpose
and the dangers of the undertaking. It is expected the Rebels will do
their all to slow us once we leave the Mississippi. Most the men say
we'll be continually fired upon.*

*It is mindful of this that I write you My Darling Harriet to say
that you shall be in my thoughts and heart all the time though it is
unlikely I'll get to send another letter very soon. Try not to fear for I*

am not afraid. I have faith that God will spare me and our comrades in our cause.

As for John and me I may as well inform you we have pretty thoroughly fallen out and I am afraid it was needful I teach him a hard lesson. I do not care to paint you the picture and trust you would not care to see it. That was regrettable business. I am not proud of it though John being his way I cannot but see that all had to pass as it did.

It does pain me going down to Vicksburg with these troubles between myself and him. I can't however see us mending matters. We have talked scarcely at all. As our scrape caused a little stir the command judged fit to transfer him to a different company. I fear it's what it is and no changing it.

But now I must close and get aboard my boat. I think it very certain I will kill or aid in killing a Rebel Man before I write again. Pray with me Harriet that God may weigh the worth of our cause against this evil act. I am

Your Adoring Husband
A. Bauer

The regiment had stayed put the winter long. Helena Arkansas shrank in army parlance to "Hell in Arkansas." Mud in camp to top a man's boot. Deplorable hole. Tentlife put soldiers away to sickness. Gravesites grew, neighbor to buried negroes. General Gorman, commandant and object of much ill opinion in the ranks, instructed the regimental guard in a "negro position" of great simplicity: *shoot every second one that gets in your way.* Though scarcely fond of the general, some in regiment made excuse of the policy. So passersby in Helena's crooked snowcrusted streets had frequently to overstep or drag aside corpses of runaway slaves. As many as four were sometimes dropped to Union guns in a day, conditions which gave little pleasure to the officers charged to raise a colored company there.

Save for dead blacks and daily rumor of Rebel assault, the 36th had done this drill before. Bide your time in camp and don't get sick. It was crazing business to even the coolest head. Some had begun to look anxiously toward a negotiated peace — even at cost of Rebel dominance in the north if that meant release to quit and go home. Things were verging on a Rebel north anyhow, Iowa Copperheads rising in alarming numbers. This at least was the word in letters from home. There came report of a new riot at Keokuk. Soldiers there smashed in the office doors of *The Constitution*, thrashing the place in answer to the paper's anti-Union screeds. So the Iowa boys squatting sick and frozen in southern muck, oathed to putting down treason and preserving the life back home, learned how Rebel favor only propagated in their absence.

Come late February, faced with a demoralized force, the field officers saw fit to draft a resolution of unqualified Union allegiance and submit it to the 36th for vote. Taken by company the ballot seemed fixed to narrow down and finger out dissenters. So the 36th discovered itself democratically coerced to unity in its commission. If Helena remained a prison to most, if this war seemed leached of purpose now, each man voted to evade hanging by shutting up about it.

But finally that month General Gorman was relieved of command. On Washington's birthday the regiment assembled to hear his successor General Benjamin Mayberry Prentiss, hero of the Shiloh Hornet's Nest, address the garrison. Time of inaction was passed, said Prentiss, and vowed to get them out of mud. The hurrah that answered was of volume to shake the fort.

Two days later the 36th was dispatched aboard steamers and gunboats to trawl reconnaissance down to Moon Lake and through the narrows of the Yazoo Pass. A levee dynamited some days prior promised smooth passage from the Mississippi.

Turning out upon the floodplain they met a torrential downpour. The men sat shivering about deck. They raised gum blankets the few that had them. In thrash and splatter the boats glided amid crowns of drowned trees. Fugitive property of all description had snagged in the limbs: fenceposts, haybales, barn doors, wagon wheels, headboards, candelabras. On the slant berms of sunken roofs, goats and dogs stood castaway, chickens and pigs beached neighbor to weathervanes. Sheep, cats, and in one place a lanky foal near starved and resting on its barrel, scrawny legs sprawled fore and hind like Scottish pipes. A soldier asked leave to shoot it from his boat and was permitted. The man was a good shot and the foal just dropped its bony loaf of a head and rolled over into the water making hardly a splash. These scenes slid behind and gone as the fleet drew into the narrows.

The banks grew thick with willow and cane, the width of passage constricting till soon the men at starboard and port had continually to fend at wet fronds. They passed early into Moon Lake where they would overnight on deck, but the wildly crooked route below would strangle them more.

No sooner had they anchored in the rain-ragged lake than it was determined the steamer MARINER must turn back to Helena for supplies its drunken quartermaser had neglected. J.M. was aboard that boat and Alfred could all but hear him cussing disgust.

Last they'd spoken was two or three days after their scrape when

J.M. had stomped into camp spouting venom on Capt. Phillips.

"Son of a bitch got me transferred, you heard?"

Alfred said he had. "You're not glad of it?"

J.M. was swatting together his belongings. He stopped and stood with toes to stovefire, looking down upon the coffee tin. His nose was still unset and plum dark. "What, you sayin I oughta be?"

"Well, seein as you don't care any for the captain—"

"You're glad of it then. That your gist?"

Alfred didn't care to hurt him that way. "Glad for you, sure."

J.M. shook his head, still staring low, mind grinding behind fallen lids. "Son of a Rebel bitch."

Alfred flinched. "John, goddammit—"

"No," said J.M., locking his eyes now. "Don't say he ain't, I won't hear it no more. Scoundrel ain't fit…" He halted to swallow or catch his breath. He looked winded of a sudden. "Ain't fit to fight longside likes a you and me — and he damn sure oughten give us orders!"

Surprised, Alfred saw how Phillips would focus J.M.'s ire, even after their scrape. To John's thinking the fool captain stood to blame even for their burnt-out brotherhood.

"You hear he wears a kinda shield under his shirt? The coward!"

*

Come morning on Moon Lake most of the boats proceeded on the Coldwater River down the pass, a few remaining against the MARINER's return. The rain had not stopped all night.

Aboard the LAVINIA LOGAN Alfred and Needham watched the trees webbing branches over the channel. The boat in passing peeled bark off the trunks. Whenever it wedged to a stall they swung axes by team, chopping loose and shoving. In this way each steamer dragged onward.

Inchwise down that tangle, they gained but four miles from the lake by nightfall. They tied to the willows — hardly necessary — and slept in the weather. Yazoo City, reckoned their first major appointment with the enemy, lay yet seventy-five miles downwater.

"Alf. Hey Alf?"

It was Needham, his voice a quiver close in Alfred's ear. The men were huddled on the deckboards guarding meager bodyheat under topcoats and blankets. A feeble awning of canvas flapped above. They'd been asleep, Alfred had anyhow. How long? He'd dreamed himself standing far back in line at a telegrapher's window, a penciled message to Harriet on a scrap in his hand: *We mean by God to come through to open country.* The agent worked the key in a frenzy — Alfred feared he'd snap the lever in two. Then waking he realized the noise was Needham's jaw chattering.

"Alf, y-y-you got the feelin I got bout this?"

"Mm?"

"F-feelin we're headed where there's no g-g-getting out of? I mean, h-how we s'posed to turn round in this wormtrack?"

Alfred made no answer, numb in his cave of blanket. The night dead black about them, rain rustling the willows, and in the cane the coughing of frogs. Needham was quiet a while but for sibilant breath.

"You and J.M.," he said at last. "You suppose it's all sh-shut tween you now?"

Alfred grunted inconclusively.

"Sorta sh-shame, ain't it. Way things shape up? You ever think that? I mean, l-l-look at poor Jim Sh-Showkwiller. He never reckoned to die of his own r-r-rifle I bet. Dead already half a year and we hardly think of him. I d–don't anyhow. We used to race each other out on the N-n-north Road after school me and Jim. And here we are the rest of us, ain't had a g-good fight yet and now set to get ambushed almost certain and n-no way out. None of it's how y-y-you pictured it to be huh? Ain't like you thought h-hardly at all."

*

By morning some soldiers went ashore a few from each boat. In the woods about thirty yards off was a homestead with a neat little cabin vacated of Rebel occupants, poultry plentiful in the yard. Soon the trees were raucous as men began jumping at random from deck to chase and rustle chickens, turkeys, whatever birds the place would afford.

Lt. Miller debarked to call them back. There was to be no "promiscuous pillaging," or so the command had put it. But when confusion settled the men returned to the boats bearing between

them a strangled poulard goose and a good dozen chickens or
turkeys neatly wrung of heads.

From deck Alfred spotted J.M. for one of the last. Unhurried, he
swaggered from the trees dangling a rooster by its bloody gullet,
red still spurting about his hand and frantic wings batting his
legs. He turned a smile to Lt. Miller as he came.

*…Remember the pains they took to keep blood off the sheets, slitting
palms by turns and clasping them tight. Autumn, eight or nine years old.
The air in Perpetua even after dark spiced of woodsmoke and mulch.
Under the snug sash the scent would creep to hang in the bedroom all
night draping their dreams. The single bed upstairs in Uncle
Thornton's house. Shared it long as Alfred could remember. No more
than three when he came there to live, his short life before all dark,
mother dead, father of no account, least that was how they liked to put it.
Perpetua in those first seasons seemed one vast cornfield, the clatter of
stalks like breath drawn and let out, drawn, let out. He heard it even
after harvest, when the fields lay fallow, even when the farmers set fire
to great sections.*

*J.M. always kicked at night, Alfred's shins and heels perennially
bruised. He would wake with nose pressed in J.M.'s musty hair or with
J.M. breathing oblivious in his face. They were sixteen before they slept
separate, a narrow bedframe and pallet dragged upstairs between them
and into the room to twin the old one. Even then their sleep at night was
rhythm and anti-rhythm, confederacy and conflict, a syncopation
unspoken but understood as only spouses or nearest siblings understand.
They were bloodbrothers, which seemed higher than natural
brotherhood. Placed them on a plane of loyalty somehow empathic.*

*They used J.M.'s jackknife. J.M. did it first then sat crosslegged in
the sheets with blood pooling slow in his palm, watching. "Hurry up
before I drip, hold it tight like that, cut down and back." J.M.'s blood*

looked black. Beforehand Alfred wondered was there something occult in the act. And he shivered to feel the bladetip going in, the line of red appearing. But then their slick palms adhered warm and he knew what they'd done was innocent, wonderful, powerful strange. Whatever the years would bring they were mingled and fortified against it now. Each stronger than his own solitude forever. Before they could stain the bedclothes they brought back their hands and sipped from them like saucers ...

7.

Feb 12, 1888
Peters, CA
Dear Alma,
Much as this piece of California agrees with me I am eager to set out again. Regretful though I was in leaving Appanoose to leave a certain somebody, I begin to remember myself suited to this lonely life or if not suited then destined no matter my leanings. I guess I have truly taken the "Traveling Cure" though used to be I couldn't see the meaning of that phrase.

Yesterday brought a single awful letter from Will Cummins at home reporting: — 1. that Emmet Scudder our old schoolfellow has died and 2. that Will is booked for matrimony for May the 1st. Well, already all but these two spoke of me at home as the hater of women who elected to live a Bachelor's life (did Anna Miller never paint me that way?). What now will be said of me gone off alone while others my age go marrying or married already and dead? Do I postpone my own life? I wonder sometimes if the chafed and itching spirit inside me is not meant to instruct me in just this. Wonder the same about this country of ours which goes on forever. Can a country be too big? I see cause to ask if ours is not.

As one of the boys in our corps, Clute, has family in this spot, I have stopped with him here. Clute's relations have 1500 acres of wheat and it makes a beautiful scene at morning the sun hoisted up behind the fields and all things lit with gold.

The trip we're preparing for will be from this Central Valley as they call it north to Portland. We will go by land along the Coast

Range most the way. Will start in 2 or 3 weeks with a 6 horse team, one horse and a half to a man. It will take about 40 days to reach Portland they say, given the surveying we're to do. Then Tacoma WT, and from Tacoma it's over a mountain RR to the eastern territory, then on to a place called Walla Walla (a funny name, they tell me it's Indian for Many Waters).

Out here, lost as I may be, I begin to know myself some way and see how little they ever knew me at home. I have never yet found anyone that really knew me. Even you, Alma, I've often asked myself if you could understand my temperament by which I can hate with the most bitter hate imaginable, but yet also I can love so fully.

Love brought me almost out of the grave this winter past, and were I without it I would soon give up my enterprises. "Out from the Valley of Death rode the six hundred" — but know there was not six hundred this time, only one. I have learned I believe to love with my whole life. Though I fear it hopeless sometimes, this is making a better man of me. Shall it continue to do so or will it prove my curse? Such thoughts follow me far away out here.

In Sacramento I found you an embroidered toilet case I'm sure you will like and have sent it by express. The agent could not say positive what the charges would be. If I haven't paid enough please say in your next. Hoping the case pleases you, and wishing you well as ever.

Benjamin

Feb 24, 1888
Dennis, Iowa
My Dear Benjamin,
It snows and snows here. I already feel it a very long time since that white day we last walked together.

Today I laid out your letters since I've known you. They show me a man who's shy of life's better things. He looks at the muddle that made *him and believing himself a lesser kind of person judges himself unworthy of joy or friendship. So he runs off, afraid to muddy what might bring happiness.*

Is my guesswork correct?

Oh Benjamin, haven't we both been too timid in these letters with bashful answers to questions no less bashful? Isn't it time we talk different? Do we not understand each other better? I do understand you Benjamin, doubt me though you may.

Now, like most girls I was brought up to stand by and wait and be careful, and though I don't think that sort of teaching awful I do believe it cannot suit every circumstance. Life surprises, is what I mean. Times come that call for different manners.

What I think, Benjamin Lorn, is you wish to ask me questions of a kind but being a doubtful soul (see above) you don't know how to go about it.

So I ask, hadn't we better make a promise between us? Your letters have become so many, and we've come so far getting to know each other, it only seems proper. You see I do have properness in me.

Let me give you my promise, Benjamin. Here it is in your hands.

Alma

8.

In sickly twilight he rolls and looks from his blanket past embering fire to the long horizon east. Lavarock plain coursing away razored blue with sage, fifty miles or more, and beyond that the same. Ride of a hundred miles to the nearest railroad. They're camped somewhere above El Señor. The boys have gone in search of deer and cinnamon bean. Benjamin reckons they'll stay out the night and doesn't mind if they do. He props himself, drags his haversack closer. He will write her, by God. He's erred to keep her waiting. *Hadn't we better make a promise between us?* Ah, his dumb tormented nature. Well, no more. Paper laid flat on the lid of the flour tin that's served them since Redfield, he dips his pen.

Apr 14, 1888
Dearest Friend,

    That history, or rather biography, that I said I ought to tell you I will relate here and now. I don't think you have any idea of what it will be, and I would to God I had a better story to tell. I could not blame you if you should say when I've concluded, all is over between us. I will say however that it concerns nothing I've ever done. But you shall understand after this those things which are always too much in my mind to let me stay at home. From you, since as you say we ought to make a promise, I wish to keep them no longer. You will be the only person in my life to know them. Not even J.M. Lorn their main subject can guess what I have learned. Read on if you will, and expect the worst.

    My mother on her deathbed sent me searching after a set of letters, a packet of them she'd hidden in our barn ...

He shudders as he writes. In El Señor he saw the cowboys skin cattle with hooked ropes and draft horses. Crude fitful business, the bleeding hides jerked inch by inch. That scene disturbed him to his soul — the dead animals lay, stupid with mass — and his shudder now is the same. For he's thought the letters, his and hers, back and forth, are changing him. Should have known it couldn't go so easy. Thickest of animals, his hide coming off will not be pretty.

. . .

"Heard this chatter bout Peru?" said Mike DeGoram, nudging, breath of fiery vapors. They'd stood at the dingy bar in El Señor, two doors from the boarding house. Floor varnished in tobacco stains, a half-hairless dog curled by their feet. "Thinkin to go on down myself. Course can't know for certain till word at Walla Walla."

"Peru you said?" Benjamin looked dumbly into a cocked eye glossed with liquor. A good fellow, DeGoram, younger two or three years. Bred in Bismarck North Dakota and well traveled already, he did a stint in Louisiana or someplace for half a year and found the lazed intonations catching, so he talked like a southerner.

"Very place. You ain't heard yet then. Mister Wren's lookin to recruit a whole outfit. Operators, engineers. Don't know what all he's got runnin but he needs fellows. Word is they're to start up early as midsummer."

"South America."

"Very place. Thinkin to go on down myself. If the chance stands come Walla Walla course."

They leaned in weary thoughtfulness. There was suddenly a warmth in Benjamin's chest, weirdly pleasurable. It felt a little like fright — the spark to send a person fleeing — but broader.

He keeps writing.

In all truth I fear what I may do to the man if I go home again. You see I have a sort of duty in that matter, though I could wish it weren't so. ...

He devours distance, insatiable for it, and distance grants him this pure union impossible through other means.

You have the whole of me now. I wished you to have it some time ago, but you understand my stunted ways. …

He's told her. Done. To write a letter to one's love is to write to oneself, he knows it now. What a marvel how the soul will speak, and seek its own face in letters.

Here is my promise, Alma, in answer to yours if you will still have it. …

And yet he hasn't told her everything, he's left out his widening plans. And knows with stark certainty, stretched on the ground in this country seemingly created for no purpose but to let a man's loneliness hum at strongest pitch, that he must go to Peru. He thinks sometimes that he would take a running leap off the world if he could.

9.

Apr 30, 1888
Dennis, Iowa
My Dear Benjamin,
I got an atlas and found where you are camping and I should think it would be rough country. I don't believe you take good care of yourself, do you? I'm at liberty to nag now we've made promises. You see I mean to keep my promise. I am thankful to have your "biography" and can well see what a test it was to write of such business — but didn't you know it wouldn't change my feelings? How could it now?

Had a letter from Anna Miller the other day. She went back to Glenwood to teach. She has gone and said Yes to her Omaha fellow and come Fall plans to move there where they will be married. Are you glad to hear it? I recall you held out some sympathy to her poor suitor.

There was a regular cyclone out at Mystic last Monday night.
They're telling how it lifted and carried off the Methodist Church. One
house had a bedroom window torn away and two pillows stripped of
their shams without their hardly moving. A certain oak tree was
impaled by a piece of straw. Nature creates the impossible all the time.

  Write to me from Portland, won't you?

Alma

10. (1863)

Yazoo, contd.—Guerrillas—Burning cotton—
The Rebel Ft. Pemberton—A shelling—A wife's letter—
No reconciliation.

They crept on along the narrows and the country clutched them harder. By the sixth day out they'd crawled but eighteen miles. Deep in the trees on either side, something fateful paced them.

When rain gave way they faced obliterative fog. It hung like cheesecloth through the day. The boats shouldered forward, scraping canebrakes. Axeblades stuttered and hacked. More than once the steamer wheels jammed on floating deadfall and the fleet made halt while timber was painstakingly hauled out or rammed through or sawed apart.

Come March the tenth they'd lived more than a fortnight on the boats, all but a day or two in that sleeve. That day, just where the channel broadened to ease passage, the fog-hung trees at left awoke with riflefire.

The Lavinia Logan up front took the brunt of it, the men crouching as woodchips sprayed like sparks off the pilothouse. Bullets pinged boatmetal and slapped the water just below. It proved guerrilla fire — not a battle sally — for once the boats behind rallied guns in answer the trees fell quiet. They passed on.

One man aboard was hit. Alfred heard him moaning at stern and saw the clumping of bodies gone to aid. Word came up it was John Bland, an Ottumwa boy of nineteen, shot through the wrist — clean enough and so pronounced lucky, for they were sans nurse on the boats and nothing like a hospital nearer than Helena. Bland was laid out in the floor of the pilothouse and fetched a strong ration of whiskey. By and by he managed to chuckle of his luck. The men took that for permission to do likewise and felt grateful.

They came down out of the fog. They'd passed into wider waters almost certain. The woods thinned and started to separate. At points the men saw cottonfields churning under braids of red and black smoke. The Rebels had fired them in retreat. The smoke accruing over the water dressed the boats in a dread shroud.

Near twilight they closed upon a Rebel cotton steamer and a single gunner. Their own gunboats opened fire and in no time the steamer's gingerbreading lay demolished, chimney staved in, paddlewheel maimed to splinters. Yawing she showed the name on her flank: PARALLEL. Aboard her decks heads bobbed and darted in silhouette, swarming up from the hold. Small fires appeared and multiplied. Torches.

"Mean to burn their cotton stead of give it over," said someone standing to Alfred's rear.

Belatedly now the Rebel gunner started booming, muzzles spitting blue and yellow. The crew was scurrying off the PARALLEL into the shadow of the gunworks, steamer smoking black from sides and top, flame lashing from the rails.

The gunner fled downriver, pursued halfheartedly, then gone. Muzzles fell quiet in the dark. The blaze of the abandoned PARALLEL brightened as she dizzied to sink, rafts of fire chunking off her sides to drift in the hundreds. Cottonbales, they turned and rocked like scattering planets. The river was soon a mirrored beltway studded with fire. Each shore borrowed the glow, bright in superficial dawn, black smoke opening in parasol above.

Southward under that dark, through unnatural firelight, the 36th proceeded. They were closer than ever now. Alfred felt fear in the palms of his hands, a faraway itch.

Late night they landed the fleet and slept aboard. All was quiet, but ashore in the distance they could hear a banjo frailing. They lay in the cradle-sway of the Coldwater, lulled to the music. On the LAVINIA LOGAN a few kept awake naming tunes as they came. Ducks on the Millpond. Pataroller. Bonaparte's March. The last was played very finely, and slower than most had ever heard. A dirge-like reach in the bassnotes, a druidical trill.

A voice said, "Reb can play, I give'm that."

Listening over the low grousing of Needham's snores, Alfred remembered porch musicians he'd heard in Perpetua, Mister Farrows at fiddle or Jed Turner at guitar. The changes he'd seen the music conjure in those players' eyes and mouths — blank looks, their faces in surrender, a coming open of the gaze. He imagined the man in the trees that way, no longer Rebel, not soldier or civilian, hardly man anymore at all, just a door ajar and music unreeling through him, the tune a thing that always was.

*

In darkness shy of dawn the 36th was underway again. With guns at shoulder the men drank scalding coffee. Black river faded to purple, maroon. The waters were littered and the men soon busy fishing up the sodden cottonbales that hadn't burned. A jaundiced sun sulked up over the trees.

Then cannons ashore set to pounding. "Howitzers," judged Lt. Miller, as the men ducked about him. They'd gained range of the Rebel Fort Pemberton.

At a place called Shell Mound they veered to land. The companies marched quickstep toward the thunder. They had eyeshot of the fort when they halted with orders to drop back. The gunboats would fire over from behind. So they stood under screaming shells and trees began to burst about them, scattering like dandelion fluff but raining down in racket.

Once started it was a barrage, the shells relentless. "Oh Lord," said a voice through gritted teeth. "Caseshot," said someone else — it screeched and hit, repeating "Now Now Now" — and on impact Alfred heard grunts and oaths as the men gripped down.

You were mad to stand there, but they held line, knees locked, hands to caps. Gouts of dirt and mud geysered up till the sky seemed to teeter.

They stood it for two hours. Before it was over the De Kalb's big gun took a shell in the muzzle — a blast to shatter the boat's casemate, it launched four dead men into the river. Ten more were badly torn up.

All that night the regiment was busy planting batteries. They could hear the Rebels beyond the walls hard at work much the same, and felt the oddity. How mutually scrupulous they were. But with dawn came only skirmishes. Reports from night-scouts led the command to judge it useless putting infantry closer than six-hundred yards. They planted further batteries. Day dragged down.

Next morning artillery fire woke them and carried on through sunrise, a noon bold blue and springlike. Again men stood out in lines while the gunboats did the work.

Next day they pitched camp on shore opposite the fort. Twenty days they'd lived adeck. The big guns traded further fire.

More than a week this tedium, the soldiery all taut at arms, orders never given. Sergeant Henry Swallow of Company F died of black vomit on the thirteenth and was buried in a glade between canebrake and swamp. Many had fallen sick of the crowded boats, of the weather, many sick since Helena. Scouts went out daily, waistdeep in swampwater for hours at a spell only to come back numblegged and pale of face, nothing to report. Water surrounded the regiment in every direction, sulfurous bog much of it. There were snakes the width of a man's leg amid the cane, leeches in the mud and shallows. Still the 36th sat. Many presumed they awaited reinforcement but there was no word.

Finally on the twentieth they decamped, abandoning the siege, if siege it ever was, to begin the long recoiling creep to the Mississippi. But on the Coldwater they met another division coming down, several thousand men under Gen. Quinby, so the following morning they turned about for a second go at Shell

Mound. Camping ashore again, they sat a fortnight more. There was more noise from the guns, nothing decisive.

On April the fifth, mud-damp, riversick, hagridden and temporarily deaf, they drew out again. This time they were under plain order from Maj. Gen. Grant to leave the fort and return north.

The Yazoo, cut clear for passage now, did not badly deter them, and in three days they were back at Helena. Alfred found a letter awaiting him.

Trillium, Iowa
My Dear Affectionate Husband,
O that you'd sooner known you would go to Vicksburg! Then this might reach you before you left. I fear it will go lost at Helena but maybe by some grace it will get to you at the battleline. You must know what I have waited till now to tell. We are to have a son or daughter before summer is through!

Just lately as it became impossible to hide I told my folks everything plain. They know now about our marriage. They were not pleased to learn any of it but we never expected otherwise did we? Every day I'm made to hear what shame I do them, how will they answer the neighbors after this? &c. Cruel and stubborn as they are they will not put me out, they do count themselves Christian. But you must come back very soon and retrieve your Adoring Wife. I so want to go, Alfred. They wait upon you as well for they wish to be rid of me. They've talked a little or father has of sending me to family in Indiana but I don't fear too much he will do it, it would shame him the more to burden kin that way.

Do not worry too much my Darling. I am well and so is our child. It has the hiccups some nights and then I like to put my hand at the place and imagine you laughing inside me, for we do have much to rejoice. O we are blessed.

Now you need only to stay well and come home. Write to tell me you will.

> *Your Loving Wife*
> *Harriet*

What boy and girl names do you like?

Sluggish snow was falling. In moonlight for moments it silvered the mud between tents, then dissolved to black ground again. Striplings lay out to make a corduroy walk. They wobbled under Alfred's boots as he jogged along asking, "You seen J.M.? J.M. Lorn?" He was in a kind of panic and almost set himself alight hurling around a tentwall upon his cousin's campfire — he'd kicked in amid embers to his heels before reining back. J.M. was squatting with palms to flame. He levered to his feet.

Alfred had the letter in hand but held it along his side. He saw he wouldn't say it aloud. He held out the letter instead. With a dead glimmer of the eyes J.M. stepped and took it. He tilted the paper to firelight. After a moment he folded it and passed it back.

"Well," he said. "I'll be damned."

Alfred doubled the paper carefully and put it in a pocket. "Last November," he said, "when I took Showkwiller home ..."

Behind the smoke J.M.'s face was a mask of shadow.

"Didn't tell you about the marriage," said Alfred. "I'm tellin you this."

"So you are."

They stood a minute, but no more would pass. Alfred turned back the way he'd come.

11.

May 17, 1888
Portland, OR
Dearest Alma,

Portland at last and God bless the place. And yet no sooner do I come to a pause somewhere than I set about scheming to get elsewhere. I wonder what you will think this time when I report my destination. Well, meantime-wise it's Tacoma, then Walla Walla. But from there I aim to board a steamer and — can you guess it? South. South beyond the Tropic of Cancer past the Equator to of all places — Peru! I'm applying to Mr. Wren's engineering corps for surveying a new RailRoad and hanging new Telegraphs across the continent. They judge it will take at least two years. I must contract to stay that long and there is no way of getting out unless I should get sick.

I am not overjoyed to go so far from you — and after I'd thought I could go no further. And yet pain alone cannot keep me. That I must go seems very clear. You understand, do you not, Alma? Do I mean ever to come home to Appanoose? Too early to say, I must be honest. Of course I will not demand you wait upon me. If you wish, I willingly release you from all promises. Of course I do not wish that.

When I was young at home I used to hear a man say in his prayers at church "Pity the People in the Beggary Elements of the World." I would laugh and wonder where that was but wonder no more after the wilds I've seen out here. Would you have recognized me riding into this town tonight, inch-thick in dirt, some bloody bearded cowboy, chaps and all? I crawl this earth like a fly, and half as fly-brained maybe, but looking at the matter I may say that I came West, Alma, and will go down to Peru for one single reason.

I believe most days I oughtn't have been born, and if I'm ever to return to you it must be as man improved, man who's pried the lead from his spirit and buckshot from his heart. You deserve such a man, for you are good and untroubled and clear.

So there is a paradox as the old Greeks would say in this state of affairs. That is, I'm going away in order for a single thing to happen if it may: that I return to you and know myself worthy.

I Am Yours

Benjamin

P.S. I will receive word from you at Tacoma.

June 4, 1888

Dennis, Iowa

Dear Benjamin,

I think you would not write the way you do, so quick to make up your mind, had you any notion the unpleasantness it causes me. Did it never cross your mind to ask my opinion? The fact is I am clean out of this business of Peru. We all have our pains, regrets, and troubles, but hoping to relieve yourself of yours by going down the very globe — and to no better purpose — is sure to prove a lost cause. Why will you not be truthful with yourself? You can write very harsh sometimes, but as I have given you my promise Benjamin Lorn, you have given me yours. Do you forget it already? I hope you will reply very soon and with good sense. — Alma

June 17, 1888
Tacoma, WT
Aboard Rail to Pasco
My Own Dear Alma,

Have patience. I am an ill-mannered unpracticed fool. I am sorry I alarmed you. And yet even apart from the reasons I already gave, Peru persists to make itself necessary.

This letter will turn out a mess for I'm now crossing the Territory southeast to a place called Pasco. We are winding upward upon the new Railway of the Cascade Branch. The track they say is the steepest ever built. I have just finished talking with another passenger, a coal miner from Wales employed at a company town hereabout, who tells me the smashups came regular as they laid and tried this line. We have a time yet before we gain the upper peaks but the land is very mountainous already, crags and cliffs everywhere all snowed over. There is glorious country here Alma. Mountains like you never dreamed. Were you here and could you see it you would better understand me. There's grandeur at every turn and it puts grandeur in the heart. One's feelings get bigger. I don't know how to say it. My coalminer friend told me of a son he left in California some years ago, a boy just of age, and called Asher. How's that for a name? Told me he thinks of that boy everyday. Has never seen him since their town down there went under and might not recognize him today, yet all the time keeps him in his thought. This man buried a wife in that town too and supposes not even her grave survives. Well, I listened to this quiet miner and felt just as if a veil dropped away between us and it was all I could do to master my emotion. So it is out here in this country where the scale of things expands and in these summits the atmosphere thins and stone is stone and grass is grass and a man is a man like any other. It gets into a person. I doubt however that I can write of it.

I've examined my feelings. We oughtn't fear my going down the globe. Surely not. So long as I'm given your promise I'm given a sure future which I shall carry in heart and memory till the day it finally comes to pass. And Alma let us now avouch our promises and put a seal on that homecoming.

The way to do it is with a question: Will You Marry Me?

If you will I shall strive the more to come home to you repaired and an abler student in such stuff as Faith.

I never did tell you about my Grandfather's rainbow did I? There is much we have not told.

I will await your answer and if you will have me,

I Am Yours

Benjamin

P.S. All told I am yours no matter what.

July 3, 1888
Dennis, Iowa
Dear Benjamin,

I have quit this business of opposing you, seeing how little use it is. This time has proved for both of us an education of the heart.

I have your letter beside me. There in your hand is the question, so I have not imagined it. I sat down believing I knew what I would answer. "If it keeps you off this Peru idea, then yes I will marry you." But now I know that's not my answer. Even as I think of you blindly boarding ship I wish to say, I Do. No matter the circumstances that's my wish. I Do, and I am

Yours Forever

Alma

You now know beyond excuse that I am waiting for you.

12.

"Come in Mister Lorn, come in."

"Thank you sir."

"Sit down amigo. Will you smoke?"

"Don't mind if I do sir."

"There you are. Mexican cigarillos these. They clear the mind. A cordial to the lungs."

"Very pleasant sir."

"And how do you find Walla Walla Mister Lorn?"

"Right fine sir. Right pretty."

"Lay your hat upon the desk, man. Free your hands. Here, tap the ash in this pouncet box. Your journey was very satisfactory. Sanderson, Clute, DeGoram, they're unanimous in praise."

"Well, we made good time sir. Made a good outfit altogether."

"Indeed so. And they tell me you would go to Peru."

"I would Mister Wren."

"You have never been as far south."

"No sir, me nor any of the boys. I expect we'll feel the distance."

"Good. Tres bien. I should expect nothing less. It is to be, you understand, an excursion of spirit as much as flesh. Mind and soul must go down those latitudes as one. Wire in hand we descend the ladder to the very wellspring, verstehen Sie."

"I see sir."

"Do you know the power of a full moon, Mister Lorn?"

"I … I believe I do sir. I've camped under several in my time. This is a very good cigar sir."

"It tugs at the tides. The full moon. And the blood in our brain no less, amigo. It thins our thoughts. And an equatorial full moon? Oh-ho what may better balance the scales in a man? Or better unpin his potential?"

"I don't know sir."

"They harnessed the heavens just so Mister Lorn to raise their Incan temples from the rock. How else could they have done it? We too shall harness. He drew from heaven the strange fierce fire. For us of course we build of matter immaterial. The heart and spirit of man — there's our matter in every mile of wire strung. You follow me Mister Lorn. Yes I knew it upon our interview in Pendleton."

"Excuse me sir, I seem to have seeds in my mouth."

"Tobacco seeds Mister Lorn. Pluck them out if you care to or chew them right down. They are Mexicana de primera calidad."

"Chew them? Mm I see…"

"Another cigarillo?"

"Thank you sir."

"My my Mister Lorn is it not a marvel to sit in this office and bend one's mind upon the magnet of the world! Mystery Mister Lorn. This lodestone of the earth, the hum of our magnetized wires, the shooting polestars of man's thought in every message transmitted. And who can tell the force down *there*? The power in those mountains where earth is fattest? Water whirls counter-clockwise in Peru, mein Freund. *Against the clock* Mister Lorn."

"Mm mm … and you yourself sir. You and Villard, Holladay, Hunt, they call you *magnates*. Ever thought on that?"

"Ah a capital insight amigo. You see there are no bumps in eternity ah no it is a fluid matter all things run together at the ultimate — eternity being gloriously inert a gliding without terminus — are you feeling well Mister Lorn?"

"Yes sir. Might we open the window?"

"Of course ... No, we are more than guests of ancient time."

"Excuse me sir?"

"The llama you know is a creature much like the camel. A ruminant..."

"Mm ... yes."

"Spits to dry his mind of too much thought."

"Mm ... mm."

"... new Corps of Discovery amigo ... we must have a nigger too. And Indians. The latter plentiful in that South. Find us a competent few ... needn't reason but ought not be vulgarly stupid ... How are your bowels Mister Lorn? Their issuance? Sound? You will need fortitude of those organs in the tropics ... dine on dog you know ..."

"Not to worry sir I'm fine. I'll just stand here by the window a minute if I may."

"A matter of mescal Mister Lorn nothing more. The Indians roll it in these cigarillos. A fine spell they cast agree? In Peru it occurs somewhat less I'm told. *Ka-kow* is their choicest magnet to the meandering brain. Your observations ought be taken with pains and accuracy down there. You've heard have you not of certain Indians in this country that designate time by the pointer finger. Ahead being futurity. Behind past. Upward the moment at hand — how would they do it down there? how especially in light of the wires? Do observe them Mister Lorn and if any should wish to have their young brought up with us and taught what arts may be useful to them we will receive instruct and take care of them. Better now Mister Lorn?"

"Better sir?"

"What was it he died of you say?"

"Of lightning sir. He'd gone to mend a break."

"Mm yes. Puffing smoke from the tips of your fingers toes roots of your hair. Imagine!"

I shall strive the more to come home to you repaired.

"Wind ran down the funnel of his throat sir."

"The power!"

"His jagged nerves were lightning—"

"Where does it come from? The sky in a gash—"

"We tune ourselves entire—"

This time has proved for both of us an education of the heart.

"Power!"

"The signal must be broken. My mother would count the seconds—"

"Imagine amigo. Imagine!"

I am waiting for you.

13. (HELENA, 4TH OF JULY 1863)

Gunroar, God — and cannonblasts fit to shatter the sun. The war will use them after all. No doubting it for the grayclad bodies fall between the trees below. Alfred in position firing at will with Needham nearby working rifle the same. Ramrods pump and clatter and black smoke pops and Capt. Phillips shouts in rear — and how the rebels drop between the trees, picked off from here.

From the river the gunboat booms. In short matter shells explode down front, oh the bodies will make a pile in those hollows before they see sense and quit. Rebs like tin men down there — and the bright little bursts when they come apart. How man should ever dream up a mortar!

The 36th fortified in four places and it's goddamn good to take high position. Rebs are making for the levee, not returning fire, and from their backs it cuts them down. Reb sharpshooters try, a few. Little use. And their other guns take position on the hills across to send volleys though this is but a gesture for still the gray bodies pour over that open place to get harvested better than half.

Yet they may take a Battery after all, numbering such a plenty and driving hard from their center — but what can that win them for they must take the Fort to get anywhere and will never take the Fort with this fire at their backs.

Down the levee southwest four more companies of the 36th join fire, a web of gunwork, Rebs can't throw it off, oh the echoes are enormous, a kind of warping drone, and they're littering the gullies, gray bodies to number a thousand before this is done, and they'll be walked upon, no way around it, slaughtered three deep some places.

Morning wears on. And by God, Rebs have taken the Battery on that hill and fight in earnest from there even cut to a fraction. Their shots are coming over now. The rifle pits dig down and some men are hit.

Morning ages. Alfred ramming and firing and every chin and cheek upline and down blacked of powder, they reek of it, all, that and the sweat that flows in this glare. But at last comes Phillips's call to fall out. Next company will refresh the line. So they're letting down guns and stepping back, the other men surging forward, Reb bullets still whistling past.

Alfred looks to Needham and meets a weary smile. Phillips is passing at Needham's shoulder calling orders — and just then Needham's head cocks aside and he blinks large and a plug of his skull flies off misting blood and hair upon the blue shoulders around him. He drops, eyes still seeing as he goes, down amid boots. Alfred tilting across the line as if to catch him, kneeling in mud, glancing behind — did the shot come from back there?

Then, in the rear amid parting shoulders Alfred sees J.M., stricken, his rifle coming down, barrel smoking. J.M.'s face blanched in guilt, his glance skates left in disbelief to where Phillips just passed. The captain moves along the line still calling orders. J.M.'s mouth mutely says No. The guns don't stop.

PART FIVE

It is impossible that old prejudices and hostilities should longer exist, while such an instrument has been created for the exchange of thought between all the nations of the earth.

— *The Story of the Telegraph,*
Charles Briggs & Augustus Maverick,
circa 1858

Somehow we don't get along right in the management of this war. There is a screw loose somewhere.

— Soldier's diary, 36th Iowa Infantry

1.

Asleep in the grandson's room, old Benjamin Lorn dreams Edwin Mueller's death.

Mueller fallen along the right-of-way, arms and legs outflung over railroad ties, shoesoles smoking, the tracks themselves ember-red from the thunderbolt. Rain falls slant in tree and weed. Hush of summer green, steam, wet haze. World newly boiled but simmering down. ...

The dream shivers, jumps, and now Benjamin walks the right-of-way with dead Mueller upright and walking beside him.

—*Where we goin?*

Already they've walked long. The tracks curl back underfoot, changeless, crawling behind forever. Ahead.

Mueller says they're going to a family reunion.

—*I'm afraid however we've lost our way.*

—*Should we turn back?*

—*No. Track's no better that direction.*

From a bulging jacket pocket Mueller brings forth an igneous rock large as a man's fist. Tan pumice. He raises it between them on the bed of a scorched palm.

—*Never without it. It's geology and mine, my heart's geology, they're the same.*

Black smoke trails from his fingertips.

By and by in a crescent of trees off the tracks stands a large banquet table. Five, six people seated there, men and women talking German. Mueller suggests pausing to ask directions. At the table he shows his rock around, ransom for their good counsel. Benjamin gets his first long look at the rock as it's passed. In the contours of two sides, the shadowy suggestion of skulls. The Germans note this also.

—*Schädel. Schädel.*

The rock rests at the table's center. Go back, say the Germans, five miles. Then turn again and start anew. You'll get there by sundown.

The track looks much the same in reverse. Mueller grows distressed.

—*Did we turn about? How far did they say?*

Benjamin, alarmed, realizes Mueller's hands are empty.

—*The rock!*

—*No, no. It's just here. Don't fret.*

But he's lying. His coat pocket hangs flat. The tracks tick past beneath their shoes.

—*Was it this that killed you, sir? Walking the rails this way?*

—*Yes my boy. Lightning lit them up like beams. Thought I saw the world soaring past, but that was me. I zoomed ahead, all else was still.*

—*Where were you goin?*

—*Where? Up Down East West, that's not the question, no such things, nowhere to go no matter where you go. After a while out there the land gives way, then deep green sea. Push and push any direction that's where you're going.*

—*And us? Now?*

—*East West North South, it's always there ahead. Got our reunion first though. Have we turned about?*

—*Yes.*

—*You're sure?*

—*I think so. Should we…*

—*No, no. Don't stop. Don't stop.*

· · ·

Benjamin wakes to his daughter's silent house, Benny's room drawn tight around him in the pre-dawn dark. He thinks, almost, he can hear the ocean from where he lies.

2.

July 20, 1888
Seattle, WT
My Own Dear,
Changes since last I wrote have started me to running around again. You wished me to understand you are clean out of this business of South America. Well so am I and gladly.

I went to Portland last Thursday. There were eight of us from Walla Walla. We arrived late and as I'd grown an awful headache on the train I went straight to sleep hardly glancing at the Hotel except to see that in my room were three beds. About 3 o'clock that night in come some other fellows. They had been down at drinking and began to go on at an awful rate. Finally they spied me. One came over and said, Clerkman wake up and join the circus. I said I was already awake and if they didn't tamp down I'd pitch them out the window. Well that was the Bloody Cowboy in me and all it did was get them riled. They began to curse me, keeping it up till I jumped from my blankets and tugged the bell to call the nightwatch. And then, I almost fear to report it, they made for me and I found myself tumbling around the room in a scrape like you only read about. I fear to tell you also Alma that I did not come out so badly. Since my mother's death I've had, as you now know, a bitter business at work in me and it was the mistake of these

roughscruffs to stir it up. By the time the nightwatch got upstairs I'd
paid out some notice and was given some too. You'd think me a sight.
The watchman took them to another room and I was granted my peace,
yet failed to sleep much more having gotten so wound up.

In the morning I learned these fellows, Californians mostly, were
going to Peru with us and that they'd been up and down the neighbor-
hood spoiling for a run-in before I supplied them one.

I guess they did me a favor to show me the harebrained layout I was
in with. Now you may blame me for going into the fight but surely you
will not for quitting my contract. I've had sense knocked into me. And
now must close for I'm in an awful hurry. I start for Iowa by rail
tomorrow. Have concluded I must face my situation at home if we are
ever to have our happiness.

If you wish to write me anymore before you see me address me at
Perpetua.

Benjamin

Coming back the town looked very tidy, houses stacked along
platted streets. But from the minute he arrived he felt a
hollowness in that arrangement of porches, dooryards, lanes.
There was an aging about the place, a blind idleness that gnawed
on him some way. He'd come for something altogether different,
but here everything he looked at seemed to say, Who was he to
think he'd make another life?

He did not go to see J.M. And steered wide of the store. He
roomed in the widower Hacker's house, on recommendation of
Will Cummins who'd boarded there himself till his wedding day
two months before. He rode to Albia to see about the telegraph.
To Centerville. No openings.

He was in Dennis three times a week, and soon he'd broached
his idea to Alma. His earnings from his months away made a

princely sum but wouldn't last. Buy out J.M. while money was in hand, else leave the future uncertain for who knew how long.

"I want us married before we both pass a quarter century."

"But the store?" she said. "Do you want that?"

"It'll get me what I want."

"Oh Benjamin."

"What?"

"Listen to yourself."

"Don't you want the same thing Alma?"

"Of course, but at such a price…"

He bit his lip and studied her. He believed he'd pay any price.

"Lorn and Son," she said.

"I aim to change that sign."

She kept her fretful look. He knew, in a way, she was right. But what could he do?

"It's a start, Alma. A start."

He called on J.M. at the store — dared not set foot in the old house. Whatever the grievances between them, he knew the man could not refuse his offer.

In figure and voice J.M. Lorn was now wholly a stranger. Shopkeep, nothing more. Standing at the counter, Benjamin saw how necessity helped to distance him from all he'd once known of this man, all he'd come to know. Deal only in the present now. Shake the hand coldly — better than seizing the throat. And yet Benjamin's duty, his purpose, was not blunted, and he told himself this was his means of vanquishing. Buy the man out. Dispossess him of all he ever was. Wad the cash in his humiliated fist, then strip every trace of him from the store.

J.M. as they talked pretended no parenthood. Knew well enough what things old Thornton Lorn had told before he died.

He hardly blinked when Benjamin came in. Did not say, Wondered when you'd turn up, nor, Heard you was out at Hacker's place. He stood listening to Benjamin's terms and said he'd think it over. They both knew though it was all but settled.

Benjamin paced the worn boards to the door, man's eyes on his back. And coming into daylight, turning down along the square, nodding to neighbors, he kept expecting the conclusive rush, the winner's relief, the calm he'd heard could come of justice.

Two days later he had his date of possession. At once he wrote the news to Alma. But sending the letter he felt ashamed. She wouldn't say he ought to, or name a better way, but she saw.

3. (San Francisco, 1944)

Benjamin sits at the table in his daughter's kitchen, bent to a sheet of paper, the house around him as dark as the coffee swirling steam in his cup.

Daughter Avis,

A long time ago after my mother died I began to ask myself Why? Why do these things have to happen? As years went by the Whys were more numerous for age in my experience does not bring Wisdom. Your own mother used to ask me, Why was it easier to do the wrong thing than nicer things, but you know Mother just lived her nice things, could do no different, was in her nature. I wish I was like her and had lived a life so satisfactory. I begin to feel the loneliness of having lived too long. I heard of an old soul once said that. For me it's true as words get about now. I know I never showed you like your Mother did how I have loved

you and what a daughter you have been. Like I say she was naturally
good that way. — Your Father

Finished, Benjamin leaves the rest of his coffee undrunk. He
stands from the kitchen table and puts on his coat, props the
envelope, marked *Avis*, against the vase on the entryway table,
and slips out the door.

Morning fog. Across the street a woman walks a small dog
on a leash, her coat collar high. Benjamin buries fists in pockets,
leans into early chill, down the steps, and turns along the
sidewalk like a man with an appointment to keep. Minutes later
he's standing in Geary Street watching the B-line car squeal to a
halt. The car is already stuffed but he finds a windowseat close
behind the driver. A red-eyed man in rumpled suit and cocked
fedora slides in beside him, folds arms atop paunch, and promptly
begins to snore. The car jerks along smelling inside of cold
jackets, newspaper, shoe polish. The riders waggle and sway at
the turns but Benjamin's sleeping neighbor stays upright.

Benjamin peers out the window at the awakening city, cars
backing slow from the drives of narrow stucco houses,
deliverymen pushing handtrucks, mothers trundling prams.
Thoughts drift and scatter. He looks without seeing, thinking of
nothing. He's aware only of soothing absence, a blankness like
dreamless rest.

The streetsigns tick by, avenue numbers going up. The seats
around him steadily empty. The sleeping man has gone. Ahead
through the windshield the pavements seem to soften and pale,
air thinning to an unmistakable roominess of atmosphere.
Another turn and he's looking out upon breaking waves, white
curlers in a field of gray.

He gets off at the next stop, beneath a painted arch that reads
in unlit colored bulbs PLAYLAND AT THE BEACH. A bright

carousel stands asleep, a ferris wheel towers motionless against cement sky. He crosses the highway to sandy sidewalk, then down a set of creosoted stairs to beach. The roar is in his ears. Twinge of salt in his mouth.

He plods in sand, slow, toward the water. Going further into openness he can feel the shrinking of the city at his back and this gives him new lightness. The world hazes away ahead, nothing but gray and white, a blurring at every edge, a plunging out and gone, no horizon at all. To left and right, even, nothing but fog.

Now he feels a quickening in his breast, a new hurriedness. Heat clusters at the breastbone, in neck and shoulders and sides. Prickles down his legs till he feels it in his shoes. Like he's stepped into a thermal pool. False heat, he knows — the sand cold and yet he breaks a sweat.

Still blank, trembling slightly, he comes onto glistening wet sand and stops to let a wave rush up around his feet, chill water flooding shoes and socks. He unzips his coat, strips off and tosses it to the dryer sand behind, bends to unlace his shoes. Soon he's undressed altogether. Slack breast and arms quiver in the frigid morning. He knows his bent shoulder is a sight but there is no shame as the water rises about his bony knees.

Now he's high-stepping into spray, rollers surging with gasping cold at his groin, thin drawers clinging. He plunges on till he's immersed and paddling, the sandy bottom fallen away, heavy water drawing downward against every kick and the earth not even a rumor underfoot. Just greeny darkness below. Slick fish wide-eyed in the void. Vines of seaweed or tubular kelp bob at the surface, dangling like ropes. They brush at his legs.

He tightens every limb against the water's drag, swimming out, out, over swelling lungs of waves, out into ice-gray merge of sea and sky where no tongue of land can taste him, where sin and memory drop and sink, the long homesickness of years lets go.

Somewhere close by is the Golden Gate but you can't see it for the fog. Was maybe never there at all.

Just once his eyes stray back, head turning to see the rim of land stretching off in the south. A weak beacon of color blinks in the haze. They've lit the Playland lights. Beneath them, on the thumbnail beach, people are tiny smudges.

He lies back and thinks, The Pacific, Peace — and numb saltwater laps to cover his face.

4. (1863/4)

Namegiving—Little Rock—A spy hung—To Camden—
Massacres—Moro Swamp—An ambush—
A riderless horse—Cowardice.

Harriet wrote him at Helena to say the baby was born. A son. He would be Benjamin after General Prentiss, as Alfred proposed following the Fourth of July victory. The Rebs were driven off the Mississippi up and down its length, Grant having taken Vicksburg the very same day. Alfred had written her nothing of Needham, interred at the battlefield, nor of J.M.'s vile act, nor of the dead and dismembered so thick in the ravines, nor the time it took to bury them. Some had lain with arm or hand upraised in rigor mortis. Ants coursed their faces. He saw he would write with large omissions after that.

The 36th, in a force under Gen. Steele some six thousand strong, was to move west for Little Rock. Up the White River they reached DeVall's Bluff some twenty miles from the city and bivouacked in the heat at the mercy of summer insects. Alfred had let his news be known in company and that night there was merriment on his behalf. Flasks appeared, glinting hand to hand in firelight. The Majors, grinning, looked the other way.

Returning from the latrine in the late dark, Alfred was stopped by a voice.

"Congratulations cousin."

J.M.'s shape dripped shadow to shadow coming nearer. Alfred was soused. "John?"

"Heard your news. A boy they're sayin. What you name him?"

"John, you keep away, hear?"

"Hear me out now Alf—"

"No John, you clear off." Already Alfred's fists were clamping.

J.M. watched him, seeming to measure further words — but when Alfred stepped he slunk rearward into the dark, one hand raised.

*

By September the tenth they'd taken Little Rock. It needed but brief fighting — done in the main by other regiments. They stripped the Rebel flag from the Capitol dome, up went the Stars and Stripes.

They were still in the city as winter arrived. In January most the regiment stood to watch the public hanging of young David Dodd, a Rebel spy of seventeen. Dodd was made to stand to the noose on a wagon tailgate, raw coffin at his heels and Union troops squared out around him. A chaplain said absolution. Then an officer's silent nod and the tailgate clattered down.

The crowd was dispersing when somebody cuffed Alfred's wrist. Before he could turn J.M.'s voice was at his ear. "See what they do to'm cousin! See how I'd swing if y'ever think to talk."

Alfred shrugged hard to free himself but the voice stayed locked at his ear.

"I never meant to do it you know it. Not poor Needham."

"But you did and now Needham's gone."

"No, but it was Phillips I—"

"That's no better, John."

"It's on your head though if I hang for it."

"Get off!" Alfred broke the grip and stalked away.

*

Late March the 36th moved south from Little Rock under Gen. Steele. It was hostile mudswamp country teeming with Shelby's guerrillas, but by April the fifteenth their brigade reached Camden on the Ouachita River. They'd been on half rations since Arkadelphia some sixty miles and two weeks before. There was no fleet to bring up supplies, foraging all they could do, but the barren country demanded they range as far as fifteen miles either side just to keep the stock alive — treacherous business.

On the eighteenth came word of one of their parties ambushed and cut to scraps at Poison Spring not ten miles west, a train of two hundred wagons captured and more than a fourth of the escort — three hundred men — slaughtered along the road.

Accounts passed down the ranks of Indian Rebels screaming

forth from the trees with scalping knives. Victim to those blades were many of the colored soldiers, 4th U.S. Infantry.

Four days later the 36th Iowa and 77th Ohio were ordered to set out with two other regiments for Pine Bluff seventy miles north to retrieve supplies, a train of two hundred forty wagons in their charge.

The roads were a slog. The wagons sunk halfway to the axles in mud. Negro recruits got busy corduroying and the detail crawled along. By the twenty-fourth, two days out, they hadn't covered half the distance. They camped that night in Moro Swamp west of the Saline River. The woods were thick about them.

At dawn they were inching onward to Mark's Mills when the noise of guns surprised them and suddenly Rebels were coming en masse. The 36th, rear of the train, doublequicked to the front where the line had scattered. The trees already hung with smoke, Rebels pouring on in a roar. Alfred and the men fumbled to fire.

But already men were on the ground, bluecoats torn open, whites of their rolling eyes. Balls whistled amid the trees. Noise of cracking wood. Horses splayed legs and screeched. Above, the morning sky hung in blasphemous cobalt.

Officers were shouting, men aswirl. A hum in those woods like a hive. Someone plucked at Alfred's coat shoulder, curious thing to do. Quipping his head he saw the neat hole threaded with smoke where a ball had passed — and in the mud to that side of him a boy lay fingering his throat, a little spyhole ejaculating blood down his jacket.

Now the artillery was coming up from the rear, thank God. Six big guns altogether, a sight how soon they got in place. Alfred dropped prostrate in front of them, all the men sinking by a sort of telemetry — though they must have heard an order — and the howitzers opened in unison such a blast that the mud where Alfred lay splashed up as if awakened to consciousness. In the smoke his line sprang to fire and along his rifle he saw the graybacks near as thirty yards, a few fallen in heaps from the grapeshot. Their charge was broken but already they were rallying. They seemed of impossible number. A short minute and they'd be at hand.

Someone was crying. Doubled over at the cannonwheels, a man dug fists at gut, a kind of jelly blobbing over his hands.

Another roar and Rebs were closing amid the fire. They came breaking through in numbers and men were grappling in mud. Up close these invaders seemed actors of some outlandish dream spilt over into day.

And here came one in butternut tearing through the thicket with sidearm popping, yards from Alfred's right. He blasted two men in the face from an arm's length off — their caps flung back and features pulped at a blink — before a third man lunged and the pistoleer slumped atop him in a sound of cotton splitting, a bayonet spiking him at groin to fin out his ass.

More were coming on, jogging with rifles at shoulder or pistols out or waving knives. They screamed as they came, every one. Wagons began to fall, horses bucking. The men kept firing where they could, other men throwing back their guns and dropping like rucksacks or just crumpling over in a kind of boneless relief.

Somehow the cannons boomed on. The smoke a great net, and all these men within it like eddying fish. Alfred could not have guessed at the blood. In a howitzer blast he saw a man come apart at the waist, his upper half unfolding in a spray, and the soldier behind him faltering, gored head to foot with his fellow. Punch of bullets, crackle of canister shot, blat and groan and everywhere the splatting meat. Very soon the smoke seemed red. They were slowing them now, he could see Rebs turning backs, ducking heads, clumps of men uncoupling. They would fall back and regroup — but they were five times the bluecoats in number, easy.

Behind the cannons, shooting at where they hid in the trees, Alfred's sight glossed the bodies in blue flung down in mud: a hundred already. Two hundred soon. They may drive the Rebs back a minute but no, this was it — done for.

He turned at a galloping noise to see the decorated horse of the Lieutenant-Colonel careering riderless into the trees, the closing smoke a curtain drawn over its path.

Could hear no officers now, no voices calling orders making logic of the skewed bodies or mud-devouring faces.

He spotted J.M. under a wagon. Doubled up fistwise, hands clamped in terror atop his head, J.M. was gritting his teeth and staring out with darting eyes.

Then the Rebel cavalry came thundering upon them.

5.

Her father is gone, his coffee cup warm at the kitchen table. She heard the click of the front door, muted from her bedroom. In the entry she found the envelope.

Down the steps into morning fog. Already she's in her coat, Mother's old mackinaw, stuffing the letter in a pocket then pulling on gloves and with hardly a thought starting toward Geary. Can't see past Anza for the fog but she hurries to the corner. If she doesn't see him from there he'll have gone the other way. Coming to the corner she spots him graying away at the end of the block. She slows, relieved. She'll follow just fast enough to keep him in sight.

The streetcar is all but packed. She spots him again amid the hats and jackets crowding in the front window. Hurry across Geary, board by the rear door. The bell clangs. She grips a lanyard as the car rocks forward. He's found a seat at the front. Over fanned newspapers, between swaying bodies, she watches the back of his white head.

Outsized some in his wooden seat, he sits upright, left shoulder drooping despite his posture. Single hatless head among the riders. Time to time he glances out the window. A disheveled man in fedora slumps in the seat beside him, drunk probably.

The car rumbles west, gears squealing, bell sounding at every stop. Last night she re-read the letters in the box, the last two newly clear to her.

Aug 15, 1888

Dear Alma,

I have bought out Lorn & Son from J.M. Lorn. Will take possession Nov. the 1st. This step undoubtedly binds me and I'm afraid it won't suit you considering what time and energy you've poured into making me think better. But if we're to get married — and you know how I want to speed that day along — this is the best I can do. I will come as usual day after next.

     Benjamin

P.S. The Everyday Guide says for Nov. 26th "Court, <u>marry</u>, and ask favors in afternoon and evening."

Nov 1, 1888

My Own Dear Girl,

It is now 4 a.m. and I sit down to write you with heavy heart. The store has just been burnt out. The building and most all the goods were burned. I was to take possession this morning.

I hardly know why I write you so soon about this. I suppose because I think you would like to know anything that has a bearing on my future.

     Yours,

     Benjamin

They're halfway through the Outer Richmond when the drunken man wakes at a stop, rises unsteadily, and totters down the front stairs to sidewalk. He's leaning to rummage in a trash bin when the streetcar starts again.

All but half a dozen seats are empty now and Avis is sitting on her father's side some eight rows behind. He peers out his window, patient passenger. Seems to know exactly where he's going.

In the shop's dark he moved without question, knowing the length of the narrow back hall, number of paces to the counter, width of each aisle. The large canisters stood eight in a row on the bottom shelf, sides turned out below the belt leather. Neatsfoot oil. Linseed oil. Varnish.

They're clear to the end of Cabrillo, and there's the ocean ahead. The car swings slow in its final turn to the PLAYLAND stop. Benjamin gets up, one hand braced at the seatback. Avis stays seated watching him shamble down off the car and over the tracks in front to cross to the beach.

He found a feed pail and upturned one canister into it. Stood in the pungent, deathly waft as liquid gurgled, invisible but for the glimmer rising along the wall of the pail. Canister empty, he upturned another, half of a third after that, sliding each back in place on the shelf. He'd bunched and tied a big rag to an axehandle. Now he soaked it and swabbed all the canisters. Left them to sweat to the floor as he went down the shelf swabbing leather, canvas, tins of talc, boots, bridles, cottoncloth.

"End a the line, ma'am," says the driver, starting along the aisle with whisk broom and pan.

Already her father is down at the sand.

"Thank you."

Crossing the highway she gathers the mackinaw under her chin. Fog thinner out here, air very cool. Benjamin is moving straight out across the sand, not quickly, but not like a man on a beach. More purposeful, as if where wave and foam hurl ahead he sees a bridge. Avis stands on the sidewalk atop a tarred set of stairs, watching, till he's small at the water's edge.

Coming to the ropes he cranked each spindle by turn. Let the braided lengths slacken into the pail, soaking. Turned the handle till the rope filled the pail, then cranked back to watch spindle fatten again, heavier now and pattering like rain. He was very thorough, going one side of the shop to the other, unhurried, loath to make a mess. Took what must have been two hours.

Now her father starts to shed his clothes. With a jolt of fear she hurries down the steps. Her shoes immediately flood with sand. She kicks them free, scoops them up, hurries on in stockings, feet quickly chilled and dragging in the little hollows and dunes.

Already he's stripped himself of shirt and trousers. Ghastly pale. She calls but ocean static drowns her voice.

Everything ready, he stood behind the dark counter unwrapping the long woolen bundle he'd brought, hands turning it with shopkeep calm as if unwinding a bolt of burlap. Black wool fell away and the cutlass blade arced darkly against countertop. He left it.

He was dizzied a minute coming through the rear door from the stink of oil to cold black air. Stood in the open door's shadow, breathing. Black sky wide open above him, stars layered to depths. Nothing but distances, a heaven's breadth of readiness, vast advocacy of kinds. He lit a cigarette. Already he was thinking about the letter he'd write once back at his room.

My Own Dear Girl, I sit down to write you with heavy heart...

She sees him walking ahead into the foam, pushing through waves in a horrible marchstep, lank elbows pumping.

She keeps calling against the roar — but by the time she's reached the water's edge his white head is bobbing far out, lost here and there amid the waves.

He smoked the cigarette down to half. Then, turning about, sent it twirling through the door. It bounced sparking along the floor, fell still, and with a small blue whoosh caught a puddle.

He did not particularly hurry walking back. Let the wet grasses wipe the scent from his shoesoles.

His mind strayed to Old Man Wills on his farm west of town, who made and sold the neatsfoot oil. How he boiled in vats the shinbones of slaughtered calves, filling those green canisters slowly with the awful skim...

Her father is gone beyond sight, lost.

Avis moves about the sand collecting his shoes and clothes. Then with the clothes in her arms she stands looking out, like a mother expecting her child back from a swim.

6. (1864/5)

Captives—Forced march—Rebel prison—
Commandant's declarations—Hard weather—
A scheme.

Twenty days they were on the road. Fifteen hundred captured, trudging south under heavy guard. Graybacks at the battle's end had swarmed amid them busy in spirited slaughter of the negroes. The remaining men were started marching but hours later. Several hundred Union and Rebel lay dead in the swamp.

Under a Captain Delbin they marched without rest or ration all the first day. Stragglers were roped at the neck and dragged behind the captain's horse. They'd gone fifty miles and seen two men made such example of before the column was halted to billet along the road, permitted to eat of whatever could be foraged at hand.

Men succeeded pawing up roots and rotted kernels from the soil under a field of hickories. Alfred was scraping dirt from his findings when J.M. came up and murmured, "Got a treat here cousin." J.M. turned to let him see the ear of corn tipped into one cupped palm from his sleeve.

"Where—"

"Stole off a Reb mule they was feedin back a ways." He ticked his head. "Come away some. We'll share halves."

"They mighta shot you," said Alfred.

They sat against a stripling fence and ate discreetly facing the field.

"That Delbin's pure Rebel scum," said J.M. when they'd finished. Behind one hand he worked the bitten ear in little dagger thrusts upward. "I'd treat'm to this cob a certain way."

Alfred chuffed and rose to move off. He'd pinched his abhorrence in order to eat but couldn't sit close anymore.

"Hey, where you goin?"

Alfred turned. "That's some dander, J.M. Far as I saw though, didn't help you fight much given your chance."

He didn't wait to see his cousin's face. He'd gone a few paces down the fence when something struck his shoulder and twirled to fall just ahead. The cob. He stepped over it. Settled among some men near a stile.

Behind, J.M. had stretched himself in the grass.

∗

They were not much better fed in following days, as they crossed down into Texas. More stragglers, more draggings. And Delbin, at every little creek and watering hole, took care to prance his horse through and cloud the waters.

On Sunday the fifteenth they came through pinewoods to the Camp Ford palisades. Inside the gates they were met by sight of a tattered man hung from his thumbs on a rope.

They'd arrived on appointment day for the new camp commandant, Lieutenant-Colonel Borders. His predecessor, a Colonel Allen, had been deemed rather too fraternal toward the prisoners, reprimanded, and removed. Borders, lest his guards should still think well of Allen's habits, would make his own policy known, issuing a writ immediately: *"The Yankee prisoners have assisted in burning thousands of homes and turning out the homeless and suffering Widows and Orphans of Southern soldiers upon a Country filled with armed Negroes, commanded by inhuman ruffians who, often by force, violate the sacred persons of our women and make them the victims of fiendish passions. They treat our soldiers whom they hold as prisoners with the greatest brutality: three thousand Confederate Soldiers at Johnson Island have not had anything for meat rations but the foreshoulder of poor beef for months. The Confederate Soldier who in face of these facts can hold intercourse with these prisoners, can trade and traffic with them, is unworthy the name of Southern man. Your duty to your country demands you guard them vigilantly and treat them as Enemies."*

The newcomers heard tell how Borders had stood packing his pipe and smoking while the thumb-strung man, for mouthing insubordination, was hauled up screaming. None would have called life in the stockade pleasant before, having faced no scarcity of disciplines — withheld rations, bucking and gagging, the sweatbox — but this Borders, together with the crowding of all the latest prisoners, brought them dread anew.

*

They lived like moles. Shebangs, they called the hovels. Some were modest as burial mounds, red clay humping over a door of size just fit to crawl through, the dank interior too narrow to let a man turn about. You backed out bearwise. Or, unlucky enough to die in camp, were hauled out by your ankles.

Other huts were somewhat bigger, sided in roughcut wood, even done up with little stoops or glassless windows on hinges. But those were few, cobbled early by some of "The Old Seventy-Two," first Camp Ford prisoners. And all were but meager, floored alike in mud, the occupants grimed and fed on darkness, more burrowers than persons.

Men innumerable had no shelter at all but slept in rags in the weather. A third or more went trouserless, bootless, crudded blankets or patchwork articles fastened skirtlike at the waist.

All ate but scantily — half a pint of cornmeal a day, sliver of beef if lucky — while being much eaten at by grayback lice, chinches, mosquitoes. At morning the men would shake blankets or coverings and watch the maggots pitter out.

There was a little spring that gave sulfurous water. Latrines were not much considered in the overcrowded pen, such that offal and other waste lay out in the sun, or moved in rain with runoff to bring slime to every door and sleeping spot. The stench hung amid the rowed shebangs.

Scurvy, typhus, yellow fever, lung fever, sunstroke, frostbite, the ague: men succumbed in scores to fill the pesthouse beyond the stockade. Little the Reb doctors could do but let them lie in awhile till their outcome — better or dead — was plain.

*

Days of clay: empty, earth-dark, motiveless. Rank days of men sun-drunk, mud-drunk, like flies. Some paced rounds with tin cups outheld, whiskey they'd spat out and stored from months before, when there was still a ration allotted for work detail. Wanted to sell it now. Buy a little bread off a guard maybe. But the guards these days were not of mind to spare any extra.

Through summer in the sun-hammered pen the men baked and thirsted, red skin cracking like lobster. They raised canopies where they could, of meshed pine boughs or garments knotted in a piece — but the guard would not permit too complete an obstruction from where they watched at the sentry boxes. Along about first of July three prisoners died very fast of the sun. That night three men loosened a place in the stockade wall and fled. Before midnight the hounds had tracked them down and by morning the men were found buried to their necks at the front of the pen, squint-eyed and sniveling in the sun. Upon a board behind them was posted the commandant's newest order:

> *Hereafter, any Federal prisoner detected in trying to make his escape, either in the act or after his capture, will be shot by the one capturing him.*

*

Come the bracing days of fall men huddled together at mean fires amid the huts, stood rotation at the few iron stoves set out in the open, tall pipes venting smoke overhead. They would not survive winter this way.

A Capt. McClough of the 176th New York made appeal to camp command and parties of ten were permitted under heavy guard to cut and gather wood outside the gates. Until the cold came in earnest the whole pen was busy at raising new shelters, all crude but sufficient most of them to house fifteen men asleep in close file. Clay chimneys could give a little heat when there was something to burn.

In November the guard caught a man of the 48th Ohio taking double rations. His arms were stretched and lashed to an enormous pine limb borne across his shoulders and for three days he walked about camp that way.

*

At a morning rollcall a young Pvt. Winsler from Indiana came up missing and a search was put on. Two days passed and some saw fit to laud his success — but on the afternoon of the third day Winsler came back a body slung sackwise behind the saddle of the chief tracker Chilicothe.

The camp adjutant announced, for edification of the prisoners, how the boy had wandered the best of sixty miles without ever getting more than fifteen from prison, had never even crossed the Sabine River, and was shot where they found him.

Two men of his regiment were given leave to bury him in the prisoners' boneyard north of camp.

*

The cold was well upon them. The wind roared some days, needled with frost. They piled through mean little doors to sit thick amid one another, barely room to bend knees, while the weather threatened to scalp their crude roofs right off. Men still outdoors formed up in clots, embracing ten or more against the howl, and took turns at the sheltered middle, shivering all.

There was much talk of Christmas coming. On more sufferable days some kept busy whittling holiday trinkets and setting them out. They bound pine branches in wreathes and even modeled the camp's red clay in rough nativities. They would sing and feel holiday warmth, circumstance be damned.

One frozen morning at mess J.M. got into place behind Alfred and as the line inched toward the mealbox he pressed close.

"Got a scheme you'll wanna know bout cousin. Reckon you're as full up with Texas as me."

Alfred wanted to shove him off but only shook his head.

"I got a compass sense better'n Winsler's. Gun comin my way too."

"How's that?"

"Guard called Grayson comes from Illinois, born there. Had an uncle died in camp, all things. Says it's evil how they treat us. He's helped some boys, Winsler last."

"Winsler didn't go so well."

"No compass sense. Come with me Alf."

"No."

"It's only you I'm askin. Nobody else."

Glancing back Alfred was pained to see in the hollow, bearded face and cracked lips his cousin's old smile — even under scurvy-swollen gums. He turned forward again and said, "No, I need no part a that."

"Too late Alf, now you know." He felt a jab at his ribs behind. "January cousin. We're goin."

Alfred heard the edged threat in the voice but shook his head again. They spoke no more.

It was December the twentieth.

7.

Avis sits in the sand. What can be done? May as well wait, don't ask for what.

The ocean rolls in crashing layers. Her fingers move in the fabric of her father's shirt. Near the collar on one side she feels something. Lifts it closer: there's a little scab of cotton and thread, a spot her mother mended.

—*Told your mother all of it before she married me.*

—*She never told me.*

—*No. She promised me that.*

Avis sees her mother now, alone in the house of an afternoon. She's leafing through old letters, tucking them in a shoebox as she cleans and tidies the cubbies and drawers in the old telegrapher's desk. Does baby Avis lie mewling on a blanket nearby? Alma, unfolding, refolding by turns — till one letter makes her stop. Sitting back she reads for several minutes. Finishing, she knows it mustn't stay. She lays its aside and goes on tidying. Cannot tear it — or burn it, surely not. But later, rolling out the fresh drawer lining, she saw what to do.

And wouldn't Alma Lorn know the cause of the fire too? Benjamin never tried to collect insurance, wouldn't have wanted an investigation. And J.M. was dead before they married the following February...

Avis remains sitting in the sand.

8. (1864/5)

Thoughts of wife and son—A pistol—Flight—
Guards and dogs—Fallen—A goodbye.

Walking the pen by day, Alfred's mind was much on Harriet and the boy. He wrote them letters in his thoughts. He would send assurances and not dwell on life in captivity, at pains to suggest a dominant boredom, *nothing going here, I am well enough, and how is it with you?*

Little Benjamin is taking steps, he imagined reading. *He's grown so sure on his feet he's all day running he can climb now spry as the squirrels I fear sometimes to look away or I may look back to see him in a treetop.*

He knew her voice.

And do you know he calls for me now when I am not at hand and at supper he'll use a spoon and fork with just the smallest encouragement. He has had some fevers and some falls and the other morning burnt his thumb and finger so bad at the kettle as to make a blister over all the knuckles, but these things as much as they pain me with fears for him do make him stronger and more knowledgeable about life as we live it, you see we are as well as could be hoped though we do worry and miss you awfully. I show him your Photograph and tell him of his Papa and do you know he will stare at you and tell you his mind for a spell of fully half an hour sometimes...

Again these days Alfred dreamt himself standing in line at the telegrapher's window with urgent message in hand, fearing the mechanism would break before his turn had come, agent pounding too hard at the key, wire gone dead, electricity itself wholly drained from the world and the system everywhere shut down, deafened, dumb.

From the dream he woke one deathly January night to J.M.'s pistol at his ribs. J.M.'s lips puckered large against one finger, stern warning in the eyes. A tick of the head commanded him up.

His hutmates didn't stir, though Alfred thought he saw the open eyes of one watching from a dark corner as they crept out. Well, what would he do were he the watcher? Stay out of it much the same.

It was pitch black in the pen. Stepping along amid the huts and huddled sleepers, J.M. prodding him ahead, they were not even shadows. They were moving toward the rear wall. At the last hut they squatted waiting.

"John—"

"Sh!" The barrel dug cold at Alfred's cheek. He saw eyes crazed silver in the dark — murder in them sure.

He was made to crawl ahead into the open, keeping low amid bodies curled on the ground. Twice J.M. grabbed his heels and they lay waiting three minutes, four. Quiet from the sentry boxes. Then up to crawl again.

Prone faces watched blinking as they passed. Some nodded good luck. No stopping to correct these witnesses. At the last man Alfred was pushed to his feet with J.M. clinging behind all but piggyback. The gun buried at his spine between them, they ran as one into black across the deadline.

*

The wall so black ahead J.M. can't see it at first. Could almost think it the open darkness — must look to the top to remember. Never been so close is why. Now they're right up against it huddled at its base and working like mad to get the piling loose. But that goes quick and they're all but out, Alf squeezing through on his side ahead, bare feet snaking and gone.

Don't you run without me goddammit! No saying it aloud though he would scream it for he does not want to shoot him but cannot doubt in this moment he will do just that should Alf abandon him and run. Whole plan's dead that way, for they're to go together.

But he squeezes through and there's Alf laid flat in the grass waiting.

All clear to go they run doubled over through grass toward the woods. And Alf is in it with him now, they're hustling for the trees — hellbent in freedom like allies again but rushing rearward in time outrunning the changes the war the last two and a half years. They are shadows in the flickering black wood, scattered parts swarming together into a piece. They stop in a hollow under the pines, catching breath.

And J.M. before he knows it takes a slug to the jaw and crashes backward in brush.

"Goddamn you," he hears, and scrambles to sit up, reeling. But he held the pistol tight going down and now cocks it and aims at Alfred standing over him.

"Put it away you fool."

"No, we go together Alf or I kill us both I swear."

"Course we're goin together," says Alf — says it in rage but better than not at all. "Put it away."

J.M. lets the pistol down but keeps it gripped.

"Where'd you get it?"

"Grayson got it off another guard. Was Winsler's gun. Grayson said it's only right it comes back to us." Touching the numb jaw as he talks, fingers come away slick. Blood looks black in the dark. "Got only but two shots. We better keep on."

"You oughta left me there, John."

"You ungrateful shit. We're cousins. Bloodbrothers."

"I won't forget Needham, John. What you done." Alf shaking his head, bitter stare, like he'd hammer that fist again. "Don't even hope."

Now why'd you say that, now of all moments? You really want I should suffer a mistake all my life? Oh cousin you have no idea how bad I wish not to kill you. What is it we need to repair us, if such a thing as this night ain't enough?

They hurry deeper into the woods. Must reach the Sabine by daylight if they're to have any hope.

*

But before they were an hour in the pines they heard the guard trumpet, then the dogs, the far-off yipping a clatter in the trees, strange misshapen sound like heavy chains dragged and tossed.

Alf was tearing ahead, black shape dodging to and fro, the paler pulse of his feet at a sprint. J.M. threw himself hard behind, trees whipping by. They knew the scent sticking fast at their heels — smell of their own escape pursuing them. No outrunning it.

Then came the roll of drums from the pen. Damn closer that noise than they cared for. Prisoners jarred from sleep to stand for a count.

It seemed very soon that the closer woods were rustling, crackling. And J.M. heard the dogs' hot breath, the snarl in each bark, and still running twisted back to fire and the pistol sprayed light upon the trees. No dogs in sight.

"John!"

Beyond the screening wood the guard rifles roared reply. Each flash a sheet of light to send the tree shadows leaping.

They kept running. They could feel the brush clutching harder to stop them, dogs in uproar and gaining.

Then came a single report and Alf with a grunt was sprawling down, scrub and leaf splashing around him. "No oh no I've had it now John."

J.M. skidded to his side, "Damn it man get up," dragged him hard by the arm.

"No I've had it John. I'm done for."

"Get up man they'll kill us both." He hauled on the arm, the body a heap in the dark.

"No no can't run," said Alf. "The hip, oh God I'm spillin out."

"Goddamn you Alf." Groping along the coat and down, J.M. felt his hand cave through, the hot gout welling from the top of the leg. The splatter fell everywhere when he drew the hand back.

"John don't leave me for em damn you, finish me."

J.M. curled down and clapped a hand at the blubbering mouth. "Sh." The dogs were weaving now, and men's voices on all sides.

Alfred's muffled words: "You'll keep goin John, I'm done and don't you leave me for em."

J.M. was clawing up the gun, his hand all smeared.

"You're saved me talking now huh?" Alf sucked breath in a grim kind of laugh.

The pistol was very hard in hand. "I'm doin it for you Alf, not for me."

J.M. arched back and put the barrel to Alfred's ear. His hand was shaking badly. For why was he doing it? And had he known one way or another he would? As he cocked the hammer there came a sound in the wood. Turning he saw in the haze of a lifted torch the shape of horse and rider coming along. He slackened and let the gun down. Seizing Alf's hand he shoved pistol butt against the palm and empty-handed began to crawl back. "Forgive me cousin."

"John."

"Forgive me." *He'll do it himself.*

"John wait — my wife, the boy, see they're cared for huh."

But up and running already J.M. could not answer. His feet met a sudden rise and then they were firing from behind and with a blaze in his leg he was pitching headlong through the thicket down a slope, wet earth and brush ripping his brittle clothes as he tumbled. They had him now, had them both, they could even go slow about it. *And Alf will do it now, do what I could not.* The dogs were coming on, slavering loud, paws thrashing in the forest floor.

And before he'd scuttered to the bottom the dark wood exploded with Alfred's pistol shot.

9.

Green water comes apart in foam, a frothing injury, edges folding over to spray, to shuttle up along the sand, dragging it smooth. The beach records nothing. Iridescence. Dust.

Avis stands to go. What use waiting longer?

But she's been watching the water so intently he's come halfway along the shoreline before she sees him.

Benjamin Lorn, gaunt-shouldered and wet, his gray brow dripping brine, walks toward her across enameled sand, ankles wavering in the sinkholes. Returning to find his clothes, he finds his daughter.

From behind, watching from the Great Highway, say, you would see a spry old man come back from a bracing swim, his daughter hurrying to help him into his shirt. She's the fretful, mothering type, protector and adorer, and embraces him almost recklessly. He stands, good-humored, as she mops at his face with her sleeve, rubs and blows on his hands, embraces him again. Carefree old swimmer, he's learned to suffer her demonstrative ways.

They stand talking a minute, the old man drying off, getting dressed. The fog is clearing up, sun breaking softly on the sand, but she gives him her mackinaw. Then they sit together on the beach, father and daughter passing a pleasant morning by the water.

. . .

Or maybe old man and nursemaid, thinks Avis. But no, turning to look at his face she sees her own profile there. They are father and daughter, unmistakable.

He's still catching his breath, hard jaw unhinged to show the brown-edged bottom teeth. He squints ahead into the shimmer on the waves as if trying to reckon what distance he swam coming back. Says, "We're the last of us, you and me."

He doesn't turn to say it, doesn't carry the thought into further words, but Avis understands. He means that's why he came back. Means he's sorry about Benny.

History, you see, it troubles the soul. She all but hears him. In her mind, her father talking around the silence between them, his voice the one she's heard in the letters. *A fellow's past is not his own. Something comes forward making him.* She sees her hands, her scissors and paper, scrolls of scrap falling away till space can draw the outline tight.

—*That store was all he had. I guess I knew it too.*

—*You mean you knew it would kill him to lose it? Or knew he'd kill himself? Did he kill himself, Daddy?*

You think you can save even those who don't seek your saving. You think it's your role, your place, being daughter, mother. Blood binds you to this duty. She couldn't swim to save him, she'll save him by talk. But it's folly. Nothing can spare you your experiences. You bear their weight — alone if you wish.

Looking at her father's profile, Avis sees she doesn't need to know some things. No, it can free neither of them to talk these matters out. He's too old.

So she asks him nothing. Better, she sees, to let him be.

POSTSCRIPTS

Then we looked closelier at Time,
And saw his ghostly arms revolving
To sweep off woeful things with prime,
Things sinister with things sublime
Alike dissolving.

— Thomas Hardy

(HARRIET, 1886)

She burnt the letters when the cancer came back. At Keokuk,
St. Louis, Helena, Little Rock, Alfred had written one at least
every month. She burnt them all.

Now, seeing her Benjamin such a man, so much anger in him,
she could wish she hadn't. Of a mind with Alfred himself, who'd
felt much the same at the end — though she couldn't know it —
she'd thought, What good for Benjamin to know his real father
dead — and dead under such terms?

She wasn't long for the world now. And those other letters
still in the barn. … She supposed she'd meant to tell him all
along. Something, if not the whole of it. Enough to help him.
Cure him, some, of bitterness. J.M. was all the father he knew.
What good the boy going on angry, hurt? He and J.M. would
have to make a peace. That or let the household fall apart. She
wouldn't be around now to bind them.

Life demands you make a peace, Lord knows. What sort of
life could she have expected, for herself or the boy, had she never
made peace with Alfred's death, his wish that J.M. look after
them? Had she never accepted J.M.'s hand or come with him to
Perpetua?

But Benjamin's had been, she knew, an unhappy childhood so
far as J.M. figured in it — could she hope to lead him so late to
happiness? No. That wasn't her aim. In a family, she'd learned,
happiness has to come by way of blessing. Despite other things.
Anyhow, as family matters go, day to day, happiness is hardly the
main concern. Like in marriage your work is bigger. But make a
peace — that you must do…

She would tell him something. Sick as she was it'd have to be soon. She would tell about the packet in the barn. If those letters proved half as much help to him as she'd found them, maybe things would go better between him and J.M. And he could still find a father in him.

Finally she saw she was going. Benjamin came to her side. She had some moments alone just him and her. Breath wouldn't come right but she talked. And suddenly saw she must say all of it. Alfred and everything. Was only right, Benjamin needed to know, and J.M. would never tell.

She said, "Forgive your father," and meant Alfred — the early secrecy, the wish that J.M. take custody — but breath wouldn't come enough. And she still had the barn to tell of. Well, she managed that. That was done. Breathe. But she'd meant Alfred, meant to tell it all, was only right he should know now... no, no breath ...

Alfred.

Last she'd seen him was the night they conceived this boy — Alfred so broken up — that friend he'd carried home in the army wagon. And after that just his letters, sent from ever deeper south, and two years later, away that whole time: killed.

For twenty years, more, she saw him in her boy everyday. While Benjamin, in himself, saw only J.M.

And Alfred buried in Texas all the time — a marked grave? She never knew. J.M., long ago, single time he talked of it, called it a *boneyard.*

She saw in her mind a field of stones. And reckoned that more than there ever was probably. Field of stones. Of stolen names.

... And his name in his own fair hand, singeing away in the grate where she stirred the fire. *Alfred.* All black around the edges, vanishing.

(MAY 1865)

War's end—Blind sutler—A souvenir.

They were conveyed down the Red River to Shreveport for exchange, then on to New Orleans where they found mucky streets aswarm with tattered Union veterans, pacified Rebels dazed in whiskey, barmen keen to keep them at it, freed slaves, stevedores, boat captains, fishwives, auctioneers, tintypists, cobblers, ragged thespians and squeezebox players, tinkers, itinerant dentists, and sutlers of all description. A market of mud and confusion to follow the four-year melee.

The officers of the various regiments out of Camp Ford sat grouped for portraits in photographer studios, barefoot to a man, still garbed in prison rags.

From a sutler specializing in war souvenirs J.M. bartered for a gorgeous Rebel cutlass. They'd settled a price — fully two-thirds of his back pay — before he made out that the man was blind. Had supposed him to be squinting in the late-day glare.

"Twas a Lieutenant-Colonel's sword no less," pattered the man, and climbed up to untie it from where he'd hung it for display along the front of his cart. He was agile as a sighted man, his grimed hands as dexterous undoing the braided cord and tassel.

"All right all right," said J.M., "sold me the sword, don't need to sell me a story."

The sutler climbed down with the blade. "Oh but the story's no extra." One squinched eye spasmed — a wink? "Buys ye a mite of heroism's all I meant."

J.M. shot out a hand, seizing the fellow's faded lapels. In his fist he felt the brittle give of seams popping. "What do you know of heroes?"

"Easy, easy. Meant nothing by it. We're all heroes to've slopped in this blood, that I believe. All of us or none of us, could see it both ways." Trim sightless fingers were plucking at J.M.'s grip. A pained and dimwitted smile.

J.M. released him. "And what way do you see it?"

"Me, I can't say I see much of anything. No, I have no way and therefore want no eyes. I stumbled when I saw."

J.M. counted off the fee. Crutching away along the mud-caked sidewalk with cutlass shoved in a beltloop, blouse pulled over to disguise the hilt, he was dreaming of a house, a hearth to hang this, a respectable life.

(NOVEMBER 1944)

Benny walks in a dimlit wood, bent at the waist, the load on his back dragging at the meshed pine boughs above. Fragrant needles shower his neck and shoulders, some going in under the collar to tickle down his spine or along his throat.

It's not yet noon but these trees create an evening, a splotchy gloom, the sun ground down to pepper and sprinkled stingily. For years as a little boy in his mother's lap he stared at the ink-drawings of the Grimm Brothers book. Loose dark lines, crosshatched for shading, sketchy around the edges. The Hansel and Gretel wood was a thick fabric of penstrokes. He felt its sinister enchantment as a knot that pulled tight in his chest. He knew what would happen but the story always lured him inside. He wanted to be frightened though he hated it. Though the story's restoration, its conclusion in sunlight, never fully relieved him. He got up from her lap tattooed somehow. The forest shadows clung to him, the day vaguely scarier afterward.

He can all but scent her now. Her arms washed in Ivory soap, open to entrap him in the story's world, and her voice the story's voice close at his ear, and the breath of coffee along his cheek that was the dangerous exotic smell of his imaginings. *Deep and dark the wood.*

He weaves onward amid stenciled trees, hunched over, going slow in tangled undergrowth off the trail toward where they said. There are voices but the wood hides them, nothing but pines pressing near in front and everywhere. Still, he can feel he's close. He'll find a spot, settle in, get to know the others.

He's just raised his foot to step over a pile of woodjunk and sod when something catches his eye and he swerves to spare a man a kick in the head.

"Jesus, sorry."

It was the ear he saw first, the man reclining on his side in the brush. *Am I there? Where are the others?* But stopping, Benny sees clear. The man's head, turned away to nuzzle in mulch, is half of a head. And there are no shoulders. And what he glimpsed as rather long black hair trailing down the neck is something else.

Benny's eyes shift away. He wants to walk on but something holds him. *Don't look down.* He turns, to put a few paces between himself and his discovery. He must still stoop for the trees but wants very badly to stand up. He swings the M-1 in that direction, ridiculously thinking he must aim there. Another step and his cheek grazes something soft, something bright. Snapping back he immediately knows the remnant for what it is. It dangles at the bottom branch, purplish red, coiled in the green boughs still springing where he brushed them. He swipes a sleeve at his cheek, the slime of the thing. *Don't look up.*

From his right a man materializes amid the trees, zigzagging closer. The 9th Division sergeant.

"Keep movin soldier."

"There's somebody—"

"Aw yep. Christ. Well they'll clean'm up. Keep movin, go on, ain't there yet."

They both felt the presence of the torso snagged in the trees just above them, its ragged sides in the ripped field jacket. They saw it without looking. *The living are complicated, the dead have lost all meaning.*

. . .

R.T.C. *meant Replacement Training Center.* Benny had tried to write her from the Training Center before they shipped out:

> *As they sure are in a hurry to get us over they tell us there's no time for much beyond basic. This makes some of the fellows groan but they are mostly draftees or ASTPers and hoped if anything to kill Japs. As they see it, what the hell should they care about France, Europe, etc.? As for me you know how I am eager to get over. Hitler is pretty well stopped I guess but I don't mind helping to keep him that way. I do not tell these bums in barracks what good fun they'll have talking Nazi German in the soda shop and football stands if he is not stopped for good!*

REPPLE DEPPLE *meant Replacement Depot.* In the first Repple Depple in France he tried again:

> *Dear Mom,*
> *Mostly waiting here while they figure out how they'll use us. I say "us" but actually we're likely to get split up as soon as not. They send men where they need them in the numbers they need. The idea is to "fill in." A chaplain here talked to us on Sunday about Decisiveness, capital D. You could say he made an impression, and not only on me.*
> *I see how I wasn't decisive enough, at first, about joining up no matter what (so easy,*

once I did it!), and this I believe is what
caused much of the trouble between you and
me. I should have gotten it over with and not
put you through so much. I am sorry.

After that sermon there is general
agreement here that a guy ought to make good
before going into the fight, meaning if you left
anything out of sorts at home you had best do
your all to clear it up.

So I am sorry.

But this letter too he left unfinished, unsent. There seemed to be some missing prologue he couldn't patch together.

REINFORCEMENT meant, as far as you could tell, the same as
REPLACEMENT, and pretty soon everybody just went back to the original
word.

Finally, in Bastogne a few days ago, he tried again. This time he started *Dear Dad*, but the attempt proved just as useless.

RETIRED, when you're talking about combat, meant you ran away.
Hauled ass. Outa there. Gone. Up on the German border in Belgium, the 28th Division had been cut apart in the Hurtgen Forest. Now Benny and the other replacements are the 28th Division. *Is a "unit" still a unit after one hundred percent losses?*

He'd heard some of the rap about replacements. Handy bullet catchers, all that. But he knew he was a quick learner. Wore his chinstrap in back his second day in France. Read the Woods Fighting Guide the 9th Division put out. *When the shells hit the trees, don't dive. Hug a pine.*

Now in the black Hurtgen night he's squatting down in a foxhole waiting out a neverending shelling. In the light at every blast he cannot believe the bodies. The woods a deafening wheel of splinters, shrapnel, exploded soldiers. On the ground a few feet away one dead private's face gapes back at him every time he looks out. Half the night, that face. Till debris rains down to hide it.

Benny digs in.

From his small New Testament he's taken the oddly shaped black paper, his five-year-old silhouette. He clutches it curled around his fingers all night.

And the shells never end.

Dawn. Small-arms fire opens upon them from the trees. Those left along this side are all of one mind, jumping up and running for the rear, dumping rifles as they go. An officer's screaming from a hole, a single voice goddamning them, ordering them back. And here's Benny on his feet and running with them, right past the officer who's holding a phone in one hand, mid-call for more replacements, a gleaming telephone wire uncoiling back through the woods. Benny's running for all he's worth — *follow that wire!* — with bullets sawing the forest all around, runners dropping dropping dropping to both sides of him, Benny still going, stooped for the trees but going, and every one that drops cuts down his chances — and the silhouette slips, floats, flutters back to tumble unnoticed along the forest floor behind.

(FROM A FAMILY HISTORY, 1893)

As a general thing they were independent, frugal livers of their day and generation. None made themselves widely known either by wealth, political attainments, or in the arts. We have discovered sixteen names of the direct line who served in the Union Army. Standing for the vanquished minority were three, so far as we have discovered.

That several lines of this family are entirely dead to us, and that we leave them so, is not a pleasurable feeling. There were two Bibles holding the family records but both have been destroyed. We regret that the present record is not a more perfect one.

But so deeply interested have we many times been in our researches of the people of the silent generations that we have lost ourselves until it seemed they were visible forms, and we were holding discourse with living beings, and we were one with them.

Of the younger generation who are pushing upward to a higher plane intellectually, morally, spiritually, as well as a higher civic and social standing, we have a pardonable pride. Their opportunities are great. Good blood, much is expected of them.

Acknowledgments

Perpetua's Kin incorporates phrases from Shakespeare and Thomas Jefferson, and also contains the following quotations and adapted lines: Page 90: "He cannot bear to possess a past" is a variation upon a sentence by Paul Zweig in his book *Departures*; page 194: "We have learned irreverence toward sun and season" is a quotation from Neil Postman's book *Amusing Ourselves to Death*; page 278: The lines "Wind ran down the funnel of his throat" and "His jagged nerves were lightning" in Benjamin's dialogue are adapted from the novel *Voss* by Patrick White; page 288: "I begin to feel the loneliness of having lived too long" is a quotation from Joseph Severn, cited in Stanley Plumly's *Posthumous Keats*; page 328: "The living are complicated..." is adapted from a line in Leo Litwak's book *The Medic*, cited in Paul Fussell's *The Boys' Crusade*; Fussell's book itself was immensely helpful to me. Also particularly helpful was the book *Love Amid the Turmoil: The Civil War Letters of William and Mary Vermilion* edited by Donald C. Elder III; the book *Camp Ford C.S.A.: The Story of Union Prisoners in Texas* by F. Lee Lawrence and Robert W. Glover; and an unpublished document known as *The Civil War Journal of Walter S. Johnson*.

Extraordinary thanks to: Catherine Segurson and Elizabeth McKenzie for publishing a portion of this novel in *Catamaran*; Linda Swanson-Davies and Susan Burmeister-Brown at *Glimmer Train* for the honorable mention; Diane Prokop for sharing her gifts and for unwavering confidence and trust; Jason Headley for friendship and faith; Harriet Chessman for encouragement and generosity of spirit; Judy Heiblum at Sterling Lord for giving it her all; Marion Abbott, Janet Boreta, Justin Hocking, Eowyn Ivey, Carolyn Kulog, Scott Nadelson, Gina Ochsner, Peter Rock, Ann Ronald, Nancy Scheemaker, Sunny Solomon, Laura Stanfill, Hans Weyandt, and Leni Zumas, for the power of their kindness; Nathan Shields, for his artistry, inspiration, and loyalty in the cause; Robert Antoni, for his wise friendship and example; Dave Roth, for fraternity in the art; Peter Turchi, for selecting my work in *Perpetua's Kin* for an Oregon Literary Fellowship; Ken Hobson and the Oregon Legacy Series at the Driftwood Library in Lincoln City, Oregon, for allowing me to speak about this book and the Oregon landscape; all the editors, besieged by the spirit of the times, who sent kind notes and said "I wish"; all the booksellers who go the extra step, read a little further, write the recommendations, and make room on the crowded shelf; Paul and Lois in Wichita for sharing the family papers; Betty Reno in Cameron, Missouri for unlocking the depot; Anne Repp, Sharon McKee, Lisa Eddy, and especially Virginia McDonough in Appanoose County, Iowa for hospitality, knowledge, and time; and, for her patience, faith, empathetic indignation, and steadfastness, K, of course.

Love and respect to the memory of Mary N.

Finally, the Oregon Arts Commission, Literary Arts, the Corporation of Yaddo, and the Regional Arts & Culture Council provided invaluable support during the writing of this book or for its production, for which I am very grateful.